THE CISTERN
SONGS FOR ABANDONED NESTS

THE CISTERN
SONGS FOR ABANDONED NESTS

Abduh Khal

Translated from Arabic by
Mira El Hayek

THE CISTERN
SONGS FOR ABANDONED NESTS
Abduh Khal

Published by Nomad Publishing in 2023
Email: info@nomad-publishing.com
www.nomad-publishing.com
Cover design: Lucie Wimetz

ISBN 9781914325564

© Abduh Khal 2023

 The Publishers would like
to thank the Harf Literary Agency

Disclaimer: The content and any opinions included in such content reflect the views and opinions of the author and do not reflect the opinions and beliefs of the publisher, the translator, Tarjim program, or any of their affiliates. The author is solely responsible for any statements made in such content and any translation is made based on the perception of the author from the original language or source of information prior to any translation or adaptation made.

Dedication

*Asmahan, we have become two separate branches.
I will go away, so don't be sad.*

Abduh

Critical Situation

Al-Yaridi and Muhammaduh converged at the Qishla market, eager to intercept King Faisal's convoy and plead their cases for a resolution that would ease their troubled minds. Life in the scorching heat had left them with dreams that seemed beyond reach, only to realise they were just mirages.

One of them was like a man who dreamed of a bird pecking at his head, while the other was closer to offering wine to the divine.

Just a few steps away from the royal palace gate, they stopped running, panting heavily, and cried out, "Your Majesty the King... your Majesty the King."

Neither of them could catch up with the convoy and Muhammaduh stopped as Al-Yaridi's shouts continued to follow the royal car, "Give us back our slaves, Faisal."

****

In front of the palace gate, Muhammaduh's situation was dire. He yelled,

"I am more worthy of citizenship, otherwise give me my leg back."

He sat down, defeated, a few steps from the palace gate, lost in thought, wondering where the line was drawn between dreams and reality.

EASYGOING PERSONALITIES

ASHOUR'S FAMILY

Chapter 1

The tranquillity of the neighbourhood was disrupted at dawn by a commotion that caused many of its residents to become uneasy.

And as the night got darker, the cries of terror became more apparent.

People began to move around and the air was filled with the sound of anxious breathing. Close to the garbage dump, the residents gathered to see the remains of a child who had been killed and eaten by wild dogs.

The smell of death hung in the air and, as it grew stronger, the air became thick with the stench of rotting flesh. The dogs were tense as the proximity of the crowd made them nervous.

Despite their distress, the dogs were able to use their claws to turn over the corpse and excavate the intestines, using their sharp teeth to feast on the succulent flesh.

From time to time, the dogs would flinch and growl with a thick, lonely urgency as they sensed the presence of people getting ever closer.

The dogs' unbridled aggression caused near panic among the onlookers, who muffled their screams to avoid further inciting the dogs. No one in the crowd dared to step forward to retrieve the victim's body.

But even if someone had plucked up enough courage to to come close enough to attempt to save what remained of the corpse, each dog would still have received a sizeable portion of meat to satiate its hunger.

The numbers of the crowd were swelling although they remained rooted to the spot in fear of the dogs that seemed to be threatening to mount a horrifying attack on the crowd.

"Are these dogs or donkeys?" asked Mahmoud Kabeini.

The onlookers' screams rose to a deafening level, causing the dogs to lose whatever composure they had left. They stood upright as they focused their attention on the crowd, with their tails between their hind legs, their eyes scanning the area, letting out blood-curdling barking howls. They were poised to jump at the sight of any prey advancing towards them.

Two of the canine cannibals turned round and faced the crowd with such an air of menace that some people started throwing rocks at them.

No one was able to get near the body until Ibrahim Ashour arrived.

He jumped off his motorcycle, took a large stick from one of the onlookers, and held it high.

"Did I not forbid you from doing this?" he screamed at the mob. The dogs then retreated, running towards a road that leads to some ruins and settled behind Ashour's house.

Relieved by Ibrahim's masterful intervention, the crowd cheered happily. Amid the cries of joy, Youssef Maghribi shouted,

"These are not just dogs, they are Ashour's Jinn."

He cast his gaze over the faces of those around him, as if searching for validation for his words.

"Didn't you notice what Ibrahim said, as if he were speaking to humans?"

The volunteers, relieved that the dogs had run off, swiftly

gathered the corpse. Covering it with a shawl, donated by Muhsin Abu al-Hamayel, who removed it from his own head revealing his bald head, still obscured by a yellowed hat.

The body parts, in a terrible state, were collected by Abou-Assida and Wahib Abou-Nokta. What helped them to overcome their fear was the fact that they were butchers and accustomed to being covered in blood on a daily basis.

The corpse was wrapped, and some of the crowd headed directly to the mayor's house, preceded by an outburst of anger over the current situation. They threw the wrapped corpse into his hands.

"This is the third time that the bowels and limbs of a newborn have been cut off, and we don't know what can be done."

In the previous two cases, the neighbourhood had been combed in search of a woman who had given birth. Eyes were put to spy out the neighbourhood and nearby areas, looking for a woman who had lost her baby. But all attempts at espionage and research were to no avail. No one had lost a child or heard of anyone who had.

Panic and gossip took over the neighbourhood about a woman who emerged from the ruins of Ashour's house carrying her child, as the cacophony of cats meowing and dogs barking echoed through the air. She had thrown her newborn as a feast for them and quickly went back to one of the ruins of the big house.

Rumours circulated that it was a "Jinn's son" and the news spread like wildfire, filling the residents with fear. But the muezzin, Yahya Qassem, dismissed these rumours as mere attempts to cover up the adultery that had infiltrated the community.

Two previous, strange and terrifying incidents had occurred and the neighbourhood's leaders had attempted to sweep them under the rug. However, the repetition of the act and the discovery of a third mutilated child brought the search for the perpetrator to the forefront once more.

The mayor carefully removed the shawl from the newborn's body, the sight of the torn body parts causing him great distress. The brutality of the injuries, the removal of the bowels and the mutilation of the features, along with the copious amount of blood, was a sight to behold. His face was pale as a gleam from the foot of the corpse caught his eye, a golden anklet stained with blood nestled amongst the shredded flesh and broken bones.

On examination, it was revealed that the anklet matched the anklets from two previous corpses. A calm and composed Aletha Al-Harbi meticulously examined the corpse, removing the anklet from the decaying flesh and washing it clean. He presented it to the mayor, who placed it alongside the other two anklets, all bearing the same inscription and curved shape of a boa, with turquoise eyes.

Their words came out in a rush as they made observations,

"This is certainly a clear indication that the perpetrator is the same person."

"All of the bodies have been found close to Ashour's house."

"All of the bodies were devoured by dogs."

"All of the corpses had dark skin."

"In each of these cases, only Ibrahim Ashour had been able to keep the dogs away."

The mayor pretended to maintain his composure and rationality, urging those around him not to give in to their emotions. He offered encouragement to Aletha, reminding him of the great reward that awaited him if she took on the task of washing the corpse and performing the appropriate rituals before burying it.

The mayor, facing opposition from Nasir Ba Nakita who reminded him of the need to inform the authorities of the events, stood up and spoke firmly to silence any objections,

"I remind you, Ba Nakita, that what I approve, the authorities approve. So, do not worry."

His sudden display of authority silenced any further comments from the attendees. The mayor raised his hand, addressing everyone,

"After the burial, we will have a meeting to discuss the new body."

The meeting adjourned with a promise to meet Aletha at the cemetery to wash, pray over, and bury the body.

****

Among the graves in the cemetery, Omar Al-Yaridi incited the people with a strong oath,

"These dark-skinned children are nothing but the offspring of a Jinn, punished by Ibrahim Ashour whenever women refuse to obey his orders."

It was said that the women's wombs had been cursed, giving birth to children of sin for marrying a Jinn.

Chapter 2

As evening fell, Ashour's house was plunged into complete darkness and no one dared to venture near it or walk on any street leading to it.

The street overlooking the house was full of fear and a challenge for anyone to be brave enough to venture there. The street was considered too dangerous to be crossed at night, except by the reckless or those who were not aware of the strange events that frequently happened there.

Walking at night became one of the unspoken taboos, and people warned their children of the consequences of going out after dark. With the onset of night, people avoided Ashour's house like a flock of birds avoiding a shotgun.

To prevent the street overlooking Ashour's house from being shrouded in darkness, stray dogs and cats roamed the district and the air was heavy with dampness.

The neighbours quarrelled with the municipality workers, who were frustrated by the constant complaints and unchanging responses,

"Someone keeps breaking the lamps here."

The supervisor, apologising to the complainers, expressed his surprise that the lamps were being repeatedly broken as soon as they were installed.

It seemed that no one knew who was responsible for breaking them. The residents were asked to be patient as efforts were made to find the culprit and hold them accountable. Several months have passed and the identity of the person breaking the lamps remains a mystery, leaving the area shrouded in darkness and the street poles damaged.

The street, now isolated as well as dark, was populated only by the eerie presence of Omar Al-Yaridi peeking out of a broken window, casting a dim light.

It's said that Omar Al-Yard had encountered a Jinn, which drew him back every night to sit comfortably, while warning anyone who dared to pass through the eerie, isolated street.

Chapter 3

Omaima Ashour was no longer interested in the happenings outside her house. She had become detached from everything and spent her days alone in a home that was once filled with joy but now felt airless and suffocating.

Word had spread so that people avoided walking on the street parallel to her house or near its walls. Rumours circulated that a Jinn emerged from the walls and ceilings, preying on unsuspecting passers-by, devouring their flesh and leaving their remains in the narrow streets.

Nuria, the wife of the sifter, swore that at midnight a dispersed flame oozed out of the depths of Ashour's house, turning into a huge fire that captivated the gaze of those who looked at it, only to disappear with the sunrise.

This sparked Omaima's curiosity to come and see the flames for herself. She searched the rooms of her house for the fire but found nothing but an empty house and her own loneliness. She missed her sister Jumana dearly and didn't know where her brother Ibrahim had taken her.

From time to time, she called out "Did you miss me, Jumana?"

She laments her loneliness and the fact that her brother is often absent throughout the night. Her solitude has led her to develop certain obsessions, as if she has discovered that her mind is a factory producing persistent thoughts. One morning, she caught her brother Ibrahim returning home with the sunrise,

"The spirits of those who lived here have gathered from all corners of the earth and returned... to be among our family once again."

Ibrahim did not want to discourage her interests in the rumours surrounding their house, so he winked and gently held her fingers.

"It seems that our Seljuk heritage has a connection with the Jinn. Your great grandfather returned to establish their empire, taking the allegiance of the Jinn," he said.

"So, it would be best to focus on your aspirations or dream of becoming a Seljuk princess instead of dwelling on memories."

For a moment, she felt proud as she remembered the stories about her grandfather who, after 130 years of striving on earth, did not die until the arrival of his Seljuk ancestors in Mecca.

He passed advice to his sons to continue with their dreams, so that someone can wear Tugrul Bey's sceptre again.

At first, she was thrilled to see her friends who were unable to visit her due to concerns that they may be possessed by a Jinn who dwelled in the palace's back alleys. And she was not allowed to leave the house, as Ibrahim had sworn to her that she must not leave even if the world was on fire.

When news emerged that their house was being inhabited by Jinn, she was delighted to see her friends and when that eagerness subsided, she found solace in watching the street through the holes and cracks in the shutters almost covering her window. To compensate for her small stature, she would often jump to catch a glimpse of passers-by beyond the walls of her home.

Meanwhile she took pleasure in mending her clothes, and

when she couldn't find any tears to mend, she would create new designs on her dresses by cutting and re-sewing them.

Her obsession with sewing every piece of clothing brought back memories of the past, and she regretted ending a relationship with her cousin who had emigrated from Jeddah to join his relatives in Istanbul. She was consumed with a desire to reawaken that relationship by any means necessary. This preoccupation consumed her, and as a form of purification, she silently cast a spell upon her emotions,

"Please do not linger in my mind any longer."

She yearned to hear a human voice breaking the silence that had settled in her heart. Occasionally, the thought of seeing the lonely young man sitting across from her home would come to her mind. Though she tried to suppress these desires, she couldn't help but blame herself for having such "childish" thoughts, Sometimes she would reminisce about her sister Jumana and the times she would jump up to try to catch a glimpse of Omar Al-Yaridi, who lived next to their outer gate. He was like a steadfast rock, unaffected by the world that surrounded him, and never once swayed by the sight of a young woman.

Chapter 4

Ibrahim Ashour always had a fondness for adventure and the unknown. He never liked to return home before the last star had disappeared from the sky, preferring to spend his evenings out, exploring and experiencing all the world had to offer.

The passion of youth was still strong within him, and he felt compelled to seek out new and exciting experiences.

He didn't want to waste a moment, being always on the lookout for something to fill his days, even if it may not prove to be as fulfilling as he had hoped. He was constantly restlessness, as if he was afraid of missing out on something important if he stayed in one place for too long. Even so he became easily disenchanted and moved on quickly.

His family's history has taught him the importance of not becoming too fixated on any one brief moment, regardless of how joyful or ecstatic it may be. He understands that all moments are fleeting and that those who dwell too long in the past are at risk of being left behind. Instead, he focuses on constantly discovering and embracing new opportunities in the future without becoming trapped in the past.

He appeared to relish living life on his own terms, without a care for the consequences of his actions. He didn't dwell on the chaos of his life and had no desire to put it in order or make amends for any mistakes he may have made.

He spent his days riding his motorbike through the streets

of his neighbourhood, looking for a fight or an altercation to keep him entertained and avoid boredom.

He had a penchant for getting involved in conflicts, whether as a loyal ally or a fierce opponent. He had many labels attributed to him, but none that truly defined him.

His ultimate goal was to have a one-on-one fight with Muhammaduh, without any interference. Every time his friends criticised him for not seeking revenge for what Muhammaduh had done, he would simply brush it off with a promise to show them vengeance like none other.

Ibrahim Ashour smoothly navigated the bend of the street leading to his house on his motorcycle, and silenced the engine's roar by disconnecting two wires. He had taken to this simple method after losing the key to his bike, and had grown accustomed to dismounting from the seat without using the brakes, allowing the wheels to coast to a stop as he arrived home.

After quickly dismounting and testing his agility as he landed, he rarely lets his motorcycle rest on its own stand. Instead, he carefully leans it against the wall of his house, making sure not to damage it.

He turned the key in the lock of the outer door and opened it with a gentle push. A noticeable crack in the wooden frame was becoming more prominent, revealing the damage that had been done over time. Ibrahim stepped inside, calling out for Omaima as he made his way through the dark.

His voice echoed through the dimly lit room, illuminated only by the faint light filtering through the closed curtains.

The grand house, once a symbol of prestige and luxury, now stood in a state of disrepair.

THE CISTERN

Crumbling bricks and fallen ceilings were a common sight, windows were missing and the elegant marble columns had lost their shine. The gypsum was cracked and the inscriptions were faded. The lanterns that lined the sides of the corridors and passages leading to the back stairs were no longer working.

The floors of some rooms had become obscured, and the wooden ceilings showed signs of wear and tear with gaps of varying sizes. The house, like its inhabitants, had grown old and fallen into neglect.

Omaima emerged from the light, holding a plate of bacon and said softly, "I'm here."

Behind Ibrahim a soft light illuminated his path as he made his way to the room, discarding the worn scarf draped over his shoulder. He sank onto a sofa whose upholstery had frayed and whose cushions had lost their plumpness. Ibrahim's gaze wandered to the sagging section of the ceiling, where cobwebs and caterpillars had taken up residence, their webs ensnaring insects in their sticky traps, unable to escape from their hanging death.

Ibrahim had made a promise to himself to restore his and Omaima's home as soon as he received the deferred payment. As the house fell into disrepair, he felt a sense of urgency to fulfil his promise to her. Time had been rough on Omaima. Her face was littered with wrinkles and other signs of debilitating hardship. Ibrahim felt a growing impatience as the days passed without definite news of when the compensation money would arrive.

Despite the challenges and setbacks he faced in his travels to Mecca to retrieve the funds, Ibrahim remained steadfast in his belief that perseverance and determination would ultimately lead to success. Five years had passed since he first sought the funds in court but he never lost hope. Each time he felt discouraged by the sluggishness of the process he reminded himself of the magic word: perseverance.

Even so he was feeling the burden of the long wait for government correspondence to be processed. The uncertainty of when a decision would be made was oppressive. Omaima, his sister, watched him with a mixture of confusion and concern in her eyes as she followed him.

She bit her lip and gathered together the hair that had fallen over her face, trying to make sense of her brother's behaviour. He gave her a reassuring nod and attempted a quick smile, asking, "Do you have something I could eat?"

Omaima turned her face away to hide her disgust and her hostility, before placing a plate of smoked meat in front of him and leaving the room. Her verdict on the meal was "This meat would break my teeth."

He didn't match her anger with insults of his own.

Instead, after he told her not to leave the house and threatened her with punishment. He was confident he had instilled fear in her.

He waited for her to disobey him, hoping that one day she would push him too far and he would be able to break her bones and put an end to his own tumultuous life.

He struggled with the responsibility of caring for his sister, not knowing how to balance his own needs with hers.

He was lost and didn't know which path to take. Whenever he looked at Omaima's fading beauty, he felt the weight of that responsibility more strongly, opting to control her with crude threats. Satisfied his menaces had peaked Omaima's fear of punishment enough for her to remain in the house.

He spent days waiting for her, hoping she would disobey him so he could break her bones and rid himself of the final obligation in his chaotic life.

He struggled with his conflicting feelings towards her. Sometimes he was tender; at other times he terrified her. His fluctuating emotions convinced some that he had multiple personalities.

He couldn't help but recall the painful memory of his stepmother and Jumana leaving the house, forced to quit because of his own cruel words,

"If you want your husband, follow him to prison."

Omaima's ban on leaving the house was now in its twentieth day and she hadn't even once considered crossing the threshold.

She contented herself with watching the outside world through the cracks in the windows.

She taught herself to spin and sew, taking up needlework as a way to complete her tasks until she could afford to buy a sewing machine. She didn't feel sad about her stepmother's expulsion, although Jumana's tears broke her heart as she begged Ibrahim to let them stay, offering to work as a maid to pay for her and her mother's keep.

She let out a deep sigh and massaged her temples, thinking to herself,

"How can a brother be so heartless?"

She couldn't stop thinking Ibrahim. At times she saw him as cold, cruel and totally free of feeling. At other times she viewed him more sympathetically as someone who had been worn down by need and hardship after falling off the pedestal of an indulgent life of luxury.

She spent her nights spinning wool and thread, confining

her life to her silent thoughts, barely able to steal a few hours of sleep to make it through the school day. Each morning, she found Ibrahim pushing open the gate, looking at her with eyes that seemed to reflect loss and helplessness, and telling her to get ready for school.

In fact, her daily school routine was the only activity she was allowed. The thought of his preventing her from going to school preyed on her mind and often she silently implored him not to. Interactions between Ibrahim and Omaima were limited in any case. They primarily revolved around his needs and her requests for the household. She didn't press him to remember her requests, understanding the difficulties he faced, and she kept her frustrations to herself, while striving to perform her household duties flawlessly.

One day he came from Mecca at noon, having accomplished nothing from his trip. She had returned from school just moments before he arrived, and before he could make his presence known, she prepared a meal of okra and rice, placing it on two clean dishes with a cup of cold water. She laid out a worn tablecloth in the middle of the room, and waited for him to sit and eat.

It was difficult for Omaima to reconcile the Ibrahim she once knew with the person he became. He was a seasoned traveller who had in the past entertained her with stories of his travels, particularly his experiences in Egypt.

He shared tales of his nights spent at lively clubs and his visits to the movies and theatre. He would boast about his connections with famous artists and even claimed to have had intimate relations with some of them. He always made sure to dress impeccably whenever he went out. Ibrahim burned brightly but briefly, like a matchstick that was ignited, caused a big flame, and then quickly vanished.

Bringing up his name became cumbersome, like inhaling smoke that stings the eyes. Unfortunately, as time passed, Ibrahim's true nature had been revealed to Omaima through her friends Mona, Aziza and Zainab.

They would spend afternoons together discussing the young men in their neighbourhood, sharing both their positive and negative traits. Unfortunately, Ibrahim did not have many positive traits according to them. Zainab shared something with Omaima that she couldn't keep secret.

On returning home, Omaima spoke to Ibrahim about what she had heard, but he became angry and swore that she would no longer be allowed to leave the house to see her friends.

She found herself spending a lot of time alone, wondering about what Ibrahim was doing during his long outings.

The thought of the things she had heard about her brother caused her great remorse. She didn't have the courage to confront him and could only speak in short, hesitant sentences, saying jut what was necessary to avoid his constant anger, which often ended in slaps, kicks and insults.

Deep down, she longed to see Muhammaduh, the person who had caused so much pain in her and her brother's life, turning their days into a never-ending cycle of bloodshed.

Chapter 5

Wounds that don't heal carry a secret record that shapes our destinies.

This is how Omaima's mind wandered as she watched her brother eat, indifferent to her presence.

Every time Ibrahim's anger erupted, Omaima's memories of the past came flooding back. Ibrahim used to be handsome, but now he had a deep wound on his face, as if a professional butcher had struck him with a blade. The wound split his cheek into two parts and ran down to his lower lip, widening as it reached his right eye. The cheek was attached to the top with jagged edges.

Ibrahim fondly remembers his former handsome features. Before the wound healed, Omaima had doubted that her brother's eye could be saved. She couldn't help but wonder what could have driven someone to commit such a brutal act.

"What drove your opponent to such violence?"

The wound inflicted upon Ibrahim was not a slight blow but rather a reflection of the malice of its perpetrator. Even after it had healed, unsightly growths persisted along the path of the blade, their ugliness concentrated in the area below his eyelid, with a protrusion that had swollen. This wound had a profound impact on Ibrahim's life, causing his once-handsome features to fade and robbing him of the admiration of young women, who no longer saw his face as a sanctuary for their dreams.

THE CISTERN

Ibrahim's confident laughter vanished alongside the disappearance of his handsome features.

He walked through life with a heavy heart, never quite finding the contentment for which he longed.

It was as though the burden of his unfulfilled desires had manifested itself in his facial features, making it clear to all that something was amiss within him.

The perpetual scowl on his face led him to seek turmoil and aggression. He became a wanderer who loved to ride his motorcycle through the alleys of the neighbourhood, searching either for a fight where he could show himself victorious to those who sought his help or simply to satisfy his own ego.

Ibrahim's once-striking good looks, a mixture of Italian, Spanish and Turkish heritage, now hung heavy, like a fruit plucked before it could fully mature.

Their sister Jumana also shared that same unique beauty that their father had passed down to them.

It's clear that the family's fortunes had taken a dramatic turn for the worse. No one could have predicted that the two siblings, once considered the pride and joy of their family, would find themselves living in a palace reduced to ruins and crushed by poverty.

The neighbourhood was shocked by the siblings' decline, with many telling tales of Ibrahim scavenging for food, even resorting to bringing home dead animals and collecting damaged fish from the market.

No one could have imagined that such a well-respected family would fall so far after the father's incarceration and the grandfather's involvement in a political scandal that resulted in his execution.

Chapter 6

Poverty shows when you've bitten your nails to the quick. A halporsh sentence unleashed a deep anger within Ibrahim Ashour's chest.

His stepmother felt sorry for his sister Omaima when her nephew refused to propose to her because of her current circumstances.

With a mocking tone, he threw his towel aside and retorted,

"And your nephew seems to have forgotten that his father used to work for mine. I am the son of Ashour, a descendant of glory and power."

His stepmother replied softly,

"That was some time ago..."

She reminded him of his family's humble origins by pointing out that he was now sitting in poverty, causing memories of his family's past rise to glory and prestige to fill his thoughts.

His grandfather was the first man in the area to fly to far-off lands with unfamiliar names, that many in the neighbourhood struggled to pronounce, calling them "places where the sun don't shine".

On his return, he would be loaded with gold plates and cloth maps wrapped around natural pearls, diamonds, and rare gems. Many in the neighbourhood still fondly remember that picture.

When the rainy seasons come, the locals still tell tales of

the gold they've found washed up in the streams, saying that it's remnants of the golden plates that were once buried in the grand palace of Ibrahim's family.

In the flow of his memories, Ibrahim's stepmother Makiya furrowed her brow, disapproval etched on her face as she spoke,

"Has the pride of your family vanished from your mouth?"

Her words were heavy with disappointment.

He was taken aback by her lack of gratitude and his mind overwhelmed with the question, "How could his father have married this woman?" As wise men do when deep in thought, he stroked his thumb over his fingertips.

This woman, who didn't seem to possess any qualities of love or sexuality, had a dark, immoral and hostile side that lay hidden beneath the surface. He furrowed his eyebrows and smiled to himself, murmuring,

"She's a man in a woman's body! How did my father get caught up in this mess, when he always had a taste for beauty?"

He straightened up, smoothing down his moustache, feeling a surge of anger at Makiya's ingratitude regarding all that her husband had done for her.

He felt a hint of betrayal in the air. Makiya's denial only added to the successive blows that weighed heavily on him. Despite this, he was tempted to taunt her by reminding her of the beauty of Omaima, a beauty that she seemed to lack whenever she spoke of herself,

"Omaima's beauty is truly exceptional, and none of your family members deserve it."

Makiya, feeling offended, jumped out of her seat, retorting,

"Do you really believe this superficial woman has any real beauty or depth of character? Look at Jumana. She's the essence of my father, while you are nothing but a dry, lifeless branch clinging onto a flourishing tree."

He could sense that his words had hit a nerve with her and, attempting to conceal his amusement, he covered himself with his scarf. Though it was a small victory, he couldn't help but feel a sense of triumph over her arrogance.

Her unwillingness to acknowledge her husband's circumstances stemmed from the decline of her once lavish lifestyle, and her anger could only be quenched through her rebellion against Ibrahim and his sister Omaima. All her actions were aimed at Ibrahim until he finally snapped and kicked her out of the house, tearing her apart by taking his sister Jumana and hiding her, leaving no trace of her whereabouts.

Chapter 7

History has two perspectives, the official and the social, each of which asserts to be the truth.

This sentiment was expressed by Tawfiq Al-Ahmadi when discussing Khairy Ashour and the progress he made in the neighbourhood.

Ashour's endeavours comprised setting up crucial amenities, like street lighting, clearing debris from water storage tanks, and removing litter from public places. He also tried to bring the community together by forming bonds between families. However, Al-Marouai could not agree with his friend and left before bringing up Mohasin Khairy. Shaking his hand in the air he said,

"You have a narrow perspective, my friend."

The residents of the neighbourhood have long pondered the pros and cons without a sense of impartiality.

If history were to record the biography of the Ashour family, it would show two barren personalities, marked by ineptitude and poor foresight. Abdul Ghafour Ashour and his son recklessly squandered a large fortune, which was supposed to provide a comfortable life for future generations. But instead, these two individuals brought a curse on the family.

The true story behind the Ashour family's wealth is not as simple as it may seem on the surface. According to the older members of the community, Khairy Ashour's grandfather was worried about the consequences of handing over the keys to the city of Jeddah, so he instructed his son to bury the gold plates somewhere in the palace and keep it secret, no matter the cost. Khairy Ashour then made deals with those around the palace to share the treasure with them in exchange for their silence.

These secrets were not revealed all at once but were passed down through the generations, kept only among a select few who had agreed not to reveal them.

It is said that the money may have come from questionable means, such as deception and fraud.

As time passed, the secret of the treasure slowly leaked out and there were different versions of the story. Some say that the descendants of Khairy Ashour approached the community leaders with the intention of opening the treasure chests and sharing the wealth with those who had kept the secret. Others say that the money was kept hidden to prevent the Ashour family from being singled out and targeted for their wealth.

The Ashour palace is steeped in legend and folklore, with many in the neighbourhood believing that a vast wealth is hidden within its walls.

The palace, once a grand and imposing fortress, now stands in a state of disrepair, its columns crumbling, its ceilings collapsed and its walls cracked. The surrounding streets have grown dark, and the palace is shrouded in mystery. It is said that the Jinn, who are said to guard the palace, have sworn to keep the treasure hidden until the promised person appears to claim it. The idea of this treasure has become pervasive in the community, with many dreaming of discovering it and becoming the rightful heir.

Chapter 8

S ometimes time can be as unpredictable as a boiling cauldron, and if its fire is not quenched, everything within will disappear into thin air.

*****

The weak sunlight seeped in through the door, crawling across the dusty bed and disturbing Ibrahim's fitful sleep. As the sun's rays grew stronger, he shifted towards the shadows, trying to avoid opening his eyes and wanting to hold on to sleep interrupted by the flood of hot sweat drowning his body. The ceiling fan, lazily circulating the air, was unable to dislodge the sweat pouring from Ibrahim's mouth and settling among the hairs of his bare chest, while the mattress absorbed the sweat that dripped from his body.

He grumbled to himself before finally opening his eyes and seeing that it was well past two in the afternoon.

He released a soft growl and quickly stood up, dressed and draped a black dotted scarf around himself, which he reserved for special events, as he considered it to be of significance.

He grabbed an old leather bag and clutched it tightly under his arm, still uncertain of how long it would take him to reach Mecca before it was too late.

He left with a suppressed growl, and Omaima's voice followed him,

"Wait, I'll prepare something for you to eat."

His mind raced through the murky avenues of his imagination, grappling with his unsteady plans.

He had not achieved the specific goal he had set for himself, as his plans had ended in disaster after his father's imprisonment and the constant setbacks caused by his own wavering mindset.

He struggled to push away thoughts of handing his stepmother over to slave traders and breaking her heart over Jumana.

As he hurried down the street, his mind was preoccupied with the potential consequences of not reaching the agreed date with his father's agent. Each time he grew weary of calculating the time, he muttered curses at no one in particular.

He passed through the wall of the fourth district on Tarek bin Ziyad Street, desperate to find a car that would take him to Mecca. An overwhelming obsession consumed him, the fear that time would not be on his side and that he would not arrive before the adjournment of the court-appointed committee to hear two lawsuits; one against the Ministry of Finance and the other against the entity in charge of endowments.

The previous sessions had been a prelude to finding a solution that would please both conflicting parties over the dissolved endowments, with Khairy Ashour obtaining bonds that preceded the Saudi era. Ibrahim's imagination was ignited by the potential of the vast funds that had been allocated within the treasury of the Ministry of Finance as compensation for his family. He reminded himself of his true motivation, pushing himself to continue,

"You will arrive on time."

He was determined to arrive at the appointed time to

avoid giving the court commissioner any justification to continue postponing the assessment of compensation for their homes overlooking the Gate of Peace, which were included in the campus expansion project.

He knew that the commissioner was skilled at evading appointments. An itch of anxiety gnawed at his chest at the thought that any lateness would be used by the government commissioner as an excuse for further delays.

He didn't know about this compensation until his father had suddenly been imprisoned. Recalling his father's words, he remembered that his grandfather Khairy had not trusted any of his family members, and he couldn't help but feel a hint of irony at the thought that he had inherited that trait from him, not trusting anyone, not even himself.

He was aware that his father had no trust in him and had not given him any responsibility for handling family matters. He heard from others that his family was quite wealthy but always responded with sarcasm,

"What kind of wealth when my sister and I can't even afford to eat?"

During his last visit, he stood in front of his father's cell, stammering as he listened to a barrage of barbed attacks.

Visitors and prisoners alike paused to listen to their conversation and shifted their gaze between the two figures; an angry face firing off insults like a machine gun with a faulty trigger and a weak face reeling from the severity of the reprimand he received.

He felt confused as he tried to deflect his father's insults by looking around but Abdul Ghafour became even more furious. Finally, he stopped the torrent of insults by asking his son a surprising question,

"What have you done about our pending cases in the courts of Mecca?"

"The situation remains unchanged."

Abdul Ghafour was like a caged animal, frustrated and desperate to break free,

"With your apathy, our entire legacy will be lost, just like a precious inheritance has been wasted."

Ibrahim's response was obscured by a stammer, so he stopped and held his breath. Before he could regain his composure, he felt someone spit on his right cheek through the prison bars.

"I am certain that my family's legacy will be tarnished by your actions."

Ibrahim tried to deny this accusation by claiming that he had no knowledge of the family's affairs, and suggesting that he was being kept in the dark, but his father's dismissive laughter silenced all the counterarguments that were forming in his mind,

"All you ever did was dress up and travel to Egypt."

"And who are you to talk..."

"Don't say anything else."

He became aware that he was speaking recklessly, he was in the company of Salem Abu al-Anayn, who he had convinced to drive him to Mecca for a double fee, urging him to hurry.

He felt that he had imprudently revealed all the reasons for his sudden trip to Mecca. Salem's eyes widened in surprise and he remained silent, pondering the potential riches that this impetuous young man could bring, and devising ways to steer him towards a mine that was on the verge of striking gold.

Ibrahim, recalling his father's words of caution "not to utter extra foolish things," regretted what he had revealed to the Salem.

He was determined to extract any information Salem may have.

"Don't worry, I've locked your secret in a tomb that will never be opened. I accidentally stumbled upon the secret of compensation, but I won't tell anyone."

However, this assurance from Salem did not appease Ibrahim and he sought to distance himself. As they approached their destination, he abruptly shouted,

"Drop me off here."

"We're still on the outskirts of Kuday, and we haven't even reached the Al-Ashraf Building."

Ibrahim laughed as he quickly exited the car, leaving Salem to fume and curse.

Chapter 9

Ibrahim rushed up the stairs to the office of his family's legal representative, where he was met with harsh words of reprimand for being late for the scheduled meeting.

The members of the committee tasked with examining official papers were already present.

The legal representative listed the details of the ongoing legal proceedings, including the case being heard by the judges of the first court, the division of the case between the Ministries of Endowments and Finance, and the lawsuit filed by the heirs of Khairy Ashour. Additionally, a recent deed had been presented by the General Investigation Department, which potentially nullified previous arguments and deeds.

The compensation money, which was tied to properties located in front of Bab Al-Salam, was now in jeopardy due to the uncertainty of the case.

Ibrahim did not offer any apology for being late. Instead, he shifted the conversation to finding a solution to their legal issues.

He asked the legal representative,

"Didn't you say there was someone who could clear up these complications?"

"Yes, for one million riyals. Do you have that amount?"

Ibrahim struggled to keep his anger in check as he sat, rubbing his hands in confusion, not knowing what to say.

The representative continued to wear a sarcastic smile, blocking any potential solution. He reminded Ibrahim,

"if it weren't for your father's imprisonment, he might have been able to negotiate with some judges."

Ibrahim felt trapped and helpless, his imagination running wild at the thought of paying such a large sum and the hardships it would bring.

He was filled with anger and couldn't find a way out of his predicament. He finally decided to turn to the family's agent for help,

"My father trusts your management, so find a solution for us."

"There is no way out save the one I told you."

Ibrahim stood up, as if to end the meeting,

"And what do I say to my father?"

Tell him what you've heard. He may know where your grandfather hid the gold plates. We can use them to pay the million and lift the ban on the real estate.

As Ibrahim prepared to leave the office, he couldn't shake off the suspicion that the family's agent was colluding with another party and that his words were insincere.

Still feeling something was amiss, he bid the agent farewell, hoping that he would be informed of any new developments.

Chapter 10

The Ashour family's history is one that has been passed down through the generations, remembered and honoured for many years.

However, in recent decades, the family's fortunes began to decline with the arrival of Abdul Ghafour Ashour. During the period leading up to the transfer of power from the Sharif to the Hijaz and the subsequent departure of the Turks from Hijaz, Khairy Ashour's family held a prominent position within the Turkish legation.

But with the departure of the Turks, the family turned its back on the past and declared its allegiance to the nobles.

The family presented its son, Khairy Ashour, as a shining example of loyalty.

He moved around frequently, Facing numerous obstacles in his pursuit, he constantly found a way to overcome them through his exceptional ability to adjust and deceive.

He formed secret alliances with both the nobles and Ibn Saud, driven by an insatiable ambition and the confidence that fortune would always be on his side.

He spent the night listening to international radio stations, to keep himself informed about developments outside the city of Jeddah. It was a habit he acquired from his father, a politically astute member of his family, who advised him to stay informed about the details and outcomes of the Sykes-Picot Agreement. He understood that the region was changing rapidly and that it was important to align himself with whoever held power.

Khairy was a clever young man and saw an opportunity to ingratiate himself with the British by positioning himself as a key figure in the Hijaz. He was willing to take risks and even put his own life on the line to achieve his goals. He travelled frequently between Arab and Western cities, and his greatest successes came from making strategic deals that helped further his ambition.

He created a secret group that pledged loyalty to him and worked to destabilise any regime that was established before he could solidify his own power. He deliberately recruited members and sympathisers who shared his vision and the group grew quickly, with branches in Jeddah, Mecca and Madinah. More than twenty people came under the banner of the group, all of whom owed their obedience to Khairy alone.

His ambition was focused on gaining control of these key cities but his path to power was narrow and treacherous, and he faced many obstacles before he could realise his dreams.

With the stabilisation of Saudi rule, his plot was uncovered.

He emptied all of his money into the columns, corners, cellars and halls of his palace, and entrusted his son Abdul Ghafour with the secret of the buried treasures, before leaving the city of Jeddah on an Italian ship during a dark night. He fled under a charge of working against the state and the fear of being beheaded.

Ibrahim heard of this story from the accounts of older people, without any concrete proof of the treasure his grandfather is said to have hidden in the palace.

Struggling to come to terms with the lavish life his family once lived and the harsh reality he now faced, he occupied himself with the legal issues surrounding his family's real estate. But as he delved deeper, he found that these issues went beyond property ownership and had implications for national security. His final meeting with the legal attorney sealed the case files, and the attorney advised him to tread cautiously. As the truth about his family's actions became clearer, the attorney became increasingly distant, expressing his disapproval and renouncing any association with the Ashour family, saying,

"No one trusts your family, Ibrahim."

The guilt and shame associated with his family's actions weighed heavily on the last surviving member of the Ashour family, renouncing, and separating oneself from anyone connected to Khairy Ashour, whether they be a son, grandson, or associate.

Chapter 11

"No one trusts you, Ibrahim."

Ibrahim's reputation was in tatters, as a result of various struggles and hardships he faced throughout his life. His grandfather Khairy escaped, his father was imprisoned, Omaima is lonely, Makiya's heart has hardened, Jumana shames him, his wounds have turned into scars that disfigure his face, and his behaviour has been bad. All these events combined to prevent him from gaining the required level of respect within his family.

Ibrahim found himself wandering around a car park in search of a taxi to take him to Jeddah. The area was teeming with taxis leaving for various destinations including Jeddah, Taif Riyadh, and other southern cities.

Salesmen were chatting and the chaotic honking of car horns filled the air as travellers came and went.

In his haste to find a taxi, he saw one leaving with only one more passenger needed to fill it. He quickened his pace to catch up with it, but as he did, a veiled woman (Hajji) carrying a newborn baby collided with him.

Wrapped in a brightly coloured towel and holding a dish on her head, in which she was carrying various goods, she offered to sell him some kola nuts. He stared at her disfigured face and saw the face of Muhammaduh materialise before him, as if it were really him.

The gleam in her wide, white blackened eyes reminded

him of his arch-rival, and he suppressed the rage that had been buried deep within him as he remembered the incident that had once brought them together.

He clenched his teeth as he always did when that scorching incident came to mind, Ibrahim's memories of the past event with Muhammaduh caused a surge of anger within him, making him feel like a dangerous and violent creature. He expressed hateful thoughts towards Muhammaduh's race. But despite this, Ibrahim refused to let his fear of facing Muhammaduh consume him, even if it meant risking his own life.

Ibrahim's gaze was fixed on the woman, due to her resemblance to Muhammaduh.

He showed her his disfigured face, pointing to the deep wound on his right cheek,

"Do you know Muhammaduh?"

He did not wait for a response from her but continued,

"That's what he did to me."

She shook her head, seemingly in confusion or agreement, and maintained her stance, keeping her plate balanced while holding out her hand offering Kola nuts with a wide smile, and broken language, trying to entice him to buy something from her, even if he did not want the Kola nuts.

Ibrahim noticed the striking lines on her face, which ran across her cheeks and were sealed with less pronounced lines,

"Did Muhammaduh cause the disfigurement on your face?""Did Muhammaduh cause the disfigurement on your face?'

He spoke in an unsavoury manner, mentioning his opponent, knowing that some African women and men deliberately strip their faces as a sign of their tribal affiliation.

THE CISTERN

Feeling the stupidity of his question, he bowed his head, realising that she may not have understood it. She placed two Kola nuts in his hand, and he pointed to the stripes on her cheeks,

"I don't want any nuts; I want to learn how to create such deep facial markings."

The woman's expression remained impassive as he gestured towards the parallel lines on her cheeks. Frustrated by her lack of understanding, he reached out to touch her cheeks in an attempt to convey his desire to learn the technique. But she responded by slapping him.

He couldn't contain his anger and let it boil over, lashing out and striking the woman. Her plate tumbled from her head, scattering her wares on the ground, while her newborn wailed in the background. Her cries of pain and distress drew a crowd of onlookers. In her distress, she removed the covering from her braided hair and sank down to the ground, covering her head in dirt as she spoke in broken, unintelligible words,

"I am a poor woman."

The men were taken aback by her presence and scolded Ibrahim for his recklessness in harming a woman.

Two men stepped forward and one of them pushed Ibrahim on the shoulder, accusing him of harassing her.

Their assertive tone and readiness for a fight sparked a reaction in Ibrahim, causing him to reach for a deer horn hidden in his pocket, in an attempt to show his peaceful intentions by gently touching her cheek. He explained that he was simply inquiring about how to make facial markings.

Despite his excuse, the men continued to disapprove of his actions and some of them quickly attended to her, providing her with water, collecting her scattered belongings and trying to calm her down.

Ibrahim, motivated and ready to trick them, pulled out his knife and brandished its sharp blade in the faces of the two men who had challenged him. The eldest of them mockingly asked,

"Would you like to finish marking your face?"

While the older man stepped back with a clear gesture of disdain, pointing at the deep wound on Ibrahim's face, he warned,

"You see your wound needs improvement, and I do not guarantee that your next wounds will be the same. I will strip your cheeks of any flesh, leaving nothing but bones."

Despite the escalating altercation between Ibrahim and the two men, the situation was not being ignored by the others and tensions between the involved parties continued to increase. A violent altercation between Ibrahim and two other men was narrowly avoided thanks to the intervention of some onlookers who managed to separate them before any physical harm could be inflicted.

Despite being held back, both Ibrahim and his opponents kept trying to break free from those holding them back in order to reach their opponent.

All eyes were on the woman who stood in the midst of the tension, shouting words that were not immediately understood. However, the arrival of a group of her own people, who came to her defence, surrounded Ibrahim and gave her words the appearance of retaliation.

This inflamed the situation yet further as a crowd formed around Ibrahim, exchanging angry words and grunting loudly. They abandoned any thoughts of forgiveness, handling Ibrahim roughly as they pushed him out of the parking lot and threw him to the ground. They seized his weakening body and rained blows upon him, striking him with fists and feet.

Ibrahim's confidence faltered as he discovered he was unable to defend himself against the onslaught or to retaliate. In a last ditch effort, he tried to provoke them,

"If you are men, let's have a fair, head-to-head fight."

However, this only served to incite them further and whenever he spoke or his body rose in rage under their hands, they beat him harder. His resistance waned, his strength drained away and he was carried off like a beaten and broken man. They flung him into the back of a donkey cart like a rubbish bag, his spirit and defiance completely broken.

Three of them jumped into the back of the cart, telling the driver to wait until the rest arrived. One of them was busy turning Ibrahim's body over, pouring water on his face, so his body convulsed, like a fish caught on rusty hooks and taken out of the sea. Even as Ibrahim continued to shout and groan in pain, he also issued threats, promising to take revenge sooner or later.

One of them leapt into the garbage heap and picked up a large burlap roll.

As they covered Ibrahim's body with the burlap, one of them spat on his face, and a loud voice ordered the driver of the cart to stop until a group who had pledged to pursue Ibrahim's body caught up with them.

The charioteer struggled to prevent his donkey from falling off a cliff as it veered down a steep zigzag curve.

The two men who had started the altercation, along with the woman and her son, soon caught up with the cart. The driver quickly navigated a flat and easy road, using a stick to prod the donkey and increase its speed. The jingling of the cart's bells rose in harmony with its rapid journey through the alleys and streets, weaving in and out of traffic.

As the cart moved down Al-Mansur Street, the aroma of strong flavoured African food filled the air. People were scattered around with some leaping between patches where bread and seeds had been spread out to dry, while others tended to Sudanese peanuts that were being peeled by boys. Women stretched their legs, busy breaking dry bread and pounding it with a huge wooden masher. There were butchers here and there, drying and selling meat. In some corners, groups of boys and women were breaking open pods and extracting their pulp, stacking it next to the doum fruit. Heaps of kola plants were covered with wet burlap sacks to preserve the freshness and lustre of the fruit.

Chapter 12

The loud clanging of bells and the creaking of the cart bore testimony to the weight of the cart attached to the donkey's shoulders. The long-suffering animal had been dawdling and incessantly braying under the crushing weight, which caused it to stumble. Even a sauntering pedestrian easily overtook it.

Ibrahim slowly regained total awareness, aided by the cacophony on Al-Mansur Street and the discomfort to his body lying on a foul-smelling burlap sack.

He wriggled out from underneath the sack and stealthily crawled along the floor of the crowded cart, all the while hoping to remain unnoticed amidst the throngs of people.

He slowly raised his head above the side wall of the wagon to scan his surroundings and try to recover his bearings. After much painful effort, he pinpointed his location by studying the monuments along the street and reading the shop signs. Knowing where he was helped to steady him, as he was familiar with the area and often received invitations to play his flute in the Al-Hafayer neighbourhood. However, this moment was short-lived.

The cart came to a stop and it appeared his stealthy movements had not gone unnoticed. A man bent down and bound his body tightly. Ibrahim felt the weight of his assailant as he was being tied with a rope that pulled his shoulders and forearms backwards. Near complete immobility was achieved when his feet were shackled.

He caught a glimpse of one of his attackers deep in conversation with someone he couldn't see and guessed there were more than three of them. Unable to do anything he tried to listen in on their conversation. Even that presented its own difficulties since they were speaking in a language he couldn't understand. He guessed it could be either Hausa or Burmese.

One of them reached over and covered his head, growling out a long sentence. Ibrahim lost track of where they were taking him.

His hatred for Muhammaduh grew stronger as he imagined all the ways he could get revenge for the pain and humiliation he had suffered. Killing Muhammaduh was a given and he considered following that up by mutilating the body. The thought was no sooner considered than rejected because it disgusted him despite his totally helpless state. He banished examination of his predicament and wondered where they were taking him.

Regretting not having used his blade during the chaotic stampede, he made a bold decision to escape his captors. He aimed to catch them off guard by leaping out of the cart, hoping to either incapacitate himself or attract enough attention to seek help and break free from his dire situation.

Though he was reluctant to rely on others for help, fearing the judgment of his community. He knew he needed to assess his oppressors and to devise a plan for self-defence.

He resolved to fight back instead of being led around like a helpless prisoner.

Details of any escape plan were still circulating in his brain when the cart came to a halt and his captors pulled him out roughly and threw him onto the ground. A short, sharp cry of pain escaped his lips as he landed on his shoulder.

Chapter 13

The chill of the night accentuated his isolation. The tall, withered trees that stood like sentinels, reaching towards the sky, added to the barrenness of the place.

Still unable to move or resist, his eyes roamed across a wide courtyard thinly populated by people of all ages. On the sides, crude rooms made of flint had been built from stones stacked haphazardly without cement or paint to hide their roughness or conceal their darkness. At the back, two rooms had been erected on wooden pillars and covered with zinc, where people were playing dominoes, surrounded by a group of people who helped in determining the rules of the game.

The chatter and cries of the people high up were abruptly cut short by the imperious voice of an old man approaching them. Meanwhile, some women started lighting lanterns, whose soft glow soon illuminated the distant corners of the courtyard and cast long shadows that seemed to come alive, creeping and whispering as if a giant had risen from beneath the earth and was now indulging in a grand feast.

As the shadows thickened, they seemed to gather like a pack of wolves, closing in on Ibrahim as he stood on a rugged surface littered with fragments of hardened cement.

Suddenly, from the depths of the back box, a figure emerged, carrying a lantern that cast a bright glow, banishing the shadows and illuminating the darkness of the night. The light was focused on an old man who stood tall, his gaze fixed intently on another, whom he dwarfed. By comparison, the smaller man looked insignificant, yet at the same time like a cowering wild dog.

Ibrahim's biggest attacker brutally crushed his neck with his foot, causing him to writhe in agony. Despite the pain, Ibrahim found the strength to lash out with the only weapon at his disposal – his defiant mouth. Ibrahim spat out a stream of haughty insults, which prompted his jailer to lift his foot off his neck. This brutal act occurred right before the eyes of the old man, who seemed to take a twisted pleasure in the violence. Instead of intervening, he welcomed the perpetrator's actions, nodding his head in approval. They exchanged a few hushed words, the meaning of which was unclear, but the conversation was punctuated by a flick of the old man's fingers. The perpetrator, responding to the signal, nodded and stepped back, allowing Ibrahim to lay there, gasping for air, as the old man gave the next instruction,

"Go ahead, Eve."

In a matter of moments the Hajji appeared. She untied the fabric from her shoulder giving her child to a woman next to her.

She was staring hard at Ibrahim, whose clothes and skin were a maze of cuts. Her face showed a mixture of satisfaction and a burning desire for revenge.

She approached the old man, clearly looking for his order. He handed her a razor, which she placed between her pearly white teeth. He didn't say a word.

With burning eyes, she advanced towards Ibrahim, her eye blaze with evil intent. His sense of impending pain was heightened by the crowd's murmurs of approval anticipating Hajji's next move.

The crowd began to encircle Ibrahim, clawing at the earth and crawling forward from all sides. They formed a tight ring around him and the woman.

In a cruel display of degradation, each person present took part in spitting on his face and allowing their children to urinate on him. The scene was a visceral act of humiliation and degradation.

As everyone stepped back, they formed a circle once more with everyone applauding the coming spectacle. Two young men stepped forward, seizing Ibrahim's body and placing him on a chair with a loose base. They re-bound him with ties.

To Ibrahim this signalled a form of collective torture and punishment he had never witnessed or heard of.

He thought about repeating his stream of insults but the anger and extreme cruelty he perceived in the eyes of those around him made him change his mind. He felt his best hope was to try to communicate with the old man.

He attempted to catch the old man's gaze but his preoccupation with finishing his task made him cut short this opening stage. With a desperate plea in his voice, Ibrahim asked, 'What have I done to deserve this?"

The crowd fell silent with all eyes fixed on their elderly leader as he walked towards Ibrahim carrying a branding iron. After planting this instrument of potential pain on his captive's head, he turned to face the assembled people. He spoke to them in staccato, harsh words, causing the throats of the audience to meld into a mysterious grumble, which ended with the old man brandishing a pair of scissors with which he cut Ibrahim's forelock hair, And with a gesture to everyone, he walked away.

The air was filled with the sound of cheers and shouts

as a flurry of dirt and dust rained down from all sides, illuminated by the flickering light of the lanterns. The grains of dirt suspended in the air looked like a warrior's army engaged in a fierce battle, brought to an end by a young boy seated on the ground, with a jug of water in his hands which he mixed with dirt and herbs to form dough. He kneaded it skillfully and handed it to the Hajji, who then took the razor from between her teeth, swallowed the dough slowly, and muttered some words that had the crowd shouting back.

The crowd gathered around her as she moved closer to Ibrahim, who was held down by a muscled man with the well-developed physique of a bodyguard. Her steady hand plunged the razor towards his body, moving from his forehead to his chin, six times, dividing them equally on both of his cheeks. Ibrahim unleashed a cry of unimaginable pain.

He writhed in agony as the audience watched, their cries of joy and ecstasy growing louder with each onslaught. He soon lapsed into unconsciousness, his life no longer in his own hands. In a flurry of activity, the crowd placed him in the cart, hurrying away from the courtyard. Eventually, they reached their destination, carelessly tossing Ibrahim to the side of the road before making a hasty escape.

****

Ibrahim did not know how much blood he had lost or how long he had been unconscious. As the sun's searing rays began to wake him, he tried to shield himself from the world, covering his eyes to fend off the sun's intrusive spotlight on his mangled body. Meanwhile Ibrahim continued to soak in his own blood.

THE CISTERN

People were stunned as they viewed the horrific mess on the ground. Suspicion and fear filled the air, as whispers urged them to move away from the pitiful creature, to be disposed of in a confined space as soon as possible.

Once the sun had its fill of baking Ibrahim's body, he stumbled to his feet, desperately trying to wipe the blood from his face.

He could not bring himself to touch the wounds that still oozed and his dishevelled and disgusting appearance served only to fuel the fear and suspicion of those around him.

Passers-by averted their eyes, fearful that they would be accused of causing his injuries.

One, however, was filled with compassion and hastily called out to him,

'There is a well at the end of the street," before scurrying away, afraid of being implicated in his plight.

Ibrahim forced himself to stand, leaning on walls, lampposts, cars and trees for support, until he stumbled on a jar of water.

He removed the lid, plunged his head into the jar and groaned as the icy water washed away the clotted blood from his face and hands. He lay down on the ground, examining the rest of his body, wincing from his ubiquitous pains...

Eventually, he pieced together his whereabouts and realised he was on the outskirts of the Al-Tantabawi neighbourhood.

Chapter 14

Ibrahim felt as if he had been plucked like a torn thread from a sewing machine's bobbin, and crudely cut loose. This left him feeling torn and discarded. Cast aside into the desolate hollow of Al-Tantabawi, he stumbled to his feet, covered in his own blood, feeling dizzy and with a concussion that made it difficult to maintain his balance. The longer he stood, the more his vision became clouded. He sought refuge in the walls, trying to avoid the attention of passers-by who could not fail to see his shaky movements and the loss of focus in his eyes. Though his miserable appearance attracted their curiosity and concern, he avoided walking on the main Al-Mansur Street. With far fewer witnesses around, he made his way towards the inner streets, looking for a change of clothes to replace his bloody rags. With blood still oozing from the razor slashes on his face it was impossible to clean the wounds. Eventually, he staggered to a space among some modest houses, whose roofs were lined with wooden and zinc crates for breeding pigeons. The human occupants were busy hanging clothes and quilts to dry on the edges of walls that had lost their colour, but were now adorned with the bright colours of African clothes.

He yearned for one of those robes to fall over him, so he could hide his hideously disfigured body. Ibrahim's stumbling movements magnified the savagery inflicted on him and no matter which direction he chose his steps faltered. He knew that seeking out his family's lawyer in his current state would lead only to ridicule and disdain. Trying to seek help from someone as devoid of emotion as a piece of charcoal was a lost cause.

He forced himself to go to the police station to report the incident, but every time he headed for the station he retreated, embarrassed to turn even to the police for assistance.

He was inspired to struggle on thanks to an overwhelming desire to seek revenge on Muhammaduh and the woman who had humiliated him by disfiguring his face. It was almost solely with this intention in mind that he pushed himself to wander the streets in search of their faces and whereabouts.

His confusion led him to the winding streets of the neighbourhood, and he mingled with groups of people, hoping to be guided to the open area where his reputation and his appearance had both been irreparably scarred, or to catch a glimpse of one of the faces that had taunted him the night before as he had been subjected to extremities of violence by a woman who had lost all sense of humanity and decency.

As he was making his way through narrow passageways, he stumbled upon a wet cupping market.

The customers sat on wooden benches, each in front of a cupping therapist and a large table, on which were placed cups made from the hollowed horns of deer and goats.

The cups had a small opening at the bottom which was inserted into the person's skin, and another larger one at the top which was used to suction out contaminated blood. Next to the table were glasses with broad bottoms and narrow tops, designed to allow the contaminated blood to be sucked out of the horn.

Scattered around were razors, threadbare towels and spools of discoloured cotton.

The area as a whole was a disorderly scene with lots of rushing around, intrusive languages and a variety of faces where everyone seemed to be in a hurry. The air was filled with the sounds of lost animals, panting dogs, playing children, and women gathered together to sell their wares.

Crows flew by, with dust hanging in the air. Amid all this, the cupping practitioners were the only ones who seemed to be organised. Each practitioner was focused solely on the customer, as if they were on guard, fearful that the contaminated blood would disappear.

Cupping practitioners are often seen focused on their clients who have become like old toys that have been neglected and left to rust, in need of some scraping to reveal their true condition.

The frequent gusts of wind scatter piles of hair which then fly around the area. The customers clearly have great trust in the barbers, who stand behind them and skillfully shave hair from the cupping sites, closely following instructions provided by the practitioner.

After the hair is removed, the head is shaved with precision, akin to gently gliding a razor over the delicate skin of a newborn. If any bleeding happens, the practitioner intervenes to finish the shave and properly position the cup on the scalp. The cupping process involves placing the client in a precise position, with the head close to the practitioner's arms, to ensure the cup can be securely attached. The cup then draws out impurities in the blood, which is collected in the glass cups. This process is repeated as necessary until the client feels satisfied. At the end of the treatment, the practitioner wipes the client's head with a soft cotton cloth and encourages them to drink tomato juice to replenish their fluids.

Ibrahim was observing the scene with eyes weary from wiping away the blood streaming down his face, making it difficult for him to see clearly.

He paid little attention to his steps, which had disturbed the crowds attempting to catch the blood-soaked particles, crushing the thick hair that lay scattered on the ground, stained with cloudy blood and littered with cleaning cloths and discarded cups. Amid the chaos, people were shouting and speaking in different languages, and young boys were running around selling cheap perfume for people to cleanse their wounds.

Ibrahim looked like someone had made a mistake while shaving his head, leaving him with injuries all over his face. Anyone who tried to console him was met with a dismissive, stuttering response, "It's not your business."

He had no desire to speak with anyone and all he could think about was obtaining some new, clean clothes. One of the practitioners approached him, "If you tell the sheikh of the practitioners, he will offer you justice."

Ibrahim received the suggestion with apparent indifference, When the practitioner saw his reaction, he handed a roll of yellowed cotton to one of his assistants and ordered him to clean the wounds.

The boy was eager to perform his task and asked Ibrahim to sit on a wobbly wooden chair. Ibrahim delivered a sharp rebuke.

The boy's quarrelsome attitude inspired Ibrahim to think of a solution,

"I'm going to clean the wounds myself. I want you to

arrange a clean gown," he told the boy.

The boy was slow to react but when Ibrahim pointed him towards the clothes drying on the roofs, his teeth shone with a sudden smile and he dashed off on his little feet into the cramped side streets of the market, vanishing down a curved alley.

Ibrahim sat in a quiet corner of the cupping market, leaning against a wall to conceal his blood-covered figure from the passers-by.

He dipped a piece of cotton, given to him by a young boy, into a nearby puddle of muddy water left over from cupping bowls. He gently cleaned the blood from his neck and chest, his mind still consumed with anger and thoughts of revenge.

He couldn't shake off the image of "Eve" the Hajji, who had mutilated his face the previous night. "Eve" was the name the old man had muttered as he handed her the razor to mutilate his face. He repeated the name over and over, "Eve... Eve..."

Ibrahim muttered the name over and over as he cleaned himself, feeling a deep sense of hatred towards her and anyone related to Muhammaduh.

The only solution he could think of was seeking revenge, not by disfiguring someone's face, but by taking their life. He was deep in thought when a practitioner approached him, offering him bread and a plate of meat,

"You cannot think on an empty stomach," the man told Ibrahim as he handed him the food.

Ibrahim felt a wave of gratitude wash over him as he eagerly accepted the meal. His stomach had been empty for too long and he quickly began to eat. As he ate, the young boy approached him and gave him a brightly coloured shirt.

THE CISTERN

The young boy's grin was full of mischief and his eyes sparkled with playfulness as he negotiated with Ibrahim for a small sum of money in exchange for the shirt. Though he was evasive when it came to negotiating for additional funds.

His smile was unwavering as Ibrahim extended his hand to give him his watch as a symbol of gratitude. Having completed his task, the boy happily accepted the watch and ran off to continue his other money-earning activities.

As Ibrahim changed into the shirt, instead of feeling refreshed he felt an overwhelming sense of disgust and distaste. The shirt was ill-fitting and smelled of wine, evoking feelings of pity and sadness in addition to the pain from his facial wounds. Ibrahim quickly made his way back to the city of Jeddah, eager to rid himself of the garment and the emotions it had stirred up.

Chapter 15

He reached Jeddah in the afternoon, carefully concealing his facial features with a stolen scarf and using narrow alleys to reach his home without passing through any busy areas or encountering any of his friends. But as he approached his home, he was surprised to find Omar Al-Aridity sitting in an electricity booth facing the house. He hesitated for a moment before hastening his steps to reach the side door, only to be confronted by the sight of a dead donkey in a secluded corner by the gate, covered in tar, with black handprints on the walls of the house. As he searched for the lost key to the gate, he heard Omar Al-Yaridi shouting at him,

"Don't sleep at home tonight."

He quickly pushed the door open with his foot and stormed inside, eager to find out the meaning of Al-Aridity's warning.

Omaima sat by the window, consumed by the panic that had gripped her since the previous night. She found no solace from her fear except to cling to the shutters and scan the streets for any sign of her brother. She saw Omar sitting in the booth across the street, and the faces of the passers-by in front of their house. She jumped up as soon as she saw her brother, her face contorted in shock and grief,

"What happened to you?"

Ibrahim felt a pang of guilt as he saw the fear and concern etched on his sister's face.

He realised he should have taken more care to conceal his wounds and cover them with the scarf. He turned away from her, ashamed his appearance had caused her distress. Omaima let out a loud gasp as she saw the extent of his injuries,

"What happened?" she asked him

His silence did not alleviate Omaima's concern, as she continued to fix her gaze on his face, biting her lips and pressing her hands to her cheeks,

"For God's sake, tell me what happened to you?"

He loathed his weakness and her fear, he shouted at her to go back inside. She retreated, crying, and he lay on his bed, stifling a groan, worried it would reach Omaima's ears. He couldn't find a way to ease his distress, but sometimes he imagined getting revenge on Muhammaduh and "Eve". He couldn't shake off the feelings that weighed on him.

Omaima, however, was kind to him. She returned with a tray filled with salty water mixed with pungent herbs, towels, and several small vials filled with liquids of different colours. She insisted on cleaning his wounds despite his reluctance and his rage.

She knew he was acting like a child, throwing a tantrum, but she didn't care. Despite his verbal abuse, she gently pulled him by the hand, making him sit. He groaned loudly as he surrendered to her tenderness and lay down. Seeing his wounds frightened her. She bent down to kiss his head and quietly cried. He patted her elbow, trying to hold back his own tears. She comforted him, telling him that his wounds were clean and she brought him maamoul, a cup of tea and Turkish sweets. She then left him, overwhelmed with love and concern for him.

The sun dipped below the horizon; shadows filled the

room through the holes in the window. The house was plunged into darkness as the internal lights flickered and failed. His wounds burned like fire, causing him intense pain. He retreated to his bed, lost in a mire of regrets and fantasies. The most troubling image that haunted him was that of his father, wriggling and slipping away like a fish that had escaped capture,

"I am certain that my family's legacy will be tarnished by your actions."

Chapter 16

When Abdul Ghafour Ashour became furious in prison and vented his anger towards his son, accusing him of falling short and bringing dishonour to the family,

"I am certain that my family's legacy will be tarnished by your actions."

He was not being honest. The truth was that it was not his son but he who had brought about the downfall of the family's reputation through his divisive actions, squandering of wealth and eventual incarceration.

Rumours swirled that it was due to political betrayals and treachery on the part of his father or that it was massive embezzlement of wealthy emirs through deceitful means, posing as a legal representative.

El-Baggio, known as Khairy Ashour, had serious doubts about the moral character of his son, Abdul Ghafour. He exhibited traits of anger, cruelty and deceit in his behaviour, and held a negative outlook towards those in his surroundings. He feared that his son's repulsive qualities would ruin the family's reputation and fortune, so he kept his wealth and property deeds hidden from Abdul Ghafour, whom he considered lazy and predicted would bring about a bleak future for the family. Unfortunately, his predictions proved to be true as Abdul Ghafour's actions ultimately led to the downfall of the family.

As his father, Khairy Ashour, grew older, he became increasingly disenchanted with Abdul Ghafour's behaviour and kept him at arm's length when it came to important matters. He saw evidence of deceit and negative attitudes in his son's actions, particularly as he advanced in social circles. Khairy Ashour kept his own actions and decision-making secretive, often assigning menial tasks to his son when VTP guests came to visit, preferring to entrust important matters to people outside the family. Despite this, Khairy Ashour was hopeful of his three grandchildren and held high expectations that they would be more virtuous and responsible than their father. Ibrahim, Omaima, and Jumana were the last three branches on the tree of a powerful and influential family. They were seen as shining examples of the family's strength and influence.

These branches grew to maturity later in their grandfather's life, not knowing that they were from a tree whose roots had been transplanted from the far reaches of Italy. That came about as a result of a double marriage between their branches and Spanish blood, whose lineage can be traced back to Seville. Their heritage was further enriched by the mixture of the two bloodlines in their grandfather Rivera El-Baggio. He had fallen in love with a Muslim woman and as a result both Islam and his wife's heart had entered his own. He changed his name to Ashour, though it was said that he did not convert, but simply wanted to write about Mecca.

During a sudden political incident, Ashour and his family made a pilgrimage to Mecca, which revealed his abilities. As a result, his government appointed him as one of the first Italian diplomats to Jeddah. There, he worked on establishing his son Khairy, who inherited all his experience and scientific knowledge.

Khairy's intellectual assets were enhanced by the knowledge

and experience gained through his travels. His father recognized his potential and worked to nurture his ambition to attain a position of power.

From the onset of his journey, he emulated his father's footsteps, engaging in various financial and political dealings and forming alliances through strategic marriages.

However, he swiftly shed these encumbrances by joining the government of Ibn Saud, feeling proud of his father for renouncing infidelity and finding solace in the sacred mosque of Mecca.

Khairy's goal was to amplify the reach and impact of his father's written work, in a book about Mecca "The Ancient House, A Close Vision" which was translated into Arabic, English and Italian.

Ashour brought a new Arab identity into the family following Riviera El-Baggio's embrace of Islam and the adoption of a unique Arab name in place of his previous Italian one.

He married an Arab woman who belonged to the coastal tribes, despite her Turkish heritage.

He met her father at the palace of Sharif Hussain bin Ali, though the details of this encounter are sketchy. Ashour built a palace outside the walls of Jeddah and invited his European and Arab relatives to visit. He also had alliances with various ethnic groups.

He constructed an opulent palace, known as "El-Baggio", after his family name, with the proviso that if it ever fell and lost its history, it would be associated with the name of Ashour. That in turn came from a family that had become estranged from its Western heritage, and vanished in the city of Jeddah, with the escape of Khairy Ashour.

Chapter 17

The residents of the neighbourhood were at a loss to explain Khairy Ashour's sudden disappearance, despite the many rumours that circulated after the decline and departure of many family members and the magnificent palace falling into ruins.

It was never imagined that the palace would sink into such a state of disrepair.

Once a symbol of prestige for both the dignitaries of Jeddah and visitors to the country, the palace had begun its decline after a mysterious event one night when a masked figure approached its gates.

****

Khairy Ashour's network of contacts had grown to such an extent that he was no longer able to control or even know all the members of his secret group. This came about as some of his associates began to align themselves with individuals unknown to him, shifting the power dynamics and leaving him blind-sided by their actions and agreements.

During the Hajj of 1935, Khairy Ashour was receiving some of his associates who were stationed in various Arab countries. He set up a camp equipped with mattresses, blankets and everything they might need. Renowned chefs were put in charge of food and drink and many pilgrims sought him out, sharing their plans and hoping for his financial support. The Egyptian delegate was particularly eager to renew their alliance, detailing the group's numerous activities and reasons for requesting his financial contribution.

As the pilgrimage was coming to a close, Khairy Ashour instructed his staff to prepare for the return of the pilgrims from the holy sites, unaware that his own time in Jeddah was nearing its end.

It was a chaotic evening when a masked individual persistently knocked on the main gate of the palace, refusing to leave until he could speak with Khairy Ashour. As soon as Khairy appeared, he was forcibly marched into a side room near the front of the palace. Khairy was horrified when he learnt of the news that would be attributed to him if a thorough investigation were to take place.

Khairy Ashour felt a sense of finality as he touched his neck, listening intently as the mysterious, masked visitor before him whispered details of a shocking event.

He was relaying information about an event reported from nearby places, leaving fear and suspicion in the mind of everyone who heard it. The visitor kept his voice low, describing an attempted assassination of an imam while he was performing the circumambulation of the ifaada by a young Yemeni man who was waiting at "Hijr Ismail". The young man had come out brandishing his dagger, attempting to kill the imam, but in a decisive moment, fate intervened and Prince Saud stepped in to protect his father, throwing himself in front of the dagger and receiving a deep stab wound in his left shoulder.

The guards had unfortunately been forced to take action, resulting in the death of two young men who had approached from the direction of Al-Multazam and the Well of Zamzam, both wielding daggers and threatening to continue their attack.

The news brought with it dire consequences, and out of fear and uncertainty, Khairy summoned his son Abdul Ghafour and spoke to him with bitterness and regret, lamenting his own perceived shortcomings,

'I understand that you may not fully grasp the gravity of the situation but I am entrusting to you significant resources to safeguard our family's reputation and ensure the continuation of its legacy."

Abdul Ghafour stood up, not fully understanding his father's words. His father, Khairy, had changed his mind,

"Given your lack of ambition, I will not reveal the location of the gold plates, which will secure the wealth of my descendants for generations to come."

Abdul Ghafour remained seated on a couch in the middle of the room, as Khairy walked over to a box filled with papers, official documents and property deeds.

"Look after our properties and put them in your name and the name of my grandchildren," Khairy instructed. The next morning, Khairy set sail on an Italian ship, leaving the city of Jeddah behind as he watched the waves of the divine beach recede into the distance.

Chapter 18

The descendants of Khairy Ashour, though not mindful of the grandeur and opulence of their family's past, retained faint memories of childhood spent in a home teeming with aunts, cousins, uncles and relatives of varying degrees of closeness in the complex web of familial ties. They recollected, albeit indistinctly, the constant stream of visitors that flowed in and out of their home without objection or reservation, and the attentive and lavish service provided by a multitude of slaves and servants in the palace.

The grand palace of Khairy Ashour, once a symbol of opulence and power, now stands in ruins. Local residents refer to it as simply the "House of Ashour" as opposed to its former grandiose name, "El-Baggio Palace". Rumours persist that Khairy had hidden a vast treasure trove, including gold plates, somewhere within its walls, leaving behind a will for his descendants that detailed its whereabouts. Some say that the gold plates were stolen by Khairy himself from the Italian consulate, where they were meant to be given as help to the Saudi state. Despite the speculation, the true fate of the Ashour family treasure remains a mystery.

The people of the neighbourhood were certain of the existence of treasure in the Ashour family's palace, as rumours had circulated for years about gold plates being hidden there. These rumours were fuelled by the occasional leak of gold coins during heavy rain, as the water would wash them out of their hiding place and scatter them in the areas where it stagnated. When it rained, it became a tradition for the locals to gather around the Ashour house, waiting for the torrents to subside, and then scouring the backyards of the palace for any coins that may have washed up. This served as further confirmation of the validity of the hidden treasure rumour.

****

Abdul Ghafour Ashour took swift action to cut the family's expenses following his father's departure. He began by turning away guests, dismissing servants, and selling slaves. He also imposed strict rules on the remaining residents of the palace, requiring they step in to do the tasks of those who'd gone. The women of the household were particularly outraged by these changes, as they felt their dignity was being compromised by being forced to perform tasks traditionally reserved for men. Abdul Ghafour also sold off family possessions, such as clothes, jewellery and shoes, further diminishing the women's status in the community. When they protested, he went even further by exiling cousins and aunts, along with their children, to their home towns.

Before exiling his relatives, Abdul Ghafour Ashour had been scheming to hide the wealth that would come to him, away from the gaze of his family to prevent them from claiming it, not as a matter of inheritance or rightful claim, but out of pure envy. He believed that having a large number of relatives was like nurturing scorpions within one's own clothing,

He presented himself as concerned for their welfare, and claimed that his father had built palaces for each family member in their home countries, and that he recommended the women of the family to travel so they wouldn't die in a land devoid of oak, chestnut and willow trees.

He tempted them with the promise of leaving and enjoying the gardens of their palaces, which overlooked the Mediterranean Sea and brimming with all kinds of fruits. He also swore that his father had deposited a generous sum in European banks for each of them. To add to the incentive, he claimed that the evacuation of the servants from the main palace was a race against time, so they could decorate their rooms with luxury furniture.

He filled the minds of his relatives, with dreams, particularly the women, as he believed that women were simply magnets to attract men.

And with an idea inspired by fear, similar to that of his father, which prompted him to leave suddenly, he gathered the members of his large family and warned them,

"You don't realise the dangers that threaten our family..."

Pausing to search for a logical explanation as to why they couldn't feel safe in their own home, he ominously added,

"You do not know the secret of my father's departure, and therefore I tell you, Leave before your heads and tongues are cut off."

This ill-advised statement would prove to be, in the near future, a booby-trap he had set for himself and his children.

He came to an agreement with his family members to leave everything behind and depart. He gathered them all, boarded them on a ship and explained that it was similar to Noah's ark, which would take them to Alexandria, and from there they would fly to the land of their ancestors, which would be a paradise for his family (the great El-Baggio).

He told his family that his father had made arrangements for the transfer of their wealth to a new location, where they could use it to sustain themselves comfortably, instead of remaining in a place he deemed as unproductive, he then reassured them saying,

"My family and I will join you as soon as I finish deporting you."

As the palace emptied, he waited eagerly for the promised influx of wealth that never materialised.

In a desperate search for answers, he scoured his father's documents in his search for the location of the gold plates. His insatiable appetite for wealth clouded his judgement, leading him to liquidate all of his assets, including furniture, paintings, dishes, gilded utensils, and even selling slaves. With the proceeds, he established a weapons manufacturing company, but soon realised the grave error of his plans as he found himself at odds with the state's legal system.

His misfortune enabled him to reach agreements that were detrimental to the country's security, which were hidden in boxes full of papers. He was unaware of the content of these security agreements, so he presented them with some deeds in order to get compensation for real estate that was within the expansion plan for the Grand Mosque in Mecca.

Chapter 19

As the evening prayer came to an end, the worshippers dispersed, while women and children stayed in their homes with radios tuned to the station broadcasting the Qur'an. The melodious sound emanating from the radios in every house created a unified harmony that echoed throughout the neighbourhood, where residents were holding a peaceful sit-in led by Sheikh Abdullah Khayat reciting Surat Al-Naml. The sound grew louder like a rumbling river flowing through a dark night. Suddenly, a commotion started to rise from the crossroads of the neighbourhood and the usually quiet streets became agitated as groups of people emerged, heading towards Ashour Palace like a disordered rabble.

Ibrahim was struggling to find words to reassure Omaima, who stood at the door of his room in a state of panic.

"What's happening outside our house?" she asked.

****

Night had descended upon the city of Jeddah, the exhausted sun having set, reluctantly bearing witness to the events that were to unfold,

"This is the night," Ibrahim said, his voice heavy with dread.

These words had been on everyone's lips since the daybreak, eager to uncover the truth of what was going on. Though many were unsure of the exact outcome, a sense of unfulfilled desire occupied their hearts, and some suggested renewing their efforts to defeat the Jinn of the Ashour household.

The community had been discussing the idea of raiding Ashour's palace for some time but it wasn't until a series of dog attacks on local children and the disappearance of Umm Al-Hassan that it gained widespread support.

Though the origins of the idea were unclear, it quickly spread through the neighbourhood. However, there was little in the way of a detailed plan, with participants simply agreeing it was time to take action.

It had been several days since the gruesome discovery of the third mutilated corpse, and despite the efforts of the mayor and his team, no progress had been made in identifying the perpetrator. However, a group of determined individuals were unwilling to let the matter rest and continued to investigate the circumstances surrounding the deaths.

The mayor had initially shown great enthusiasm in solving the case of the mutilated corpses but, as time passed, he began to neglect his duty and excuse himself by stating that none of the residents had claimed the bodies as their own.

He expressed his anger to his assistants, citing pregnant women in the neighbourhood as the cause for the men's persistent demands to solve the murders.

He spoke impulsively and for a moment became suspicious of those sitting on his council. He became very conscious of the effect any rash or injudicious words could have.

He reined in his anger, reminding himself not to let it control him.

What he stated echoed the fears of the mothers, who were

worried for their newborns. They constantly moved them from place to place, to ensure their safety, following the advice of elderly women who warned against leaving the infants unattended, as they feared a Jinn would come and silence their cries. This resulted in a surge of complaints from new mothers who struggled to get restful sleep or find relaxation, as they were constantly preoccupied with their babies' well-being.

The mayor was determined to protect the residents of his neighbourhood and was eager to take action. However, despite this, the residents were disappointed by the mayor's distinct sloth in that direction as well as the lack of information they were receiving from him. When news of Umm Al-Hassan's disappearance in the vicinity of Ashour's house spread, the neighbourhood became a buzz with rumours. Many residents went to the mayor's house and office seeking answers and to find out what action he had taken, if any.

A sense of anger and unease began to spread throughout the northernmost parts of the neighbourhood as a group of people close to Umm Al-Hassan set out to search for her. They eventually came across Omar Al-Aridity, who informed them that she had been spotted heading towards the abandoned ruins behind Ashour's house and had not been seen since.

The search of the ruins proved fruitless, and when Umm Al-Hassan's brother, Mubarak, approached the mayor for answers about his sister's disappearance, the mayor displayed a shocking lack of concern, empathy and moral decency suggesting she may have left with a lover.

The mayor quickly realised the magnitude of his mistake as he saw Mubarak's confused and bulging eyes. His companions, who could sense the anger brewing within him, quickly intervened to stop him from acting on his intentions, made clear by the clenched fist and sudden forward rush towards the mayor's throat.

The mayor stumbled over his words, desperately trying to correct his clumsy faux pas but the damage was already done. The reaction on the faces of Mubarak and the others made it clear his words had been deeply offensive. But for the quick thinking of his assistant Al-Kuraishi, who stepped in to try to smooth over the situation, it could have become even more heated.

He claimed the mayor had been referring to another woman who had gone missing prior to Umm Al-Hassan's disappearance and whose family had also reported her missing, following a family dispute with the man who had come to propose to her.

Mubarak appeared to accept the flimsy excuse in an effort to save face.

Despite the mayor's attempts at damage control, the air in the room remained tense and hostile.

Mubarak looked upset but the mayor approached him, kissed his head and promised Umm Al-Hassan would be back home before the end of the night,

"Don't worry, I have a plan to root out whoever is causing problems in our community," he said.

The mayor's promises had gone unmet before and the rumours circulating in the neighbourhood had begun to tarnish his reputation. He was feeling the pressure of the community, who had grown increasingly dissatisfied with his lack of action. Desperate to find a solution, he began to look for any way at all to resolve the situation.

THE CISTERN

On a scorching afternoon, the signal for a fierce battle against the Jinn inhabiting Ashour's house was given. Omar Al-Yaridi sounded the alarm by walking shirtless and dragging a donkey's corpse behind him. Flies swarmed around the animal's rotting flesh, and the stench of it offended the nostrils of those who followed his lead as he repeated,

"Let's use this donkey as a lure and strike down the Jinn just as "Banu Sahm" did back in the day." Though his plan introduced even more confusion, the crowd rallied behind him, their voices repeating his call to action,

"Let's eliminate them like "Banu Sahm" did back in the day."

They completed the first ritual by pouring melted tar over the back and legs of the donkey's carcass and followed Al-Aridity's instructions by dipping their hands in the tar and leaving their marks on the walls of Ashour's house, both front and back.

Some criticized the decision to entrust the task of signalling the battle to Omar Al-Yaridi, as they deemed him to be deranged but these objections were silenced,

"If you want to protect the people of the neighbourhood from the wrath of the Jinn, then Omar Al-Yaridi is the best person for the job."

On the night in question, Ibrahim Ashour was away from his home. Khalil al-Fal had prohibited the neighbourhood leaders from entering Ashour's house without informing him first. However, Al-Aridity took it upon himself to inform him. Just as Ibrahim was approaching the outer gate of his home, Al-Aridity emerged from hiding and shouted,

"Don't sleep at home tonight."

The tension was palpable as the promised night approached, with many harbouring fears of the potential harm that could be inflicted on them.

Some tried to push these concerns aside but others voiced their anxieties aloud, questioning,

"What if the Jinn seek revenge by attacking us while we wait outside Ashour's house or, worse, by entering our homes and harming our women and children?"

These fears almost caused many to back out of the plan, but Musa Falafel came up with a solution to ease these worries.

"Let's place a reciter of the Quran in every house, so the Jinn will not be able to approach them," he said.

The plan to have reciters stationed at the gates of houses to protect against Jinn during the march to Ashour's house was hindered by a lack of available reciters. In a frantic search for a solution, Saeed Al-Malabi proposed the idea of having Qur'an radio playing in every home as a substitute.

As they approached their task, the gravity of what they were about to do became more evident. They watched as the mayor dismounted from his mule, entrusting its care to a young boy who ran ahead of him. He halted at the gate of the mosque and, after performing his prayer, delivered a short sermon emphasising the importance of their mission that night.

Despite his best efforts, the detective's failure to solve the brutal murders of several newborns led to a significant loss of credibility and respect within the community. The perpetrator's ability to evade capture and continue these heinous actions without consequence drew intense criticism towards the detective, with many blaming him for the tragedy and the disposal of the bodies in the trash..

The mayor furrowed his brow, expressing his agreement to the idea of raiding the suspected location of the Jinn, following the declaration made by the family of Umm al-Hassan that their daughter had been kidnapped from there.

THE CISTERN

As the evening prayer came to a close, the neighbourhood was enveloped in a thick, darkness orchestrated by a mysterious force. The true nature of this force was only revealed through the raid on Ashour's house.

It was a meticulously orchestrated plan, whose origins remained a mystery. The commands were carried out with precision and efficiency, as the attack began with a frenzied chorus being shouted by the boys through the narrow alleys.

As they made their way through the city, the clang of metal sheets and cans, coupled with the steady thumping of a hound rod, echoed in their ears. The lamps they passed flickered brighter, illuminating their path to the Cistern hill, where their plan was set to unfold. The ruckus they created was loud and chaotic, heightening the sense of urgency and excitement.

Al-Malabi was not impressed by loud songs, but found solace in the recitation of Sheikh Abdullah Khayat, whose voice carried the words of the Most Merciful in a calm and peaceful manner.

Al-Malabi's disapproval became insignificant and meaningless amidst the overlapping revolution of boisterous voices, the enthusiasm expressed through the movement of feet, and the insistence on standing firm, regardless of the situation,

The men of the neighbourhood came out in full force, each with a light source in hand, to guide their way; a lantern, torch or flash-light. They were armed with sticks, machetes and knives, touching each other and reciting the names of their fellow marchers, to ensure that no one was taken by the Jinn without their knowledge. After the march, they would verify that all participants had returned safely by checking the names.

The crowd had expected the mayor to give them guidance but

they soon realised their assumption was wrong when the mayor lowered his head. His face appeared tired and worn under the light of the lantern held by one of his aides as he spoke,

"I have said my piece, now it is time to hear from someone more knowledgeable in this matter."

To everyone's surprise, Omar Al-Yaridi joined the discussion, speaking in disjointed phrases for around thirty minutes. On piecing together his words, it became clear that the expansion of Ashour's house, coupled with the neglect of its outbuildings and the collapse of its roofs and structures, had resulted in these outbuildings becoming ruins and a popular residence for Jinn who had broken their covenant not to inhabit living quarters.

They relished in residing in the neglected ruins of the palace and believed that ignoring them was a sign of weakness. As a result, they launched attacks on the neighbourhood, murdered infants and dared to abduct women. Al-Aridity's words were disjointed and difficult to understand but they came together with force when he yelled out to the crowd,

"Would it make you happy to have your women kidnapped?"

They developed resolve from an accusation that totally impugned their honour. They made a clear determination to take action. The brightness of the lighting created a feverish atmosphere, while the rest of the place was consumed by the darkness of a night filled with the sounds of radios broadcasting Quranic verses.

The assembled group, armed with lanterns, swords, sticks and machetes, advanced towards their destination, the vicinity of Ashour's house. They were determined to eliminate their enemy, the Jinn, and reassured by the clear recitations of Quranic verses that reached their ears.

THE CISTERN

The last groups remained behind, carrying the shoes of the participants, as they set out for battle in the vicinity of Ashour's house.

All intentions were set, and weapons were ready to eliminate their enemy, the Jinn, in any form they may take, be it animal, insect or rodent. The warning, long overdue, was to remain quiet in order to catch the enemy off guard and prevent them from fleeing.

The group surrounded Ashour's house, blocking escape from every exit. They were ready to launch the campaign under the leadership of Omar Al-Yaridi. Bright light illuminated the halls and ruins of Ashour's palace, as the first victim of the massacre was the mayor's very much alive donkey, who was set loose but quickly captured by butchers' cleavers knives before it could flee the battlefield. The killing did not stop there, as donkeys, sheep, dogs, cats, pigeons, chickens, mice, beetles, geckos, molluscs, and any other animal, bird, or creature were brutally slain. The bloodshed was relentless and indiscriminate, as the group sought to eliminate their enemy, the Jinn, in whatever form they may take.

It was a bizarre slaughter in which all the participants were actively engaged, each of them shouting out the name of the creature they had killed.

They spent the better part of the night hunting down every animal they could find, until the collapse of one of the back walls of Ashour Palace startled them.

Suddenly, a pack of vicious dogs that had been hiding jumped out to attack them, causing fear and panic to spread throughout their ranks. Their terror was further amplified when they heard a loud warning,

"The Jinn have come out to punish you."

Chapter 20

Omaima desperately needed her brother's help that night, as it seemed to her that he was unable to stand tall and his ferocity had dropped to its lowest limits. She pitied him for his arrogance, and the false bravado he put on. It was only when she tried to motivate him to see what was happening outside their home that she discovered how serious his condition was.

He struggled to stand up and, for the first time, reached out to her for help, placing his hand on her shoulder. She paused, standing beside him, and together they peered through the small openings in the window to observe the movement of their neighbours outside.

She felt the weight and helplessness of Ibrahim's ill health as he pulled her back to his bed. His prolonged silence and the absence of his gaze, hidden behind the drooping wounds on his eyelids, made her understand and forgive his weakness. She sought to conceal his inability by urging him to stay in bed. As she considered what she could do to help him, she came to realise her words had struck a deep blow to his pride. With great effort, he slowly sat up, his voice growing gruff as he spoke,

"I fear you will wrap me in your abaya and go out to meet the men of the neighbourhood, wearing my clothes, pretending to be me."

Her apologies went unheard, causing him to rise with a

clenched jaw and head towards the balcony with a vacant stare. Omaima advanced towards him with trepidation, as if she were approaching a wounded wild beast.

With a sense of cold and bewildered astonishment, they watched as light spilled over their house, unable to understand why so many people had gathered and were cramming into the backyard of their home, surrounding it on all sides. As Omaima peered through the shutters, her eyes opened wide with astonishment and shock at the sight of the large crowd of protesters outside. Ibrahim, meanwhile, was looking for a comfortable position for himself amid the chaos. The sudden fever that had seized his body left him feeling debilitated and unable to stand. Sharp pains wracked his body from his wounds and the overwhelming anxiety in his chest did not subside but he put on a brave face, hiding his pain and struggles, so as not to cause further distress to Omaima, whose steps faltered and lips trembled with fear.

Ibrahim's chest was filled with an ever-burning hatred towards Muhammaduh, and he could not help but curse "Eve" for causing such damage to his face, leaving him unable to meet anyone without feeling a deep sense of shame.

He had considered venturing out to confront the happenings outside, but his debilitating condition stopped him. He felt light-headed, and the inability to open his eyes made him aware that any confrontation would only lead to him becoming a subject of ridicule among the people. All he could do was grit his teeth in frustration.

The constant noise outside his window made it difficult for him to remain calm. He asked his sister to bring him a cane to help him walk and threatened her with severe punishment if she did not obey. Holding himself tight, using the cane for support and trying to conceal any signs of unsteadiness, he made his way to the shabby back rooms of their home.

He wanted to bring down one of the crumbling walls at the back of the house and release the fierce guard dogs he kept in the backyard to confront the attackers outside. He had previously kept them locked in a cage, but lost the key in the same yard where his own face had been brutally disfigured.

He no longer kept the dogs securely locked away. His goal was to release them from the back of the house, by dropping the back of the cage. That would allow them to spread out and drive away the intruders.

****

On the third day of the war against the Ashour Jinn, the stench of death from the rotting birds, dogs, cats and rodents permeated the area. Nobody dared to dispose of the corpses and push them to the outskirts of the city.

Rumours spread throughout the neighbourhood that the corpses were those of Jinn, causing the residents to avoid removing them. Even those who were hired to dispose of the bodies refused to do it.

The accumulation of corpses became a major concern for the local authorities.

Ubaid Ismail, along with the rest of the janitors, refused to handle the corpses due to their belief that they were not of animals, but of Jinn,

"I don't want to risk handling the corpse of a Jinn," he declared.

The mayor's troubles were compounded by an outbreak of rabies among three of those bitten by the dogs of Ashour Palace. The community called for them to be quarantined before the men of the neighbourhood began to behave like the dogs themselves.

As the mayor tried to come to grips with the series of events that had occurred, his thoughts kept returning to Al-Aridity, who had repeatedly caused harm to his reputation. Starting with his proposal to attack Ashour's palace and kill the Jinn, and ending with the outbreak of rabies among the men of the neighbourhood, the more he reflected on Al-Aridity's actions, the more he realized that he had entrusted important tasks to incompetent individuals. His anger grew as he began to shout at his aides,

"May God give you hell, Omar! May God give you hell, Omar."

His rage was so intense that he began to foam at the mouth and his helpers quickly realised that the mayor had lost his cool.

Chapter 21

The daily routine of the community had been abruptly disrupted and the only thing that the residents were now exchanging with each other were words of caution and advice.

It had been one full week since the incident at Ashour's house and the community was still grappling with the traumatic memories of that night.

That event could have joined the ranks of the countless intriguing narratives that circulated in the neighbourhood, leaving behind a legacy of resentment and pretentiousness, to be mulled over during nights of boredom. But what occurred shook the community to its core.

"The Jinn will not let our disrespect towards them go unpunished" – this statement circulated among the people, originating from Aletha Al-Harbi, and its validity was tested by eyewitness accounts of injuries sustained by some.

Stories started to spread about the Jinn disciplining those who defied them, with reports of direct retribution. Ibrahim Ashour was said to have faced such consequences, with his face so distorted that it now resembles a map, and Mahmoud Nawar claimed to have witnessed men turned into dogs running through the streets of the neighbourhood, barking with tongues hanging out like unbaked loaves.

News of the mayor having rabies brought sadness to the faces and shattered the hearts, as the residents feared for their own safety and waited for any impending harm. Anxiety spread throughout the community, and they struggled to find ways to alleviate their fears. The most common piece of advice shared among them was to flood the rubbish dumps with manure and bones to appease the hunger of the remaining Jinn. This advice was suggested by Rabah al-Kujaili, the imam of the mosque, in a brief sermon titled "The Unity of the Poor and the Guardians". Tawfiq Gharib considered this title to be vague and its meaning unrefined, like someone who wore their clothes on their head while walking around naked. This analogy made people mock Rabah, exposing his lack of leadership abilities. However, the neighbourhood's residents were too preoccupied with their own fears and anxieties to address Rabah's flawed and misguided thinking.

After leaving the mosque, the aim was to feed the Jinn until they were fully satisfied. The task of gathering dung from cow sheds, sheep pens, and donkey stalls was given to the boys.

Butchers donated an abundant supply of fresh bones, and some of them went to great lengths to spread dung and scatter bones near the decaying corpses, hoping to feed the Jinn who had come to pay their respects to the dead from that fateful night.

Women constantly washed themselves to avoid unexpected menstruation that could lead to their bodies being penetrated by a wandering or vengeful Jinn. Those who found themselves menstruating were sent to designated homes at the bottom of the city.

The neighbourhood became fixated on various rituals, with everyone offering advice and following through with it. However, they did not hesitate to curse and insult the mayor and Al-Yaridi, blaming them for the terror they were experiencing.

As night fell, the neighbourhood became shrouded in a sense of tragedy. With the sun gone, people hastened to retreat into their homes, following the advice not to go out when the Jinn were said to leave their ruins in search of fresh air. The streets emptied as residents remained in their houses, listening to Qur'an recitation, with the sounds of the reciters rising from the yards and rooms of their homes.

People huddled inside their homes, windows shut tight and hearts racing, seeking refuge from the Jinn and their potential harm. Those without access to a Qur'an reciter at home would encourage a family member to recite or move to a home where a reciter was present. The community remembered Rabah's sermon, where he forbade collective radio recitation and encouraged householders to recite the Qur'an themselves. He also granted permission for indoor prayer, eliminating the need to attend the mosque.

The night arrived with unease, each heartbeat uncertain, leaving behind restless souls consumed by their fear of the dark. Come morning, they kept watch over the streets surrounding Ashour's house, as the putrid scent of slain animals hung heavy in the air, drawing swarms of flies and mosquitoes from all corners, aided by an army of insects and bugs feasting on the scattered remains.

The decay of the bodies resulted in the proliferation of pests and the area was plagued by overpowering stenches. Upon seeing the scars on Ibrahim Ashour's face, people understood that the Jinn had taken revenge on him. It was whispered that they chose not to kill him, instead marking his face as a warning to others

"no one's loos would be left unscathed."

THE CISTERN

Meanwhile, reports of rabies cases were on the rise in other parts of the neighbourhood with individuals exhibiting advanced symptoms, indicating that they were nearing the end.

Some of the residents believed that those bitten by dogs had become possessed by Jinn, and Iyas Musa warned of the dangers of leaving the infected alive,

"If the disease takes hold of your neighbours, you will hear them barking, or we'll have to expand the cemetery," he warned.

The community trusted Iyas's expertise on the matter, and they advised against approaching the infected, instead opting to tie them up and lead them to an empty barn located outside the neighbourhood.

With the fourth rabies case being reported, the neighbours of the person responsible for keeping track of rabies cases became alarmed, realizing that the disease was spreading. The community leaders and elders demanded that all infected individuals be taken out of their homes. Hamed Al-Manfoush's wife screamed,

"Do you expect me to dispose of my husband like rubbish?"

Zainab Munawar promptly responded with a harsh reply,

"What harm would it do if we throw him away? He's a broken machine, as you say, and it's better to dispose of him than to turn us all into rabid dogs, risking the possibility of ending up eating our own children or each other.

Neighbors of Saud Ghalib, who was infected with rabies, gathered at his house to observe worms coming out of his body. He was propped against the wall, unable to control his panting and the saliva that continuously dripped from his tongue.

So, with the help of Laila Yahya, Saud Ghalib's wife

bravely took him and secured his feet to an inner support beam. They quickly left, advising others to flee before the disease could spread. Laila Yahya claimed to have witnessed Jinn coming out of Saud Ghalib's head in the form of hot steam with a strong smell. She stirred the women to tears and urged the men to take decisive action against those infected with rabies.

Chapter 22

The night was filled with fear as the residents of the neighbourhood scattered in terror, searching for the source of the loud noise that echoed through the streets. Barking could be heard coming from multiple directions and the shouting grew louder, warning that the Jinn were seeking revenge. Those who heard the warning were faced with uncertainty and fear, and felt that the only way to find stability was to leave their homes and face the situation in the streets. This was a principle that the community deeply believed in,

"to support one another and stand together as one, with everyone ultimately being accountable to God."

They gathered near the cistern hill, exchanging puzzled thoughts about their next move. There was a sense of uncertainty as to who would take charge, but Ali Mubarak seized the opportunity and stepped forward as the march's leader, guiding the crowd towards the mayor's residence. The masses followed him silently, hoping their voices wouldn't incite the anger of any lurking Jinn and provoke an attack.

The group made its way through the dark, using the light from the torches held by those leading the way. They marched down a street leading to the mayor's house and stopped nearby, waiting for what was to come. A forceful knock on the mayor's door roused him from his slumber. His maid alerted him,

"Sir, there are people at the door."

Startled, the mayor's body jolted like a boat swaying at its moorings. He rubbed his eyes, trying to dispel the drowsiness that had settled on him. He attempted to get up, securing a towel around his waist, but his wife stopped him, "Don't you want to maintain your decency by getting dressed first?" she asked him,

"The Jinn have left me no dignity," he replied. His wife rose to dress him properly, countering any gossip being spread among the people. The mayor muttered,

"May God curse Omar Al-Yaridi for causing all of this." He stepped back, allowing his wife to button his waistcoat, but a fit of coughing overtook him, and he spat out another curse,

"It's frustrating when people believe everything they're told," he said, only to realise quickly that he was also guilty of this tendency, having blindly trusted Omar Al-Yaridi's tales without considering the potential consequences.

"You're ready to go," his wife told him. He left with thick phlegm clogging his throat, hindering his ability to express his appreciation and gratitude towards her. And he continued to resent those who disturbed him at such an inconvenient hour of the night. His frustration only intensified upon hearing the loud knocking at his door, prompting him to entertain thoughts of retaliating against the knockers.

He was taken aback by the sheer number of people who had gathered, expressing their turmoil, anger and calls for help. In a moment of arrogance, he shouted,

"What brings you out on this night?"

Ali Mubarak retorted,

"Thanks to your wisdom, mayor, we have been reduced to barking dogs."

His words were spoken with disdain and it was clear that a deep-seated hatred was fuelling them. The mayor understood that if given the chance, Ali would utter words that would sully his reputation in front of the assembled crowd. To avoid this, he interrupted him and attempted to steer the conversation towards Abdullah Al-Barakati,

"What is the matter?" he asked. Al-Barakati's delayed response gave Ali Mubarak the opportunity to continue speaking, his words filled with reckless disregard.

"The matter at hand is that a large group has started behaving like dogs, barking incessantly. So, we must either kill them or prepare ourselves for the inevitable, and you will undoubtedly be with us,"

The mayor was taken aback, losing his composure as he shouted,

"Be mindful of your words, Ali, or I shall make an example of you."

The situation could have easily escalated into a confrontation, had it not been for the sudden and loud barking of people coming from all around, acting like dogs, drooling and panting to the point of exhaustion. The mayor was thrown into confusion, and the men rallied, ready to face the group of barking individuals approaching them.

Chapter 23

Everyone was horrified to witness a group of men from the neighbourhood howling with a bark of overwhelming determination, circling around them with bare feet and bare bodies. Their features were clearly visible under the lights shining on them. They were dishevelled and dusty, blinded, staggering as they made their way to the mayor's house.

"Who are they?" the mayor asked. His heart was filled with foreboding of an impending downfall. He signalled to one of his assistants to stand between him and the people, keeping his eyes fixed on their scattered steps, trying to steady his trembling hands.

He was grateful to Mohsen Aylan for his quick thinking in the moment when he turned to address the crowd and concealed the mayor's apparent tremor,

"The mayor is asking who are these? And he has the right to ask."

His statement caught Ali Mubarak off guard,

"He asks, and sleeps peacefully, while we count our patients?" He began to list the names of those who had contracted rabies and, as he reached the last name, he confronted the mayor in a sharp and stern tone,

"All of these people have rabies. Some of them have been locked inside their homes, and yet you sleep soundly?"

Nasir Ba Naqita interrupted the mayor with a raised voice, his eyes filled with disgust as he spoke,

"We were overjoyed when we heard you had contracted rabies but our joy was short-lived."

The mayor struggled to control the trembling of his hands, retracting the fiery words he had intended to say and replacing them with calm, sober words. He also remembered to add a hint of sorrow for the sick. However, this facade did not last long as he became horrified when Ali Mubarak held him responsible for those suffering from rabies, so he stammered, shouting,

"I am one of you and I agreed to your proposal to attack the Jinn of Ashour but I was not aware of the consequences."

He was interrupted as the rabies sufferers approached. Bewildered and inquiring he asked,

"What are we to do now?"

It seemed that this question was eagerly awaited by Ali Mubarak, who exacerbated the mayor's fears,

"What if the officials found out about this incident and the one responsible for it?'

The atmosphere was tense, and the mayor's neighbours flocked to inquire about what had happened by the eastern side of their neighbourhood. When the news reached the women, they panicked and jumped out of their windows, screaming and howling. Despite all the efforts, no one could control or calm the panicked groups. The mayor was troubled, and sought advice from local dignitaries, but refused to inform the local authorities or the palace of Prince Faisal.

Each time the suggestion of informing the officials was brought up, the mayor found a defect that prevented its implementation. He tolerated the foul language used by those present, but was too preoccupied with a warning issued by Qassem Al-Jeddawi, "What will we do if the afflicted come and attack us?"

The mayor was in a state of confusion, wishing that the earth would shake and remove the group of people who had settled in the courtyard of his house. He regretted his inability to use his famous bamboo stick to hit them. He felt a sense of satisfaction at the suggestion made by his assistant to line up against the affected people, stop them with sticks and if necessary, kill them.

The assembled group became agitated, their whistles grew louder, and their insults targeted the warden who had entrusted the task of managing the neighbourhood to a mayor who didn't know how to look after a chicken in its own coop.

"Kill who? Our family and friends" they shouted.

Ali Mubarak was stirring up the situation, prompting an escalation and opposing the mayor and his men. He was marching towards Prince Faisal's palace, even though deep down he didn't truly want to deviate from his aim of perplexing the mayor and causing him distress by announcing his intention to reach the Prince's palace, fully aware that they couldn't reach the road leading there.

The mayor looked on anxiously as the afflicted approached, his hands trembling as he hid them behind his back. He muttered repeatedly,

"What do we do, what do we do?" as he frantically searched for a solution to the crisis at hand. In the midst of the turmoil, the voice of Iyas Musa offered a glimmer of hope,

"I know how to treat rabies," he said. The mayor grabbed Iyas by the shoulders and shook him in an attempt to hide his own trembling hands as he implored,

"Say it, say it, Iyas. What's the solution?"

Iyas replied, "The solution is for the afflicted to drink the blood of Ali Mubarak.

The mayor was torn between expressing disapproval or rejoicing, but ultimately chose to overcome his disapproval.

Despite his inner joy, he pretended to be shaken and echoed Iyas's words, expressing his trust in Iyas's knowledge of medicine and curative abilities for many diseases.

He then shouted to the crowd,

"As long as Ali Mubarak's blood is a cure for our afflictions, let us shed his blood."

The crowd became increasingly agitated with the afflicted coming closer to them, and the mayor's aides rushed forward, waving their sticks to prevent them from advancing.

Chapter 24

The mayor agreed to Iyas Musa's proposal, who addressed the group stating that there is a cure for rabies in the form of a blood treatment.

Sharif Al-Barakati supported Iyas by sharing strange and miraculous stories from the north of the country, where only a few drops of blood mixed with water or coffee saved patients from certain death. With a dramatic gesture, Iyas shouted to the crowd,

Perhaps some of you may question why Ali Mubarak's blood is the cure. Let me tell you, he is of pure lineage and his first ancestor was blessed with this special privilege, which has been passed down to his descendants'

The crowd was agitated as they jostled to reach the front rows, eager to witness the experiment that Iyas would perform on one of the patients who had been apprehended by the mayor's agents. They forcibly brought forward one of the afflicted individuals, restraining him in order to prevent him from causing any harm, and positioning him in front of Iyas. Ali Mubarak was asked to step forward to the centre of the human circle that had formed around Doctor Iyas and the afflicted patient, but he refused, expressing a disobedient reluctance to have his blood spilled.

The crowd's voices rose in unison, imploring Ali Mubarak to provide his blood for their sick patients. Faced with their insistent pleas, Ali Mubarak reluctantly agreed but only on the condition that the mayor publicly apologise for past wrongs committed against him and beg him for his blood. The mayor, feeling remorseful, searched for the right words to appease Ali Mubarak and convince him to go through with the bloodletting. Whenever the mayor said something, Ali Mubarak insisted that he improve his request. The mayor secretly wished he could slit Ali Mubarak's throat. This desire grew in the mayor's heart, and he began contemplating a plan to shed the blood of that despicable person who humiliated him like he had not been humiliated before.

The mayor then came up with a plan to gather the residents of the neighbourhood and coerce them into drinking Ali Mubarak's blood as a way to prevent rabies, ultimately leading to the death of both the infected individuals and Ali Mubarak himself by draining all of the blood from his body.

Ali Mubarak agreed to the bloodletting only after witnessing the mayor's degradation and suffering, The crowd of onlookers grew until the space became cramped, forming a semi-circle while shining their flash-lights towards a scene they would never witness again. Doctor Iyas, with a sterile razor blade in hand, asked Ali Mubarak to extend his left arm, he swiftly made the incision, collecting the flow of blood into a cup, which was then mixed with Zamzam water.

Approaching the afflicted man, he instructed the mayor's attendants to maintain a firm grip on his hair as the cup's contents were poured into his open mouth. He then stepped back to monitor the outcome of his treatment. At this point, people held their breath in anticipation. Silence and anxiety filled the atmosphere, rapid eye movements were in action all around, and some of the onlookers buried their faces in their hands, whispering a quiet prayer that was abruptly cut off by the patient's loud and distressed voice shouting out, "What are you doing to me?'

Iyas instructed the bandages be removed and for the patient's face to be wiped down with a dark-coloured towel, declaring his recovery. It was a mystery as to why the towel had to be dark, and time was needed to procure it. Amidst the commotion, a sudden gunshot-like sound filled the air, causing everyone's voices to break out into a loud, deafening hum. This was followed by the wailing of the patient's families escalating and ululating from the balconies nearby.

However, the mayor was unaffected, still battling to steady his trembling hands and sneering at the scene. He made a vow to himself that he wouldn't rest until he had humiliated Ali Mubarak with a degradation that no one had ever witnessed.

Chapter 25

People were making their way to Ali Mubarak's residence with a strong resolve, seeking a mere drop of his blood mixed with Zamzam water, much like ants on a mission to reach their goal.

The volume of guests overwhelmed the available space, as Ali Mubarak's blood was now considered to have properties beyond treating rabies. Iyas Musa claimed that a single drop of Ali Mubarak's blood could banish evil spirits and protect against the evil eye, attracting a massive influx of both men and women seeking his blood.

"Has the supply of Ali Mubarak's blood run out yet?"

The mayor spoke this sentence with a concealed, growing hatred in his heart. His loathing for Ali Mubarak grew stronger every time he heard news of the successes of his blood in healing people, causing his chest to constrict and his hatred to be obvious to those around him,

"Ali Mubarak is the lowest of all creatures on this earth, and his blood is filthier than the drain in a bathroom sink."

The mayor couldn't express his disdain towards Ali Mubarak, who had gained a high status and won titles close to that of saint. Whenever he saw the queues lining up to obtain a drop of blood, he would mock their ignorance and resolve to plant seeds of doubt in the minds of Ali Mubarak's followers.

"If Ali Mubarak had as much blood as the Zamzam well, it would have run dry by the third day."

He felt the intense gaze of those around him and heard the pleas for Ali Mubarak. In an effort to quell the situation, he offered a show of feigned sympathy,

"I spoke only out of concern for his well-being. If you want to help him, I suggest you provide him with something to strengthen his body."

But as soon as the words had left his mouth, he regretted them deeply as they were eagerly embraced by everyone. The community came together to support Ali Mubarak, donating money and food, as well as offering the blood from butchered animals. Vegetable sellers gifted their finest fruits, and gifts of honey and ghee arrived from distant lands. Women took on the role of his cooks, preparing the meals of his choice. Some women even swore that they would donate their jewellery to Ali Mubarak if he would grant them his blessing to ward off the evil eye.

Rabah Al-Kajli declared that it was acceptable to use zakat funds to support Ali Mubarak, as he was deemed a wayfarer. However, the mayor opposed this fatwa and reminisced about when Ali Mubarak first arrived in the neighbourhood, begging for support, and resorting to steal three eggs from Hassan Moussaka's chicken coop after being turned away by the community. The act was discovered due to the chickens' noisy squawking.

He was apprehended by the mayor and brought before him but refused to confess to his crime. The mayor noticed the bulge in his pocket and squeezed it, revealing a liquid from the eggs which spilled onto Ali Mubarak's thigh. The mayor's bamboo stick left a bloody mark on Ali Mubarak's back, causing a blow to his dignity. He shouted at the mayor,

"I will drink your blood as you have shed mine, you coward."

The mayor was taken aback by the boy's boldness, but Hassan Mu'afa implored him not to pursue him. The boy went on living in the alleyways of the neighbourhood, doing any odd job that came his way.

The mayor was furious when he realised that fate would have him beg for even a drop of that scoundrel's blood. It was said that Ali Mubarak's blood could perform miracles on patients who came to visit, and only those bearing gifts or money visited his house. The area was crowded with people, including vendors who had set up makeshift stalls near his house, displaying their wares on mats sheltered by sun-blocking canopies. Naeem Jalal created a cloth doll adorned with seashells and stitched with colourful threads, which visitors could purchase to protect against the evil eye. He swore solemnly that the threads had been steeped in a mixture of dyes and Ali Mubarak's blood.

Other traders also set up shop displaying a range of goods including pants, flannels, kaftans and scarves. All of them claimed their products had been sanctified by the blood of Ali Mubarak.

Chapter 26

The residents of the neighbourhood flocked to Ali Mubarak's house in search of medical treatment for their various ailments. From treating rabies and immunise themselves against it, to dispelling evil eyes, expelling Jinn, promoting fertility, marrying spinsters, draining abscesses, resolving relationships, seeking success in their pursuits, and uncovering both visible and hidden magic, numerous health issues were combined and the only remedy prescribed was to consume Ali Moubarak's blood.

Both collectively and individually, the masses implored Ali Mubarak for a cure to their ailments except for Ibrahim Ashour and his sister Omaima.

Following the survey conducted by Iyas Musa with the help of Omar Al-Yaridi, and after reviewing the records of patients and the gifts and contributions they had made, Omar Al-Yard realised that Ibrahim Ashour's name was absent. In a loud exclamation of distress and lament, he claimed that a serious error had been committed and urgently called for it to be put right,

"Ibrahim Ashour is the only one residing with Jinn, and his body needs to be purged, otherwise, he will pass on his Jinn to us."

The crowd that had gathered at Ali Mubarak's residence demanded the capture of Ibrahim Ashour and his sister Omaima, concerned that their efforts so far would be to no avail and the evil spirits would return through the bodies of Ashour's descendants. The demand was fuelled by the news of what Basima Munawar had said. According to her husband, who had rabies, Ibrahim had sided with the Jinn during the night of the war against them, and he toppled a massive wall in an attempt to bury everyone who was around that night.

There were rumours that Ibrahim was responsible for the kidnapping of Hamid Al-Manfoush but Hamid denied these allegations, asserting that the true abductor was a Jinn with a face smeared with blood, and that on touching the wall, this Jinn made it collapse, releasing his siblings in the form of rabid dogs. Al-Yaridi seized the opportunity to assert that Ibrahim had descended into the underworld and become a Jinn and must be rescued.

Chapter 27

Omaima was in a state of anxiety the night the neighbours stormed their house. Her brother Ibrahim was struck by a sudden fever that had weakened him, leaving him unable to stand and defend their home. With the call to kill any animal that roamed the area, Omaima wished she was one of the neighbourhood's young boys.

Omaima was in hiding in the depths of their home, filled with anxiety for her brother, who had fallen ill with a sudden fever that made his strong body unable to stand.

Ibrahim ignored his sister's attempts to keep him inside and, despite his weakness, he pushed on with determination, leaning on his cane and making his way to the cage where he kept his guard dogs.

The cage was ten metres away from the worn-out back gate, standing between the street and a cluster of rooms whose roofs had caved in. Once in that dilapidated state the former rooms were inhabited by creatures seeking an area beyond human reach. Local residents used the area next to these ruins as a dumping ground for rubbish or as storage for excess possessions when the dogs were locked up in their cages. Some of the empty spaces were also used by drunks as a place to spend the night.

Ibrahim kept many things concealed in those rooms that he did not want anyone in the neighbourhood to discover, including a pack of dogs he trained to follow his commands no matter how challenging.

He would venture outside the house daily to feed and train them. He assiduously collected dead animals, unused meat from butchers, and spoiled fish from the fish market to provide proper sustenance to his beloved canine companions. Caring for the dogs was a crucial aspect of his daily routine and was very important to him.

Loud cries echoed from beyond the ruins, calling for the exorcism of Ashour's Jinn while Ibrahim struggled to reach the back of the palace, keeping out of sight of his sister. Omaima had never experienced more harrowing night than when she found herself alone, vulnerable and unable to defend herself or her brother, who she always relied on for protection. However, his current state of misery, shattered dignity and weakened strength made her understand the challenges faced by a woman trapped in the turmoil of conflicting emotions.

Her ears were alert to the sounds outside their house, filled with anger and concern, carefully listening to the soft lamentations every time her brother breathed out.

Amid the thundering noise and cries of death, Omaima was worried for Ibrahim and followed him to the very outskirts of their residence. To her relief, she discovered that he had regained his strength, as he gripped Hamid al-Manfush's throat and brandished his cane at another person whose features were unclear, commanding them to run off. The individuals promptly complied and did not pursue them further. Ibrahim was busy tearing down the wall between the dog cage and the street behind their house. As it collapsed, the dogs eagerly sprang outside in response to Ibrahim's urging.

The dogs started barking loudly. One of them bit Hamid

Al-Manfoush's shoulder, causing him to panic and scream for help. At that moment, Ibrahim collapsed, as if his energy had been reduced to just a fleeting breath. Omaima helped him to sit down and took care of him. She gently ran her fingers through his hair asking,

"What's happening to us, Ibrahim?"

She was aware of nothing but the imminent danger surrounding their lives, so Ibrahim reassured her and put his arm around her neck to support himself as he stood up.

She helped him through the hallway leading to his room but he guided her towards the outer balcony to observe the crowd who had been shouting and protesting, now dispersed to hunt the animals scattered throughout the ruins.

Omaima watched the crowd fleeing from the guard dogs, stumbling and tumbling over one another, making her happier by the minute. She celebrated and applauded the disorder and terror among the people who were running away from their home.

Chapter 28

"Time manipulates everything in its path, leaving it in the annals of memories." Youssef Maghribi sighed as he spoke these words, then wandered away to reminisce about the days and nights at the Ashour El-Baggio Palace.

The gate of the Palace was a familiar sight to those who came to request an audience with Khairy Ashour. The lock of the main entrance would open and local dignitaries would flock in, seeking hospitality and offering compliments to the owner of the palace.

Little could they know that the once magnificent entrance would deteriorate into a mere window hanging on a wall, The passage of time had taken its toll, destroying the magnificent gate, which used to accommodate many vehicles at the same time. To add to Youssef Maghribi's statement, Suleiman Abu Noqta shared a point of regret,

"Time wears down even the mighty mountains." He spoke with a heavy heart after his hair had begun to turn gray and his life of luxury had faded. He was hesitant to join the group visiting the former palace of Ashour, now reduced to rubble. Only a few simple rooms remained, and them the worse for wear, to provide shelter for the descendants of a once wealthy man who symbolised prosperity.

Some prominent members of the neighbourhood stopped asking Ibrahim Ashour to come out and meet them. Abdullah Al-Barakati was the most ashamed to carry out the task assigned to him by the community and so he stepped down from leading the group, passing on the responsibility to Bakri Obaid to approach Ibrahim Ashour with their request,

"Why did everyone agree with the views of a madman like Omar Al-Yaridi?" Bakri asked. "Is this not the right time for such a question, Barakati?" he added. Ibrahim emerged wearing a scarf that covered his recent wounds and revealed only his eyes. He greeted the dignitaries with a warm welcome and lavish praise for their leader. The purpose of their visit was a mystery to Ibrahim.

Despite their initial doubts, the dignitaries were taken aback by Ibrahim's kindness and politeness, which only added to their confusion. In an effort to break the tension, they apologised for the inconvenience and explained their reason for coming,

"We fear for your safety, Ibrahim, given the recent troubles in the neighbourhood."

Bakri Ubaid found himself at a loss for words, causing him to dig deep into a well of ancient stories, historical accounts and rumours. He seemed unable to break free from these elaborate conversations, always finding himself drawn into another equally complex tale. That was until Abdullah Al-Barakati intervened, placing a steadying hand on Ibrahim's shoulder,

"It's obvious that you have yet to learn of our current situation," Abdullah said. "Everyone has taken measures to protect themselves, except for you and your sister. We fear that you will become the only vulnerable targets for the Jinn to exploit So, we've been sent to urge you to follow our example and to request that you and your sister take precautions to guard against their influence."

Ibrahim struggled to suppress a laugh. Despite his best efforts a chuckle still passed his lips. He was curious and asked the question that had been gnawing at him.

"Who, may I ask, originally made this invitation?"

"Al-Yaridi's teachings have gained popularity in our community, and he's the one who suggested you take protective measures," said Al-Barakati.

When Ibrahim learned that it involved drinking Ali Mubarak's blood, he erupted into a full blown belly laugh. The sound even pierced his tightly-wrapped scarf. "I couldn't be more delighted," he declared "Drinking Ali Mubarak's blood in its entirety is my deepest desire."

Despite his unusual reaction, Ibrahim was gracious in his dealings with Al-Barakati and Jamal Ba Mohsen, so much so, that Jamal Ba Mohsen dismissed any rumours of misbehaviour by Ibrahim. They agreed to meet near Ali Mubarak's house following the afternoon prayer the next day, on the understanding that everyone would take part in the ritual and that Ibrahim's sister would stay away until he was properly immunised. Only then would she join.

Chapter 29

"Looks like you'll be associating with undesirable individuals," Ibrahim thought as he ruminated on Ali Mubarak's actions. The anger inside him only added to the confusion in figuring out his priorities against his enemies.

The goatskin mask created by Omaima instilled confidence in Ibrahim. She made sure it was flexible, smooth and gentle, ensuring it wouldn't hurt or scar her brother's face.

After multiple attempts to find the right size and fit, Ibrahim was pleased with the final result. It was the first time he would wear the mask in public, fulfilling the invitation to participate in the immunisation ceremony on his own terms.

Ibrahim entered a yard overlooking Ali Mubarak's house, where a large crowd had gathered seeking relief from their afflictions. He walked through the crowd to reach the group that had called for him, and saw that Omar Al-Yaridi and Iyas Musa had joined them.

Ibrahim then entered the house with them, ignoring the crowd, who were shouting at different pitches and asking him to remove his mask and reveal his face to see what the Jinn had done

"Uncover your face and reveal the marks left by the Jinn," they said.

Al-Barakati asked for a brief pause to welcome Ibrahim and pay tribute to him for his polite demeanour during their visit. He was seated across from Ali Mubarak, who was wearing a green velvet overcoat, a well-tanned leather belt decorated with antique silver accents and around his neck a rosary of dark brown amber beads interspersed with red sapphires.

The largest bead on the rosary was tied with brightly coloured silk threads. Ali Mubarak fiddled with his beads frantically, scattering incense beads into the burner in the centre of the council, causing its fragrance to permeate the room. He did not look up at Ibrahim at all, becoming increasingly agitated and mumbling to himself as Ibrahim spoke,

"Ali, have you had too much fermented grape that you think your blood can cure any illness?" Iyas Musa offered a cup of reddish liquid, urging Ibrahim to drink its contents, to which he replied,

"Iyas, are you also serving Ali Mubarak's blood?" Ibrahim's hesitation was met with frustration from the audience, which was growing tired of his avoiding to drink the blood. Omar Al-Yaridi stepped in to explain,

'Ibrahim is reluctant to drink the blood and we're asking him to reveal his face, as there's a suspicion that a Jinn may have taken control of him and that our friend may be buried elsewhere."

Ibrahim stood up, snarling,

"Omar, the books of magic and Jinn have clouded your judgment." Several members of the audience stepped in to defuse the situation,

"Ibrahim, you were not summoned here to display bravery. You came in response to our call."

Ibrahim spoke with conviction as he sought to set Al-Yaridi straight,

"I came here to expose the falsehoods of this impostor and

his accomplices…" The crowd erupted into an uproar but Ibrahim quickly regained control, "I am willing to drink every drop of Ali Mubarak's blood, as long as I can see it for myself."

He took hold of Ali Mubarak's hands, showing them to the onlookers, and declared,

"This charlatan claims to have given you his blood, yet his hands show no evidence of any puncture wounds. Is he offering you blood from his backside?'

Iyas was scared as he heard the accusation against him. He went pale and quickly looked at Ali Mubarak. Ali asked for time to go to the bathroom, but it was really a way for him to escape, which prompted Iyad to inform them that the drink was simply a blend of berry juice and Zamzam water.

People quickly started chasing Ali to return the gifts they had given him.

Ibrahim Ashour stepped away from the gathering, pondering his options for retaliation. He weighed up his enemies to determine who should be punished first, starting with Omar Al-Yaridi, who had instigated the people to attack him and accused him of harbouring a Jinn. Every time Ibrahim neared his house, memories of Muhammaduh and "Eve" resurfaced and he was certain they were the ones most deserving of retribution. They had plunged him into total obscurity, anxious that others would discern the scars they had left on his face. So, he made the decision to commence his revenge with them.

****

Ibrahim sat worn-out and humbled by his reflection amid the pile of building blocks that evidenced the disintegration and collapse of the house. He searched his mind for a positive idea or feeling that would bring him hope and a plan to improve his life and bring him fulfilment.

The mirror in the corner of the room corner had captured his reflection. He was no longer afraid of the imperfections it revealed because Omaima's mask acted as a shield from malicious gazes and mocking remarks. He embraced the notion that a Jinn had caused his deformities as these expressions lessen the shame and dishonour that has befallen him.

He contemplates by night, searching for a way to outrun time's relentless minutes and seconds. The thought of Omaima being taken and sold into slavery used to drive him to madness. Though he wavered in his determination, he stood tall, donning the mask to hide his face,

"One cannot be loved by others if they cannot accept their own appearance." He walked to the beach, gazing at the dreary sunset, visualising a ship navigating the waves, with himself as its captain

MUHAMMADUH'S FAMILY

Chapter 1

As dusk began to settle, Muhammaduh and the Indian physician engaged in a one-sided battle.

The day quickly morphed into the wild night, not lingering to uncover the result of their altercation as the sun dipped and the Divine's light faded. Under the faint beam of the streetlamp, the fight was brought to a close by the intervention of spectators.

Witnesses provided clashing testimonies about the cause of the quarrel which resulted in a severe wound to the physician's shoulder.

The investigating officer pursued his quest for answers with a leather whip always at hand, coming back to it frequently due to his quick temper. The interrogation room was located in the back of the police station, with walls that shimmered with colour. There was nothing in that room except for a window and a door that were kept shut all the time, trapping the overpowering smell of tobacco smoke used by both law enforcement officers and those being questioned.

In the corners of the room, there was a strong, stale smell along with an overabundance of furniture tossed about. Some of it leaned against the walls facing the investigation officer's desk, while the rest of the space was reserved for the suspects to stand in front of the officer, with limited movement. The room was cramped, with no spare space. However, Officer Abu Laban enjoyed bringing the suspects into this cramped room, waiting like a hungry predator, ready to pounce if any suspect dared to upset his mood.

Muhammaduh leaned forward, his eyes catching sight of the dirty floor beneath him, which was as grimy as the soles of his shoes loaded with abrasive salt marsh dust. He felt that his cheap towel only served to lower his worth and increase the officer's disrespect.

"What brings you here Ibrahim?" the officer asked.

Muhammaduh was preoccupied with this question as he stood with his head bowed, waiting for his chains to be removed or for the silence in the tight room to be broken. He tensed up when he saw the officer stand up from his desk, taking a leather whip that was lying among papers in a wooden basket on the surface. He quickly looked at Ibrahim, who stood calmly next to two soldiers, with stiff postures like two new nails, devoid of any curves or bends.

The officer walked around Muhammaduh, breathing hard and talking through clenched teeth,

"I'm fed up with you people, especially you."

His physical appearance didn't match the show of strength he put on when he quickly turned and hit Muhammaduh on the temple.

"I'm going to make an example of you for others like you, you beast."

He spit on Muhammaduh's face. It landed in his eye, making it hard to wipe away,

"I acted in self defence," said Muhammaduh.

"Let's see how you defend yourself now;" the officer replied.

The officer headed to his office, drafted an order for Ibrahim's release from detention, and before he stamped it, stopped and looked at Ibrahim.

"Would you like to be released?" he asked him.

Ibrahim shook his head, and the officer smiled slyly like a fox that had just captured its prey.

"Let's see how you defend yourself," he said, as he approached Ibrahim with an unsigned release order.

"If you truly want to be let out, you must do as I say," he told him.

Ibrahim's words asking him to explain came out with a slight stammer.

"Poke *(Slang for an action that insults one's masculinity)* the darkie, and I will secure your release," the officer demanded.

Muhammaduh was taken aback hoping that Ibrahim wouldn't comply with the officer's request. He felt a tightness in his chest, making it difficult to breathe, his throat and tongue felt constricted. He waited for the resolution of the strange case that involved him, Ibrahim and the doctor.

****

Ibrahim Ashour was detained in a holding cell following an accusation made by Muhammaduh that he had fired a shot at his mother during a bet with his friends to shoot the big toe on Al-Hajji Fatima's foot. Ibrahim's denial and the lack of a debilitating injury to the foot caused the officer to classify the report as false.

To validate the decision, Ibrahim remained in custody for a week as a thorough investigation was conducted with witnesses who refuted Muhammaduh's allegations. Misfortune struck when the two rivals, holding equal animosity towards one another, chanced upon each other during questioning in a string of unfortunate events.

Ibrahim saw the officer's demand as a means to humiliate Muhammaduh and eagerly agreed to comply, his eyes sparkled with excitement as he remembered Muhammaduh's previous displays of masculinity in the fields.

"Come on, let's go," officer Abu Lacan ordered, his voice reflecting both his anger and determination.

Ibrahim saw this as an opportunity to humiliate his rival, clear his own name, and secure his release from jail. Memories of Muhammaduh chasing and tormenting him in the fields lingered at the forefront of his mind. The thought of taking revenge and being released from custody motivated Ibrahim, who was eager to boast to the neighbourhood men about poking the black football player, in accordance with official instructions he had been given.

Meanwhile, Muhammaduh, who was handcuffed, had similar thoughts. But when Ibrahim approached to obey the officer's request, Muhammaduh, filled with anger, began to protest and threatened to report the officer to the police. The officer became even more frustrated, causing him to stand up and ask,

"Are you challenging me, darkie?"

He grabbed the whip from his desk and swung it in the air, repeatedly striking Muhammaduh's back. Trying to stay quiet, Muhammaduh was biting back his cries of pain, and was at a loss for words. Every time he tried to speak, he stopped himself, only the whip broke the silence.

Muhammaduh was in a difficult situation as Ibrahim appeared determined to carry out the order, which would result in his humiliation. He retreated to the wall of the interrogation room, firmly pressing himself against it. His eyes were filled with anger and a hidden hope, as he muttered a quiet prayer asking not to be publicly humiliated. His gaze went around the faces of the people in the room. The atmosphere in the interrogation room was tense and two soldiers were present, one of whom lived in the neighbourhood, and was known for his loose tongue and for spreading gossip around where he lived.

Ibrahim's approach showed his intent to escalate the situation, while Muhammaduh recoiled and held his ground, protecting himself by pressing his back against a wall cluttered with extra office furniture. Muhammaduh swore to remember Ibrahim's relentless pursuit of humiliation and disrespect. Ibrahim then dragged Muhammaduh to the centre of the room, yanked off his towel, and stripped him completely repeating his act, all while Officer Abu Lacan shouted in a frenzy,

"Poke him again! Poke him again."

Muhammaduh could no longer able tolerate the constant barrage of insults, and began to shout profanities, cursing Ibrahim's family line in every way he could. However, these insults only strengthened Ibrahim's resolve. Muhammaduh's rage led him to curse the officer, referring to him as a donkey that contaminates its own food.

Officer Abou Lacan was livid and instructed the officers at the library to escort Muhammaduh to the detention room and hang him by the door. He trailed behind them with his leather whip, repeatedly lashing Muhammaduh's bare skin, warning him to never cross paths again or face dire consequences.

Chapter 2

Muhammaduh quietly returned home, trying not to draw attention to himself. His home offered little privacy, and soon his family members, who were spread out in the spacious yard, gathered around him, curious about his experience in detention. Rumours of shameful events had been spread by Officer Abi Khadash but Muhammaduh denied them all and claimed nothing had happened. When later he settled into bed, he thought he had answered all the questions that needed to be answered.

The lantern light cast shadows of his mother as she leaned over him, gently feeling his back with concern,

"Every part of my body aches and I don't know what happened to you. Don't keep anything from me, my beloved," she said to him.

He sat up, unable to hold back his tears, and hugged her tightly, kissing her hands and head.

"You're exhausted, go back to bed," he whispered. Then they wept together, united in their distress.

****

As soon as the first light of dawn appeared, he cast aside his blanket and rose from bed, carefully trying not to step on one of his siblings who were sleeping on the cluttered floor, and listening to his eldest sister's warning,

THE CISTERN

"Be careful not to disturb Hawaa who's asleep at the foot of your bed."

Hawaa stretched and chuckled replying,

"I'm used to his feet pounding me."

The cramped room housing nine people had a restless night, with hearts filled with fear and worry at the delirium and restlessness of their mother Fatima. After Muhammaduh's return from the detention cell, he remained silent and was unable to shake off the tiredness that was showing on his body. Despite trying to summon confidence for what lay ahead, his tears flowed freely and would not stop. He went straight to his mother's bed, wiping away both their tears and encouraging his siblings to return to sleep.

Each person in the room let their minds wander to happier thoughts during that sad night, hoping to find solace and escape from their difficult reality. Muhammaduh struggled to suppress his sobs, gasping for air as a cough escaped his throat. A deep groan escaped him, reducing the intensity of his sobs. He eventually managed to calm himself, pretending to have woken up from a deep sleep. As he rose, the morning dew was settling on the branches of the lemon tree that nestled within the courtyard surrounded by zinc sheeting. Three families related through their common grandfather had come together in this house. They were all grappling with the loss of their aunt, Amina, on their journey to "beit al haram". Their mother Fatima's illness added to their woes and, to top it all, Muhammaduh was accused of trying to kill a representative from the Ministry of Health. Muhammaduh stood still, casting his gaze upon his family members who hastened to sink into the depths of slumber. He made his way to the tap, shaped like a cone, with water trickling out in small quantities, near the lemon tree. Dribbles of the run-off watered the plants growing in the basin, which were a variety of vegetables used to sustain the family.

Water dripped from Muhammaduh's fingers as he wiped his forehead, bringing back memories of the terrible distress from the previous night. His mother was ill and suffering from a fever that the Indian doctor suspected was meningitis. However, he refused to enter her room to examine her and instead only administered chloroquine as treatment. This intransigence frustrated Muhammaduh, who, feeling helpless, grabbed the doctor's medical bag, emptied its contents, and threw each tool in a different direction while venting his anger, "My mother is dying and you won't even go in to examine her! This is unacceptable."

In his agitation, the Indian doctor tried to gather his scattered tools while speaking broken Arabic in an attempt to condemn Muhammaduh's behaviour. However, Muhammaduh did not allow the doctor to finish his words or retrieve his tools. Instead, he used a medical scissor as a weapon and stabbed the doctor in the shoulder.

Five nights earlier, Muhammaduh submitted a report to the police accusing Ibrahim Ashour of shooting his mother in the foot with a hunting rifle. Now, with the scissors still lodged in the shoulder of the Indian doctor, Muhammaduh stood before Officer Yahya Abu Lacan, who had an electrifying voice that released bolts of electricity as he shouted.

The officer shouted and screamed while disputing Muhammaduh's charges. When Muhammaduh confronted him, his face contorted from the barrage of insults directed at him.

THE CISTERN

Muhammaduh was tempted to counter the officer's insults with his own offensive language, but he was constrained by the officer's authority and the presence of two officers. Despite his urge to react violently, Muhammaduh repressed his emotions and chose to stay quiet. However, after the actions of Ibrahim Ashour, his anger surged and he unleashed a torrent of insults in various obscene languages. He continued to curse while hanging from the cell gate, which only prompted Officer Abu Lacan to step the intensity of lashes from the whip.

Having received around fifty lashes, Muhammaduh couldn't get into a comfortable position to sleep. He kept tossing and turning like a fish being fried. He felt ashamed and humiliated by what Ibrahim Ashour had done. Growing up, he was taught that physical pain would eventually fade, but a broken soul would continue to burn and consume the remaining joys of life. Muhammaduh felt that Ibrahim Ashour had shattered his pride and manhood, destroying the boastful spirit he once had. He had always fought against the people in his neighbourhood, trying to prove that race was not an acquired pride, but merely a vessel that carried the imprint and genes of human beings throughout history.

Ibrahim was freed from detention and the officer punished Muhammaduh for stabbing the doctor with the scissors. Despite the doctor waiving his rights, Officer Abu Lacan meted out 50 lashes to end Muhammaduh's time in custody.

Muhammaduh emerged unsteady on his feet... and unable to face his ill mother. It was a restless night, filled with loneliness that weighed heavily on him. He had not slept well the previous night, tormented by his mother's moans, the pain of the lashes and the cruel act of Ibrahim. These events made him agitated to the point of hyperventilation, bottling up his anger and releasing deep breaths in the cramped room shared with his mother and siblings, while the rest of his family occupied the other two rooms. He was also oppressed with knowing what the men in the neighbourhood were saying about him. Every time he imagined their sarcastic comments and insults, he would become livid, cursing Ibrahim Ashour under his breath.

Chapter 3

After that night, Muhammaduh felt like a machine broken beyond repair. A tight knot of tension settled in his chest, creating unrelenting pressure that escaped only in the form of constant groans. He couldn't rest or forget the events that had caused his distress.

Three faces haunted his dreams, Officer Abu Lacan, Ibrahim Ashour and the Indian doctor and he plotted revenge on each of them. He couldn't help but fixate on these plans, as each face stirred a different grievance within him. He vowed to pursue the hatred he felt for these individuals he deemed impure. As the days passed, only Ibrahim Ashour's face remained in his thoughts.

****

The cackling of the chickens in the yard led him to the coop where he found scattered eggs. He collected them, cracking a couple open to eat on the spot and wiped his mouth on his stained shirt. He breathed out deeply and reached for some peanuts from a roasting pot to freshen his breath. He then took the remaining eggs to his sister Hawaa',

"Make us breakfast," he told her.

The ship's horn entering or leaving Jeddah port sounds heavy and slow, bringing with it Hajji Fatima's sorrow. She covered herself with a faded shawl, trying to conceal her trembling limbs by holding onto the quilt's edge and calling to her daughter for a brazier to burn some incense, while she hid behind the smoke to conceal her sickness.

The sound of the horn took her back to a time when her daughter Khaddar rested on her lap at the port.

"It's been a while" echoed through her mind, as flies covered her face despite the smoke and wormwood. They won't go away. She ignores her daughter's request to stay in bed,

"It's just a low-grade fever," she said, pushing herself up.

She trudged over to a wooden box where she kept her trinkets and reached for a bag of coffee, which she claimed lifted her mood. She untied the knot and was about to roast the beans over a slow flame when she remembered the bags of peanuts she had bought from the market before being laid low by the wretched fever. She turned to her daughter Aisha and asked,

"Did you peel and roast the peanuts?" She let out a deep sigh adding,

"Time passed and I never sold them."

"Once you recover, anything is possible," Aishaa replied, to which her mother retorted,

"What's possible is what you do now, not what you'll do tomorrow."

Khaddar wrinkled her nose at the sound of the ship's horn and the salty sea breeze.

"Where does this mouldy smell come from?" she muttered.

"The sea," came the reply. Al-Hajji Fatima chuckled, covering a gap in her teeth with her hand,

"Every full belly releases its rot?" she said "This smell is the sea's stomach belching, I'd say it's had enough." When her daughter didn't respond, she added,

"Your ancestors are familiar with the sea's moods. "They're from the 'kotoko' tribe, descendants of the Sao, which lived near Lake Chad and purified its fish from the sea's breath. Your grandfather (my father) always said, 'The sea brings both death and decay'."

As if emerging from an old tomb, Al-Hajji Fatima's memories flooded back, accompanied by her sorrow and shivers.

"I don't remember my father scolding me as harshly as he did when we were about to board a ship to escape the French army," she said. "My shoe fell off and before I could pick it up, your grandfather sternly said, 'The sea wants yeast to sour its guts, so let it be'."

Years passed and that incident faded but Al-Hajji Fatima's memories breathed new life into them, bringing those days back to her in vivid detail.

She is Musa Jamnin's first wife, and he entrusted her with three other women who were also his wives. He passed away in the dock of Port Sudan and left her in charge, making her the ultimate commander. She became a mother to all and was known only as "Our Mother Fatima". She took great pride in her responsibilities and sense of motherhood. The disrespect shown towards their black race by some of her neighbours fuelled her anger, and she never missed an opportunity to reclaim her pride in her roots, which once ruled the Kingdom of Kanem. She also followed in the footsteps of her ancestors by cursing the French who brought an end to a kingdom that ruled for twelve centuries.

She remembered Independence Day as a national holiday when Chad became a free country searching for roots that had been buried by French oppression. Had colonialism not left behind a legacy of civil conflict among the people and a lingering pain in their hearts, her family would not have fled to Sudan and then migrated to Mecca.

Fatima asserted her identity as an immigrant, so much so that it became a part of her name, "Fatima Al-Muhammad" (the immigrant). Despite the lack of scrutiny from her neighbours, she remained proud of her roots. She never tired of recounting the story of her family' journey, where they had to abandon everything and cross treacherous deserts to escape poverty and danger.

Whenever she faced poverty, she drew strength from memories of her home town of N'Djamena or their journey to the east of the country towards the "House of God". However, a traumatic event occurred on the shores of Port Sudan that haunted her family for the rest of their lives. Her husband's sister, Amina, was kidnapped by slave traders when she stepped away from the convoy to use the restroom. The incident devastated her husband, leading to his death from depression before they even sailed to Jeddah. On arrival in Jeddah, Fatima became the guardian of her co-wives and children and took on this role with dignity and pride.

Chapter 4

Fatima expressed her frustration with her son Muhammaduh, saying,

"This ball will only bring you harm, you're running around all day playing in the streets."

Muhammaduh had a lifelong passion for football, failing to support his mother or help with any chores. His love of football was such that he willingly accepted the consequences of deliberately botching tasks he was asked to do.

However, this love ultimately led him to a very odd reputation among his peers. As a child, he had difficulty actually playing the game. After each setback, he moved to a different position in the team.

He tried every role, forward, midfielder, defender and goalkeeper but his modest skills left him unable to fulfil the responsibilities of any of the positions to which he was assigned. This became a major weakness for his team on which their opponents often capitalised to secure victories. Despite his efforts to improve, he never became a standout player. However, Muhammaduh excelled in creating a positive playing atmosphere and it was this skill that kept him on the team.

He started his career by crafting a ball from scraps of cloth and kicking it in every direction, causing him to chase it through the streets as it never bounced back. By the time he finished, he was panting and exhausted. His cloth ball wasn't enticing enough for his peers to join in the kickabouts. Even if one of them did, the ball's laces would quickly unravel and the pieces of cloth would scatter, leaving only torn fragments at their feet, snuffing out whatever slight eagerness there was to continue playing. He sought a solution to the fragility of his cloth ball from tailors and Mutshar Qahtan advised him to buy a sock and stuff it with pieces of sponge pieces. However he found it challenging to collect all these materials. One day, he was in the middle of the Bab Sharif market haggling with vendors to buy one sock, when a Yemeni seller took hold of his ear and pulled him up, shouting,

"You're an idiot buying just one sock."

The Yemeni seller lost six pairs of summer socks after pulling the boy by his ear. When the vendor eventually let go, he saw Muhammaduh grab the socks and flee through the crowded throng of tool sellers. Despite having stones thrown at him, the boy's agility allowed him to escape the Yemeni. The stones struck the boy's thick skull, which withstood the impact without causing serious injury. Unable to retrieve his valuable summer socks, the Yemeni seller gave up the chase.

Muhammaduh went to the garbage dump to search for a sponge mattress. He went from dump to dump until he arrived at the Seven Palaces Street, before returning home dragging two flimsy sponge mattresses behind him. He then sat in the shade of his courtyard's lemon tree and plucked out sponge pieces of various sizes, stuffing them into one of the stolen socks.

The look of his new ball, with its slightly misshapen roundness and slow rolling, was much better than the old one, and he managed to coax some boys who normally avoided going out to play with him. He no longer lost his temper as before in frustration when his sock balls were crushed. He had plenty of other balls, so if one went missing or got damaged, it would be quickly replaced with a new one made from scraps of sponge.

The sock ball kept him isolated in the backstreets. He became the main and leading player among groups of younger boys who didn't know much about football apart from what he'd told them. Despite his desire to play in the big fields of the neighbourhood, his superiority over these boys made him content to be in charge. He had two advantages: he was the owner of the ball and the most skilled player. Muhammaduh gained additional satisfaction by staying immersed among the boys called "house pigeons", since the smartest of them had seen and done far less in life than Muhammaduh and wouldn't be able to prove his lies, even if he claimed to bring the sun up from under his armpit.

Muhammaduh liked the conduct of the "house pigeons". They were peaceful, obedient and giving. He took pleasure in spending time with them, playing games that made him happy and kept them as regular players.

One of the boys fell out of favour early on and Muhammaduh was annoyed when he made fun of everything he did. This boy put himself next to a wall and placed the sock ball under his foot. He thought he would get away with it, but he found his earlobe being rubbed with pebbles between the fingers of Abdul Ghafour Ashour (El-Baggio), causing him to cry out in pain.

"I wouldn't trade a weirdo like you for a bag of salt," said Abdul Ghafour Ashour.

Muhammaduh felt his ear was being skinned, so he tried to escape by lowering his head and grabbed Abdul Ghafour

Ashour's hand, pleading weakly but to no avail. In the heat of Abdul Balfour's emotions, he pushed Muhammaduh against the wall, pinning his face against a smooth wall coated with limewash, and pulled him to the end of the wall, repeating,

"You are still slaves, and even if freed, you will never escape your skin."

and ending it with a kick aimed at Muhammaduh's behind, saying,

"I don't want to see you on this street again. Do you understand or do I need to repeat it?"

Muhammaduh now avoids El Bagnio's house at all costs, taking alternate routes even if it means a longer journey, turning east or south, and taking parallel streets The only thing that distresses him is losing the smile of a child who used to greet him and bid him farewell. He still remembers the last time he saw her, tears streaming down her green eyes as she saw the marks of the limewash on his skin.

Muhammaduh did not forget the free discipline session he received from Abdul Ghafour (El-Baggio). He consistently attempted to harm his son Ibrahim by following him and verbally harassing him; on his way to school, to the grocery stores scattered around the neighbourhood, or on his way to the mosque. Muhammaduh became like a shadow that didn't cause harm to Ibrahim but always followed him. Ibrahim tried to fend off his hostility by not responding to his comments or by letting him catch up with him and talk to him. But their interactions continued to ignite feelings of anger and hatred in each other.

Chapter 5

The residents of the neighbourhood laughed at Muhammaduh when he arrived at the neighbourhood field with a home-made ball, offering to play with them. He earned the nickname "sock ball" and stopped going to the fields, instead practising in his backyard, encouraging his sisters to play with him so he wouldn't have to chase after a ball that doesn't bounce.

The ball the neighbourhood residents played with was light and snow-white, with a flat surface that allowed it to bounce and roll quickly in the direction it was kicked. Muhammaduh had never seen one like it before, and was eager to collect his pennies to get one for himself. And after a few days, he had saved only a quarter of a riyal, due to the scarcity of his mother's resources, as she strived to provide bread and food for him and the rest of the family...

One afternoon, while listening in on some boys who were gathering Lux soap wrappers and Tide soap box bottoms, Muhammaduh heard them counting and excitedly shouting that they only needed nine more wrappers to get a new ball.

Once he had heard enough, he set off to garbage dumps in various alleyways, gathering wrappers from Lux soap and Tide boxes. He collected many but was unsure where to take them or how many he would need to obtain the ball that had become his sole desire.

Exhausted from his journey, he came across Daoud

Al-Awar's water cart heading home. He hopped on the back, clutching a bag of garbage he'd gathered. Daoud was unaware of his presence.

As he reached the street leading to his house, he leapt from his ride like a stuntman and scattered the contents of his bag in front of Abdullah Al-Mahjoub.

"Uncle Abdullah, are these packets enough for me to get a ball?" he asked. Al-Mahjoub, standing outside his shop, grabbed hold Muhammaduh's salt stained flannel and shouted,

"Come and see this little thief! Look what he's done,"

Muhammaduh was taken aback by the outburst and tried to dodge the slaps Al-Mahjoub was raining down on him while inciting those nearby,

"While my back was turned, this rogue took the soap wrappers I'd been collecting," Al-Mahjoub shouted.

Muhammaduh was slapped several times before being chased away with a dire threat for stealing from Al-Mahjoub's shop. He sobbed as he pushed open the creaky wooden gate of his house and told his mother what had happened, begging her to come with him to reclaim what he had gathered. But when she refused, he wept again. Before his tears could flow any longer, she slapped him on the face,

"You know some people are like wells. Whatever falls into them is lost and Al-Mahjoub is a dark well of injustice."

For the first time, he felt wronged, and the longing to speed up his years to the point of being an adult, lingered with him whenever he experienced injustice, crushing him wherever he went. And he daydreamed that if he were older, he would have had the power to assert his rights through his own actions.

Despite the numerous moments of vulnerability that he

had to endure, dreams of becoming a tyrannical oppressor still remained with him, fantasising of becoming a grown man to face Al-Mahjoub and placate him with kicks and punches, and he persisted in his imaginings of throwing the store's items from the shelves onto the floor, to make him understand a small portion of the anger and frustration that he feels now. He shut his eyes to dreams of reclaiming what Al-Mahjoub had taken from him and of getting the ball that meddled with his aspirations all night.

Chapter 6

Since Muhammaduh learned how to scavenge the waste, he had been able to provide for himself and he no longer relied on his mother for an allowance, but instead convinced her to help him increase his income. This suggestion came not in the early days when he first found the waste dump but at a later stage when he realised that others were competing with him for the scraps and racing to collect them with their families.

He used to spend his days between books and the trash. In the former he received only continual canings from his teacher, Zainab Munawar, and he forgot the pain of her cane when he sold the scavenged empty milk cans and copper wire. He was able to save enough money to buy a ball better than the plastic ones that Bin Dawood used give to the collectors of his soap wrappers.

This made up for his lack of footballing ability and he became an essential part of all gatherings of the boys in the neighbourhood, as they agreed to let him play any position he wanted, in exchange for supplying the original leather football for them to play with. If he increased his earnings, he would buy a berry drink to quench the players' panting thirst from having spent the afternoon running on the pitches.

****

The patience of the neighbourhood team eventually ran

thin and they were convinced of Muhammaduh's poor play and gave up hope of improving his skills no matter which position he was given. Ahmad Ziab waved the white flag of annoyance after their team suffered a crushing 8-0 defeat, with the goals easily scored as Muhammaduh failed to fulfil his role as goalkeeper. Abadi Masawi swore that there were only eight attempts and all of them cost a goal. To have Muhammaduh leave the team, Abadi began to question the financial support he provided and suggested that his teammates give it up, splitting the costs of their matches instead to avoid becoming a laughing stock among other teams, refusing to let their team be an easy win for other teams because of Muhammaduh. When Muhammaduh realised he might lose his starring role, he considered announcing his retirement and offering to bear the expenses in exchange for becoming the team's coach.

****

In the afternoon, the players headed to the "Nails" field, navigating the narrow winding streets in the heart of the neighbourhood, to have a fun time playing. The fields are scattered across the city and whoever arrives first gets to claim the best one. In the absence of any preference, the unused spaces served as parking for trucks carrying a variety of goods as well as other vehicles loaded mainly with construction, electrical and carpentry supplies for the southern market. The surface was covered in asphalt and littered with nails of various sizes, as well as wooden boards, wire, barrels, pipes, massive tanks, paint containers and cables.

The area selected for Muhammaduh's team was previously

used for storing and transporting wood to carpentry workshops, leaving behind nails that made made football a difficult and dangerous pastime. Muhammaduh made the effort to secure the stadium before the other teams arrived. He chose a plot of land in the middle of the Sabkha neighbourhood, north of the mayor's house, and oversaw the removal of the nails giving his team priority for that field. He would turn up an hour before afternoon prayer to be there ahead of the players and greet them on their arrival, making it clear to the other teams that the field belonged to his team. One afternoon the team members arrived to find Muhammaduh wearing a new uniform and carrying a whistle, shouting,

"Gather round... gather round..." while occasionally blowing the whistle.

The players rushed onto the field and as they gathered, Muhammaduh tried to break the news of the ball being damaged. A nail had pierced the rubber when he kicked the ball to test his skills. The players were not impressed,

"How can we play without a ball?" they complained.

Muhammaduh felt terrible and attempted to cover it with numerous apologies, fearing that his teammates would hold him responsible for the damaged ball and take away his title. Nowhere in his string of apologies, did he mention the real reason for his failure to acquire a replacement ball.

"Let's focus on Swedish exercises today," he suggested.

His proposal was turned down flat by the players, and many of them ran off to head for the port fields to join other teams. Muhammaduh truly lacked the expertise to adequately perform the role of coach, and was humiliated when the players stared calling him "Noonday donkey". Muhammaduh took this insult as the final straw in his coaching career.

Chapter 7

Every misfortune that could befall him seemed to be directed against Muhammaduh. His only solace was to dwell on what he could have done differently. He found himself reverting to his teenage years and dreams of the child who used to greet him with a smile. She was his refuge from all his failures. He never forget the tears that flowed from her green eyes when El-Baggio had rubbed his face against a wall coated with limewash.

During his teenage years, his attention shifted to observing the faces of girls as they walked to and from school. Every morning, he would sit in a corner of a long street that connected all the narrow roads and alleys. He would sit there, scrutinizing the faces of the girls concealed behind thick black Shayla scarves. He continued this until he became fearful that one of the girls would tell her family, leading him to a fate of misery and ruin.

He wanted to continue looking at the girls but at the same time feared reprisals against his behaviour. He resolved to stand on the street just one morning a week, changing which day every week. Whenever the idea of doing so overcame him with shame, he stopped looking at schoolgirls. One day in the period when these conflicting thoughts raced through his brain, a girl who was lagging behind her friends uncovered her face as she walked past him. She gave him a smile that he recognised, which almost made his heart skip a beat. It was the same girl who had often smiled at him, but once cried when she saw her father insulting him by pushing his face against the wall.

She had eyes as green as grass and cheeks as red as ripe berries. Her hair was braided with the hue of the night sky. She awakened memories from his childhood and stirred up feelings deep within him. He couldn't look away from her but she quickly covered her face. He spent much of the night with his eyes open wide, unable to eradicate her smile from his mind. He became addicted to waiting for her and watched from afar as she went about her day. Even though he knew where she lived, he dared not follow her. Her path took her to places forbidden for him.

He was consumed by fear, content to bask only in the memory of her smile. It was enough to let him escape into a world of his own creation, where he could dream and imagine to his heart's content.

Chapter 8

On the night Muhammaduh made a pledge to change his life. He struggled to make sure the decision was what he really wanted to do. He had wasted his childhood and a portion of his youth chasing after a ball that never paid off, leaving him with a sense of failure. He failed to grasp that the winds of failure blow from the shores of our actions, for every failure-prone action sows a seed that bears fruit of our missteps, serving as bitter sustenance for those who have failed.

He didn't realise every action shapes our fate, either for better or for worse, and many people fail to recognise the significance of chance. However, it is not just luck but also the consequences of past actions that have been overlooked.

The young lads from the neighbourhood had gathered for a game to restore their pride after the 8-0 drubbing. By midday when they arrived, large cloths had been placed to block off sandy roads and alleyways and to prevent vendors and passers-by from entering. Rugs were laid out for spectators while other people squatted on flat stones, their gaze roaming over the faces of the players, either approvingly or disapprovingly. Muhammaduh's arrival sparked Hassan Sekran's curiosity,

"Who invited this weirdo?" And he saw Bakr Al Kach laughing,

"Did he come by mistake, or did he think it was a gathering to form a football team?"

The atmosphere became tense and the heat, combined with humidity, made everyone uncomfortable. Some fanned themselves with pieces of cardboard while others wet their heads at the fountain by the entrance to the square. Hussein Zumal appeared, looking for a spot to see everyone. He greeted each attendee by full name.

"In your neighbourhood there are very worthy men who guard our community's reputation... We've invited some young men to be appointed as protectors of our honour," he said.

The crowd cheered and greeted the neighbourhood's dignitaries.

At the meeting, Muhammaduh's name was mentioned due to his athletic build and muscular physique, making him a suitable candidate to play the role of a protector. His first task was to seek revenge against the "sons of the cistern", who had previously attacked Hussein Zumal's group, disrupted their dance, broke Madah's rib, injured Al-Messiri and stole their instruments. This act was meant to restore honour to the young boys of the "Zawiya" neighbourhood.

That attack brought shame upon the people of "al Zawiya" and left a mark on Hussein Zumal's forehead. Despite this, he stirred the people of his neighbourhood to take action. However, Kamal Al-Qusayr argued that it was best to wait,

"Don't attack your opponent when they're expecting it," he said.

Without waiting for questions or answers, Hussein Zumal went forward with dirt in his hands, pretending to throw it in the faces of those gathered around him. Their reactions varied but they all closed their eyes, and that's when he spoke with great enthusiasm,

"Just as they took us by surprise, we need to surprise them," he said. "But before that, we need to gather the rest of the neighbourhood's young people and choose the strongest among them."

It had been some time since the residents of "Al Zawiya" vowed to take action against the defeat inflicted upon them by the "sons of The Cistern". They took their time to prepare for a retaliation mission to wipe away the shame that had befallen their community. Abu Aisha was tasked with rallying the youth and stirring up their anger with tales of the disgrace suffered by their neighbourhood, with the belief that only revenge could erase it.

"The pupil expands when seeking a solution," said Abu Aisha as he gazed upon Muhammaduh. The group's stares seemed to be urging him to step up and join the circle they had made, so he walked around twice, then stepped forward with confidence,

"It's time for us to be proud of you, Muhammaduh," he said. The group realized the importance of structure and unity in seeking revenge. A muscular figure, sweating profusely from every muscle, stood before them. Muhammaduh had a solid stance, broad chest, thin waist, steady feet and hands clenched tightly.

"This man may have a strong body but he lacks heart." Abu Aisha disregarded the remark and challenged the speaker, Hassan Sukran, to a fight with Muhammaduh. In one flowing movement, Muhammaduh grabbed Hassan by his collarbone and threw him aside. The fights continued, and after each one, Muhammaduh emerged victorious.

Chapter 9

Muhammaduh had developed impressive muscles from lugging heavy waste and carrying it on his back for long distances. His biceps gleamed in the sun as he carried his load and even after a long day of collecting garbage from his neighbourhood and nearby areas, the gleam didn't fade. He returned home as the sun was starting to set and made sure not to upset his mother by bringing the waste into their yard. She often scolded him for being foolish,

"People take the rubbish out of their homes and you bring it into ours," she told him.

He could bear all the criticism, searching for a spot to keep his new hobby. He found the perfect place at the back of their garden, which would ease his mother's frustration and allow him to stash away things he couldn't sell or trade. He'd spend his days sorting through the rubbish he'd collected and, as soon as he was done, he'd head to the field to paint the floor before the team arrived, in a last effort to win back the trust of his teammates who'd threatened to kick him off the team.

He greeted Abu Aisha warmly, but didn't take his gaze from the tangled electrical wires. He worked hard to unravel the mess, showing his obvious preoccupation in his brief responses and lack of attention to Abu Aisha's introductions, making the latter angry at the cold reception. It was as if someone was saying to him, "Still clinging to the football dream? You're pitiful, spending your money on coaching boys and all they do is mock your failure."

Abu Aisha realised his words had upset Muhammaduh, so he kept talking to try to clarify his message. Meanwhile, Muhammaduh muttered an obscene insult under his breath. Abu Aisha pretended not to hear it by looking away and following a water cart that had spilled. People were shouting at the water carrier, Musa bin Ali, accusing him of mistreating his donkey, which had collapsed in the middle of the road.

In an attempt to stir up Muhammaduh, Abu Aisha mentioned breaking Al-Madah's rib and how Salem Al-Bouma had tricked him with a weak strike that caused the bat to fall on the his side, breaking his left rib. Abu Aisha sat down close by and patted Muhammaduh on the shoulder, saying,

"The lads are betting on your ability to get revenge for the people in the neighbourhood. Don't let them down."

Muhammaduh didn't react to all the enticements that Abu Aisha presented to make him the head of the Al-Mizmar group,

"Your foolishness will keep you as a child's plaything," he said, rushing off before Muhammaduh's wrath boiled over. He narrowly avoided being hit by a rock thrown at him. Instead it struck the gate of Abdullah al-Mahjoub's shop. Abdullah retrieved the rock and tossed it back, cursing Muhammaduh and his ancestry.

Abu Aisha was not confident his conversations with Muhammaduh would be successful until he was freed from captivity. He longed to become the leader of the neighbourhood's boys and spearhead the fight to bring turmoil to the Cistern Quarter so they could successfully fight Ibrahim Ashour.

****

He accepted his defeat and no one dared to acknowledge the hidden disappointment in Muhammaduh's heart. The prominence of his muscles tempted him to procrastinate and seek a sense of contentment that he hoped to pass on to his peers, so he went to Al-Ahly Club to join the bodybuilding competition. His physique, defined by chiselled muscles, caught the eye of the fitness trainer and made Muhammaduh a potential champion. With the first exercise, he secured his spot on the list of contestants.

He returned to his house, leaping and putting an end to the deceptive path he had taken for what felt like an eternity. Early in the morning, he woke up to paint his body with oil, massaging and rubbing his body and limbs to reveal his muscles beneath a short-sleeved t-shirt with very short sleeves and a two-piece sports outfit that showed off his thighs. Eager to show off his newly-toned figure, he set off in a hurry to reach the long street, hoping the smiling girl would catch a glimpse of his physique.

Within moments came across the young woman whose face instantly bore the broadest of smiles, filling the place with a very clear message.

As the call to afternoon prayer echoed through the air, he rushed towards Al-Ahly Club. On reaching the gate, the coach signalled for him to step back while delivering the crushing news that membership required proof of citizenship. His shoulders dropped with disappointment.

Chapter 10

Al-Zawiya took its name from its position nestled between two ridges, one stretching north from the Bab Sharif market and the other extending west towards Al-Hajja city. It wasn't always known by this name. It was originally simply referred to by its location within the walls of Jeddah. The vast expanse allowed residents to choose a place for their homes without allotting a name. They were identified based on their proximity to notable landmarks. As the neighbourhood expanded and streets were established, names were given based on other famous things, such as personalities, events or ethnic groups. With the advent of telegraph and mail, names were standardised and every neighbourhood sought to exert its influence over adjacent areas.

Hussein Zumal was the leader of Al-Zawiya. The surname "Zumal" was not inherited from his father but earned from his expertise in organising and running the "Mezmar" game. He was known for his competitive drive in rallying his neighbourhood and his talent for composing rousing battle songs that resounded beyond Al-Zawahiri's borders.

Since the beginning of his leadership, he had faced numerous challenges that threatened his position. Each time he failed to resolve an issue, rumours spread among the neighbouring communities. His opponents tried to tarnish his reputation with false stories but some incidents had a profound impact on his leadership. For example, Bard

Al-Ghoul spoke about the shortage of water, the mayor's harsh punishment of the residents, the lack of oversight for outsiders in the neighbourhood, unbridled illegal activities during the night and the forced removal of the muezzin, Yaounde Khalil. These events made Hussein Zumal's leadership appear fragile.

Among the incidents that damaged his reputation and showed his lack of resolve and disregard was the shooting of Fatima Al-Muhajira in the foot by Ibrahim Ashour with a hunting rifle, and his inadequate reaction. He visited her but failed to take action against Ibrahim Ashour, especially when Officer Abu Khaddash spread stories about what happened to her son in the detention centre It was rumoured that his cousin, Officer Abu Laban, insulted Muhammaduh greatly in a message that he failed to understand. The efforts to remove Hussein Zumal from leadership persisted, and the final straw was an attack by the Cistern Boys on the Mezmar dance stage that was taking place under his direction. This event caused him to vow to restore the neighbourhood's reputation, even though he had previously brushed off previous incidents as minor mishaps, regarding the incident of shooting Muhammaduh's mother as being accidental.

However, his claim he was unaware of the reason behind the Cistern Sons' attack on his neighbourhood was the catalyst for calls to change leadership.

As the investigation into the attack continued, reports of abuse of Muhammaduh in the detention room by his cousin, officer Abu Laban, came to light. These revelations added to the growing discontent with Hussein Zumal's leadership and eroded the reputation of the people of the Al-Zawiya neighbourhood.

Hussein Zumal was so taken aback that he was considering a rash move of his own – to take Ibrahim Ashour from the Cistern Sons' group of young men. This idea was causing him great distress.

He remembered the warning given by Abdullah Al-Battini, which carried a constant threat from Ibrahim Ashour's uncle, making him hesitate. Memories of Suleiman Al-Daksh complaining about Muhammaduh also came to mind,

"If the actions of Muhammaduh the weirdo go unchecked, blood will be the final outcome between us."

Suleiman finished his complaint with a long sentence,

"I am giving you fair warning of Muhammaduh's harassment and you know what Ibrahim means to me."

Before Hussein Zumal could respond, Suleiman rode off on his motorbike, regained his focus and posed the question,

"What does Abu Aisha aim to accomplish by nominating Muhammaduh for leadership?"

He headed home, grabbed his hookah pipe and took a few sips of strong tea. Gradually, he reflected on the events and the motives behind his actions. A web of stories and connections formed in his mind. He was sure there were hidden forces directing him towards a destiny he had not chosen for himself.

****

"Life has a surprise in store you didn't ask for."

The phrase echoed in Muhammaduh's mind, causing him deep reflections. Despite being taken aback by a sudden shock, he declined to reveal it, even to himself. However much he tried to dispel the idea, it persistently remained at the forefront of his thoughts. His actions of harassing Ibrahim Ashour had only escalated the tension and conflicts between his community and the Cistern Boys. Instead of considering the consequences of his actions, he was focused solely on improving and gaining control over the local football team via rummaging through waste, selling scrap and accumulating wealth. However, an unexpected turn of events prompted him to reevaluate his relationship with Ibrahim Ashour.

He made numerous attempts to attract Ibrahim, using all means at his disposal, in an effort to entice him to play on the team he led. With each rejection, he devised a new strategy, trying various temptations. Finally, he decided to buy a motorcycle as a luxury gift for Ibrahim to use during his travels. He ostentatiously decorated the front and back of the vehicle with additional accessories and even used the help of calligrapher Saeed Sanallah to write on the license plate,

"The heart adores every beautiful thing" accompanied by a drawing of a pierced heart that Muhammad al-Aswad disapproved of stating,

"Ibrahim was born into wealth, so saving your effort and money would be best."

Muhammaduh vividly remembered the time Abdul Ghafour Ashour pinched his ear as a child, and he harboured a burning desire for revenge. He daydreamed of replacing the pebbles that had pierced his earlobe with a grenade, which he would use to pierce the ear of that arrogant man.

As the years went by and the gap in age, material wealth, and prestige between them grew, Muhammaduh's desire for revenge shifted from the father to the son, Ibrahim. This latent desire began to resurface with each passing day, blooming like a cactus in its ferocity.

Muhammaduh didn't realise that desires can spur impulsive actions and ventures into unknown territory. The element of surprise always lingers between the recognition of a desire and the act of fulfilling it. Muhammaduh could sense that Ibrahim Ashour would be the catalyst for his descent into an uncertain darkness.

His grudge started after he left the detention cell, fuelled by his anger and eagerness to venture into the darkness, determined to humiliate Ibrahim Ashour in a way that would bring heartbreak and remorse to Abdul Ghafour Ashour, at the same time purging his pride and arrogance.

Years had passed, and as he woke up one day, he realised that revisiting the past did not erase what was but confirms one's place in it. Muhammaduh reflected on the days gone by and felt like burying his head in a trash bin, wishing to replace his shameful past with flowers to surround the life of the Ashour family. He even imagined kissing Abdul Ghafour's head daily, as a way to show closeness and connect with Omaima.

****

On the second Monday of Rabi` al-Awwal in 1373 (AH), the city of Taif was stunned by the news of King Abdulaziz Al Saud's sudden heart attack, and his body was transferred to Riyadh. The city of Jeddah was deeply affected by the loss and its leaders decided to offer condolences and pledge allegiance to King Saud bin Abdulaziz. They agreed to travel on Wednesday and as they prepared to depart, they lined up to select a spokesperson. Abdul Ghafour Ashour and Oqab ben Ali were among the contenders, but the decision was postponed until they reached Riyadh, as Fadil Al-Hamwi stated,

"Our minds will be clearer to make a choice once we reach Riyadh. Let's not delay the journey by indecision."

Wishes can be fickle and when faced with tough times can become like a strong wind that mixes up dirt and people's spirits. Muhammaduh learned that Abdul-Ghafour Ashour had been appointed to a prestigious royal delegation. He spent the entire night wrestling with his innermost thoughts and the pain of his own failure, which even haunted his dreams. "How can I wound that arrogant heart?" he asked. He wasn't striving for power but rather for his family to escape the tyranny of his arch-nemesis.

Chapter 11

At a creaky wooden gate, Muhammaduh sat listening to the humming of his friend Yasser Mohanbi, whose voice was filled with emotion. Yasser was struggling to fill the silent void, which was an overwhelming task,

"Ibrahim was raised like a spoiled brat. He comes from a family of pure bloodline and it's said that his grandfather, Khairy Ashour, owns the vast majority of the Cistern region. How can the rich and poor be equal, Muhammaduh?" he asked him.

The question hung heavy in the air and stuck in Muhammaduh's mind. He sought refuge in the corner he had picked behind his house to sort through the garbage he collected. The stench clung to his fingers and the palms of his hands, which he tried to remove by washing them with kerosene he kept close by to get rid of the grease that stuck to him from handling the waste.

He washed his fingers and palms but the smell persisted. He thought about what Yasser Mohanbi had said,

"Souls have a life that leaves an indelible imprint regardless of changes in circumstances."

He rebelled against the waste and began throwing it about. In his frenzy, he piled waste into a pyramid. With a manic shout, he leapt over the top of the pyramid, declaring,

"I am climbing to greatness through the trash."

When he had calmed down, he shook his rugs

and reorganised the scattered rubbish. As prayer time approached, he heard his mother calling him from inside the house,

"Prayer is the path to righteousness, so leave everything aside and head to the mosque."

He was often preoccupied with sorting his belongings only to find his mother standing over him, scolding him for his actions and regretting she had not passed on to him her religious upbringing. To appease her, he would kiss her hand and hurry to the mosque to avoid further rebuke. Fatima al-Muhajira's voice was always sharp when she woke him up for morning prayer. If he took too long getting up, she prodded him with a cane to rouse him from his slumber. On his days off, he headed straight from the mosque to the local dump to search for items to sell but on school days he caught glimpses of the smiling girl and headed to the dump after the schoolgirls left, his eyes heavy with fatigue but his heart filled with joy.

His daily routine started to change and, although he was still fond of visiting the chickens and collecting their eggs to eat, it was at the price of annoying his sister Eve. The sound of the roosters and their chicks crowing would wake her early, followed by the fluttering of feathers all around. This made it difficult for her to sweep the floor and remove the small feathers sticking to scattered utensils and to clean up the feathers from the seeds spread out for roasting. Every morning, Muhammaduh would receive a scolding from her, and if she ever forgot, he would remind her,

"If you kept clear of the unpleasant raw eggs, you could consume them as meat."

Fatima Al-Muhajira noticed a shift in her son's behaviour

but was hesitant to address it, choosing instead to observe from a distance. She watched helpless as her son went through bad patches, resorting to tears and prayer for comfort.

****

Al-Mallah informed him about the rumours circulating in the neighbourhood about Ibrahim Ashour's arrest, exaggerating the situation and mentioning the desire of the youth to join forces against the residents of the Cistern Quarter. However, he made clear that Ibrahim was his only concern.

Muhammaduh was eager to participate in the neighbourhood's revenge but was disappointed when he was given the task of travelling to Mecca to get news of his aunt Amina's whereabouts, who had reportedly been sold on the coast of Port Sudan. He showed a defiance he had never exhibited before.

"You're rejecting my orders, Muhammaduh?" his mother said.

He tried his best to persuade her to change her mind but she insisted he must go to bring her news of Aunt Amina.

Al-Mallah promised to give Muhammaduh the freedom to deal with Ibrahim as he wished. Meanwhile, the people of Al Zawiya finished their preparations and began looking for news on the preparations for the Mezmar in every nook and cranny of the Cistern Quarter.

He had been gearing himself up for a revenge battle, having made a promise to do so. He worked hard to make a big club to fight with and searched for days to find the perfect weapon, digging through piles of greased up guava branches. His tireless hunt was finally interrupted by Saud Al-Saidi, who gave him a club crafted from a thick Acacia branch. It had been pruned, immersed in a basin of oil and lubricated, with a silver ring in the middle and bull's skin at the two ends, secured with a roll of reinforced copper wire.

His heart was satisfied with this gift and spent the next morning practising swinging the bat in the air with two fingers, until he was able to control its movement. Then came his mother's order for him to head to Mecca. The journey coincided with the planned date of the attack on the Cistern Quarter.

****

Hussein Zumal welcomed and warmly embraced some of the members of the group who had taken part in the attack on the Cistern Quarter and began making his first recommendations before the rest were finished. Leaning on his club, he let out a hearty laugh and said,

"We chose a very dark night to spill their blood however we wanted."

This encouraged El-Messiri to show his happiness, even as he touched the wound on his head,

"This is our good fortune and it means our revenge will be crushing."

In no time at all, Al-Zawiya men had gathered together, like a pack of ravenous hyenas. They marched in the footsteps of Hussein Zumal, who had chosen to sneak into the neighbourhood from below. The band of men avoided the main streets by keeping to the winding alleyways, so news of the attack would not easily reach the people of the Cistern Quarter.

"Tonight we will entrust the neighbourhood's young people with leadership."

THE CISTERN

The thought troubled Muhammaduh as he walked at the front of the group, brandishing his club with a confidence that was marred only by his growing remorse for not fulfilling his mother's request to go to Mecca. He was afraid this distraction would cause him to fail in his mission, so he tried to dispel it by reassuring himself that his mission was only to avenge Ibrahim Ashour's wrongdoings and restore his dignity. After that, he would spend the rest of his life searching for his aunt with his head held high. However, this didn't entirely remove his regret. He walked with sadness, knowing he had disregarded his mother's wish, which was an act of defiance he had never previously committed. Every time her face appeared in his mind, he muttered heartfelt apologies that could sometimes be heard. Nasr Karim thought Muhammaduh was afraid of confrontation, so he tried to encourage him,

"Today, you will be honoured. Don't be afraid." But Muhammaduh took Nasr Karim's words as an insult and prodded him in the waist,

"I have never been afraid and I've been waiting for this day for a long time."

Chapter 12

The news of the return of the notable leaders of the neighbourhood from Riyadh, after paying their condolences and offering their allegiance, was conveyed by the senior men of the neighbourhood. They rushed to greet the delegation and most people sat on the ground, while others with houses close by brought chairs and refreshments. Some showed respect for the elderly by offering them seats and a few even provided mattresses, cold water and home-made juices. A small group simply stood by and watched the proceedings.

On the horizon, the sun appeared timidly, spinning to embrace the night and then falling silent, afraid of disrupting the gathering.

The delegation and its followers reached al-Sukkari square on the road leading to the seaport. The greeters mingled with the delegation's escorts, forming a crowd in which calls were raised for the delegation to address them.

Oqab Ben Ali appeared in the midst of the dignitaries, dressed in his finest clothes and sporting a brown dotted head wrap. He wore a turquoise bag around his waist, a cream vest and oriental shoes, the epitome of high fashion for a notable at such gatherings. His tongue faltered as he tried to speak and his face turned a bright yellow. The words were difficult to form, as if he were forbidden from speaking.

He had a huge task ahead of him, breaking the news of a catastrophe to people, who were wholly unprepared for it.

With great effort, he finally revealed details of events that weighed heavily on his chest,

"Abdul Ghafour Ashour has been arrested."

His silence after this terse announcement was followed by an uproar in the crowd though the situation was soon brought back under control. Standing upright and pushing his head wrap back, he continued to stumble over his words as he tried to carry on with his report.

He started his speech many times, apparently dissatisfied with his choice of words each time, as he struggled to find the best way to begin.

He was eager to switch between phrases and words, as per the guidelines agreed upon by the leaders, without delving into the specifics, so he stuck to using generalities in his speech, to the extent that many people grew restless with his grandiose words. He felt his avoidance of clearly describing what had happened was making the crowd angry. So he came out with a version that was far from that they had agreed,

"Abdul Ghafour Ashour was put in Al-Murabaa' prison." He refused to answer any questions, leaving one particular question hanging in the air,

"What did Abdul Ghafour Ashour do?"

The news from Riyadh reached Muhammaduh like a tune he had heard and repeated many times before, causing a rapid and feverish panting with each breath he took. He attempted to keep his feelings in check and not become too obviously overjoyed. However, the sudden happiness that shone like a star in an empty sky was a divine message in an unexpected form. Overcome, he received it with an open and accepting mind.

****

"What joy had overwhelmed me?"

Muhammaduh was consumed by this thought inside him, as if a beautiful girl had just bestowed a kiss on his cheek. A sudden and intense feeling of happiness was transformed into a powerful engine, propelling his imagination and stirring up memories that flowed like a torrent of time. A stream of events, seemingly crossing from eternity, played out before his mind's eye.

He couldn't quite remember how he got caught up in the tale of becoming Abdul Ghafour Ashour's enemy. As his thoughts wandered, he clutched at his ear, as if it held the key to a TV channel that would transport him back to the first scene. That was when Abdul Ghafour picked up small stones and pressed them into his earlobe, teasing him about his appearance and colour while splitting his face with a cruel sneer that still echoed in his ears, "I wouldn't trade a black slave like you for a bag of salt!"

He persisted in tormenting Muhammaduh, pushing him against a wall painted with limewash, as if he sought to lighten the darkness that constantly plagued him. That insulting incident was intertwined with the memory of the girl's tears that flowed like a river of love soaking into his heart, taking permanent root and branching out into the promise of a fruitful future. Despite the passage of time, the memory of such cruelty and that tear had not faded one jot. Far from it. They were rekindled by Abdul Ghafour's subsequent actions and Ibrahim's heinous deed, leaving Muhammaduh feeling shattered and degraded.

He didn't know why he had been treated so cruelly and since that childhood incident Muhammaduh had avoided roads that led to, or were even close to, Abdul Ghafour

THE CISTERN

Ashour's house. This whale had the neighbourhood as its sea, because it was owned by his father. It was once a vast empty land that communities from different countries had decided to call home, seeking refuge from hot summers and cold winters. Muhammaduh's family was among those communities that arrived from Port Sudan and settled on the streets of Jeddah. Fatima Al-Muhajira claimed a piece of land and built a three-roomed house for her family to live in.

After a period in which no one claimed ownership of that land, other communities arrived from overseas and continued to construct zinc or wooden homes, all residing in friendship and harmony.

On a chilly winter's night, Abdul Ghafour Ashour rose and demanded that Fatima Al-Muhajira leave the area. He warned her that if she did not, he would, as rightful owner of the land, evict her. He justified this action by saying he sought nothing from humanity save ownership of his land.

The following day, surrounded by the mayor's men, Abdul Ghafour proclaimed at the top of his voice that the land on which Fatima had built her house belonged to his father, Khairy Ashour. The mayor's men began clearing her belongings from the house, preparing for her eviction.

Like ants whose nest has been disturbed by a strong stream, the family emerged, carrying only the necessities for their simple life. They lacked many things, as the impoverished migrant family was unable to make ends meet. As they were forced to leave, all the members of the family carried something on their heads. Fatima, exhausted from all her hard work, made every effort to protect her family from utter destitution.

In that sad farewell, Abdul Ghafour stood with a lack of

remorse, acting like a bull only capable of attacking. He hurled insult after insult at the family, far beyond anything reasonable.

Sad memories flooded Fatima's memory with the events that happened after she had set out in search of safety. Abdul Ghafour had pushed her, causing her to fall and scatter the belongings from her head. Muhammaduh, who was 15 years old, turned to help his mother all the while trying to hold back his tears in the face of Abdul Ghafour's arrogance. What helped him was his mother's hand resting on his shoulder and preventing the demons of his anger from completely engulfing him.

That incident was the second to fuel Muhammaduh's hatred for Abdul Ghafour. In the same episode, the noble Oqab bin Ali offered his legally deeded land as a permanent home for Fatima Al-Muhajira and her family.

They were two contrasting figures, love and hate, intermingled in Muhammaduh's heart, nurtured until they bore fruit. Oqab Ben Ali had always been magnanimous towards Fatima's family but El-Baggio was relentless in his efforts to rid the neighbourhood of all those of African descent.

Some sad events befell Hajji Fatima Al-Muhajira family and El-Baggio was quick to fan the flames of resentment in those who had no justifiable reason for their hatred.

Over time, something known only to Abdul Ghafour Ashour had given rise to his intense antipathy towards those of African descent. He was wholly dedicated to upholding the power and prestige of his father, Khairy Ashour (El-Baggio), yet neglectful of his own responsibilities and not interested in fulfilling tasks assigned to him by his father. This left him with a sense of purposelessness, lacking ambition and without the drive to achieve greatness like his father. All his life he adopted his father's glory, content with this passive role until a sudden realisation dawned on him.

When Khairy Ashour said his farewells the night before he had to depart from the port of Jeddah, he left a letter with his son detailing the money, property, financial instruments, documents and some confidential papers that had been left to him. As the night settled in, Salman Lajes knocked on the palace gate. He confided in Khairy Ashour, telling him that he could not let him wait until sunrise to consider the options he had for getting himself out of the situation. Leaving the country was the safest choice before the soldiers arrived to arrest him, said Lajes, who worked as his assistant and was placed in a sensitive positions. He had brought the news of his cover being blown and his manipulation of correspondence and pledges to help anyone who sought to return to Hijaz. Khairy Ashour had been careful not to let any secrets slip, as even the smallest one could result in his life being forfeit. He remained cautious until he lost control of the secret cell that he had established. For a long time he had been meticulous in every detail, allowing leeway to some of his closest associates, which in turn led them to attract individuals whose backgrounds and motives he was unaware of.

News of an attempt to assassinate King Abdul Aziz also uncovered a plan to bring Khairy Ashour down. He became aware of this after the disappearance of his slave Jawhar, who was sent to the assistant of Osay al-Shakima, a high-ranking member at the court of the Mutawakkilite kingdom, with a vague message, filled with prayers and good wishes, but also with one line that was enough to implicate him in multiple charges, including the major one of attempted assassination.

On the third day after Khairy Ashour's departure, Salman

Ajeeb returned with news that had slipped from his tongue before it reached Abdul Ghafour Khairy Ashour. Salman introduced the matter briefly before saying in an animated tone,

"Your father and family have suffered greatly because of Jawhar the slave." Khairy Ashour's father had left instructions to burn all papers in the chest after removing the deeds and important documents.

Salman was familiar with Abdul Ghafour's apathy, and he made a commitment to stay with him until he carried out the two orders given by his master, Khairy Ashour. He was aware that Abdul Ghafour was slow-witted, as evidenced by his sluggish reaction to the news of his father's departure. He also swayed between being conscious and reckless, keeping his ears open for what was being said. But everything he heard fell on deaf ears. He was not motivated by any of them. Salman was frustrated by Abdul Ghafour's continued recklessness, so he repeated Khairy Ashour's last request,

"Your father wants you to find the slave Jawhar and cut out his tongue;" he told him.

Abdul Ghafour reclined, staring off into the distance, as if just realising that his father had finally given him a mission to carry out for the first time. Like a child who knew little of anything, he grabbed Salman's clothes and begged,

"Where can I find this slave?"

After that moment, he searched tirelessly for the slave, and when he couldn't find him, he developed a hatred for every person on earth he thought could be remotely described as a slave.

Jawhar was a slave bought by Khairy Ashour, reassured of his non-Arab heritage. However, Jawhar surpassed expectations by quickly mastering Arabic, including reading and writing. His ambition went beyond just gaining freedom. Due to his elegant handwriting and ability to write in a flowery style, Khairy Ashour tasked him with writing.

The message Jawhar carried was intended for a powerful Yemeni figure in the court of Imam Hamid al-Din, and he saw it as a means to escape slavery. After delivering the message, Jawhar began to dream of rising higher. He was trusted with a secret, but he changed course and delivered the message to the Ministry of Interior, adding a line that sealed Khairy Ashour's betrayal.

Abdul Ghafour needed time to understand a part of his father's business, and, despite this, did not act on his order to burn everything inside the chest. He kept his hatred for any slave who reminded him of Jawhar's betrayal.

Muhammaduh was delighted to learn of Abdul Ghafour's capture and imprisonment in Riyadh.

****

Abdul Ghafour continued to torment Fatima Al-Muhajira family. Like a rat, he found refuge by forcing himself into their lives. He heard a reliable rumour from Youssef Abou Khinak that Jawhar, the slave, was a member of Muhammaduh's family and that they were protecting his identity to keep him safe.

Abdul Ghafour was not renowned for his intelligence and held onto a flawed belief. This persisted until his arrest and eventual imprisonment.

He would knock on Fatima's door every day, asking,

"Where is Jawhar the slave?"

Each time, he was met with Fatima and her family's frustration at his repeated questioning,

"I won't stop until I cut out Jawhar's tongue," he would say. Despite Fatima's repeated claims that she did not know Jawhar, he persisted.

It was only when Muhammaduh's family was given a place to stay by Oqab ben Ali, to protect them from Abdul Ghafour's wrath, that the truth was revealed. Youssef Abou Khinak had made up the story of Jawhar's being from Muhammaduh's family while working for him in an attempt to pay off his debt to him.

Chapter 13

It was a night of chaos as the men of the Al Zawiya quarter surrounded the stage where their enemies were performing the "mezmar". An angry and vengeful heart was at the base of the sudden attack, as they viciously attacked the dance floor, throwing dirt onto the blazing fire.

One of the musicians encouraged his friends to continue playing, as the sound of their harmony mixed with Amro Daksh's raw voice. The dancers formed an uneven circle, with Jamal Al-Marsi in the middle, urging the musicians to repeat the verses. He brandished a stick under his arm and wore an amama with black and white dots, trying to overpower the music with his voice,

"The night, oh Sembilan**
I am from a distant land**
The night, oh Sembilan,
Between Mecca and Madinah**
The night Oh Sembilan,
I am from a distant land
The night, oh Sembilan, you thief**
The night oh Sembilan
no mercy for the dead**
the night, Oh Sembilan,
worms eating his eyes"

This was a message to the opposing teams, not to

welcome outsiders, and for their men to stand united against intruders. The mezmar players gathered around the blazing fire, propped up on their canes, watching out for any movement from the Al Zawiya men.

Kabda approached Hussein Zumal, saying,

"Tonight is my brother's wedding, it would be honourable of you not to spoil our happiness."

But nobody listened to him, as Hussein Zumal jumped onto the centre of the stage, swinging his club and hitting his enemies. He pressed his club against Fakuna, who rose to the challenge, and the two battled with sticks, wrapped around each other. With a swift move, Hussein struck Fakuna's face, causing him to bleed and shout in pain. The Zawiya men then joined the fight in a brutal show of equal force.

In a matter of seconds, the place turned into a battlefield with widespread destruction. Cleavers, daggers, rocks, and chairs were used as the participants sought to attack anyone within reach.

Wedding guests were thrown into confusion and chaos. The area became dark as lanterns and lights were shattered, furniture was broken and musical instruments thrown about, along with rocks, shoes, tea and coffee cups. The situation remained volatile and chaotic, as tempers flared and anger overtook every other emotion amidst the turmoil.

Muhammaduh was on a mission to locate Ibrahim Ashour, his primary focus being to take revenge for the insult. He searched high and low, moving cautiously through the throngs of people engaged in battle, armed with a stick and determined to find his adversary.

He continued his quest, dodging flying sticks and bodies as he sought out Ibrahim. The light was poor, making it difficult to distinguish faces, and many were swinging their weapons aimlessly.

The Zawiya men seemed to be gaining the upper hand, advancing and pursuing those who sought to flee in the narrow streets of the Cistern neighbourhood.

The triumphant spirit was buzzing with excitement, with Hussein Zumal vowing to perform a mezmar dance on enemy soil. Meanwhile, the defeated sought refuge in their homes, cursing their fate.

Muhammaduh roamed the streets like an angry bull, desperate for any clue to lead him to Ibrahim. In a sudden turn, he grabbed the neck of a violin player, threatening to end his life unless he revealed the whereabouts of Ibrahim Ashour.

He released his grip on the violin player, allowing him to speak,

"I don't know Ibrahim and I'm not from this neighbourhood," the player said. "I just came here to sing."

In response, Muhammaduh grabbed the man's throat in his hand, shouting,

"I'm not leaving this neighbourhood without Ibrahim Ashour's corpse."

In the midst of the chaos and noise, a hand touched Muhammaduh's shoulder,

"Leave him alone, I'll tell you where Ibrahim Ashour is."

"Don't you see me in this darkness?" the man replied, before turning his back to Muhammaduh and saying,

"I am the enemy of your enemy, so leave the man and follow me."

The fight had slightly subsided and shouting could be heard. Muhammaduh believed his people were winning the battle but the thought of strangling Ibrahim Ashour was the most powerful force driving him forward.

He followed the man who promised to take him to Ibrahim with the secret intention of cutting his head off if he were lying. With a long and loud exhaling of breath, he panted,

"Why all this running?"

****

Omar Al-Yaridi saved the violin player from Muhammaduh's angry grasp, telling him;

"The residents of the Cistern neighbourhood have been defeated and your folks have retreated back to their neighbourhood," he told Muhammaduh.

Despite his doubts, Muhammaduh followed Al-Yaridi as he led him through the streets towards the heart of the neighbourhood. "I want you to have faith in me and not to argue," Al-Yaridi reassured him.

Although nervous, Muhammaduh's desire to reach Ibrahim overpowered his caution, and he did as Al-Yaridi instructed. They soon arrived at the gate of Ashour's hose.

"This is his house. Knock and take your revenge," Al-Yaridi said.

Remembering the last time he stood in front of the house, Muhammaduh stepped back anxiously.

"I cannot be seen. I'll wait for you at the back. You ask about him," he said.

Al-Yaridi approached the gate and knocked several times. There was no reply but a woman's voice asked who was knocking.

"I'm looking for Ibrahim;" Al-Yaridi told her.

"Ibrahim hasn't returned yet," the woman replied.

Confused by a mixture of memories, Muhammaduh tried to hide and waited for the moment of victory.

****

The jumble of events was obstructing Muhammaduh's path to the right decision. His mind was clouded with uncertainty, like trying to choose the right dough to make a good loaf of bread.

He remembered the two men who had wronged him so deeply. Abdul Ghafour who had thrown his mother out of their home and Ibrahim his son, who had insulted him during his arrest. He was determined to seek revenge against them, to rid himself of memories that haunted him. He waited for Al-Yaridi and, on seeing him, asked,

"What have you done?"

"He hasn't returned yet," Al-Yaridi replied.

Muhammaduh gritted his teeth in anger at Al-Yaridi's next suggestion,

"What if we wait for him in the ruins behind their house? That's where he goes in."

Doubts once again consumed Muhammaduh about Al-Yaridi's motive for bringing him to a place where he didn't know what could be waiting for him. He threatened his guide,

"It seems like you're going to be my victim instead of Ibrahim."

Muhammaduh was confused. He didn't know if his people had truly won the battle or if they had been defeated and were now back looking for a perfect opportunity to take revenge.

"What would become of me if this is indeed what happened?" he wondered.

Despite feeling conflicted, Muhammaduh was determined to return to his neighbourhood before he fell prey to the Cistern people. He disregarded Al-Yaridi's pleas to follow his instructions. Before he could make a move, Al-Yaridi chased after him, begging him to slow down. But before he could rejoin his peers, he saw that the battle had ended and a group of men from the Cistern were closing in on him, threatening

"Let this black slave be our prey to make up for the victory of Hussein Zumal and his neighbours."

Muhammaduh realised Al-Yaridi had been leading him into a trap.

So he seized him by the neck, saying,

"I made a vow not to harm anyone apart from Ibrahim Ashour but it seems I won't be able to keep my promise."

He drew the blade tucked into his belt and placed it against Al-Yaridi's throat, who was frantically shouting,

"Please give me another chance, I'll take you to Ibrahim."

"I demand your life now," Muhammaduh replied.

People running away from the mezmar stage were still trying to protect the children and the elderly. When they saw Muhammaduh grab Al-Yaridi, they called out to their young men to help save him,

"Rescue Al-Yaridi," they screamed.

Their cries were lost in the chaos and all that could be heard was an indecipherable racket. They retaliated by throwing rocks at Muhammaduh, but most of them hit Al-Yaridi who was being used as a shield. Al-Yaridi shouted for them to stop the attack.

Trapped in the middle of a crowd from the Cistern neighbourhood, Muhammaduh tightened his hold on his captive and began dragging him towards the heart of the neighbourhood. Meanwhile, the residents of Al-Zawiya had gathered to celebrate their victory, forming a large circle around Muhammaduh and those who had assembled against him. Abu Aisha called out,

"I have your enemy in sight and, as I promised, only you will be responsible for punishing him."

Muhammaduh delivered a violent kick to Al-Yaridi's body before administering repeated blows with the club. Then he followed Abou Aisha's lead to reach his prime target. Ibrahim was part of a group of defenders, standing strong to protect their neighbourhood, forming a semi-circle barrier to keep attackers at bay.

The two sides clashed in a critical moment of triumph or defeat, with blows flying from all sides.

The defence line started to falter and attackers began to penetrate. Despite the chaos around him, Muhammaduh's focus was set on Ibrahim. He watched his every move, waiting for the right moment to strike. As the defence line weakened, an opening appeared and Muhammaduh seized it. In one swift motion, he grabbed Ibrahim by the shirt, threw him down and sat on his chest, brandishing a sharp blade over his face, shouting in excitement,

"You will never forget me after today."

As Muhammaduh rose to his feet, he took his club in hand and began to retreat from the battle, leaving Ibrahim badly injured and bleeding.

****

The older members of the community were not involved in the battle and viewed the events as youthful unrest. They held the view that the fallout from the violence should not serve as grounds for retaliation, However, what happened to Ibrahim was widely criticised, condemned and met with strong opposition. Jamaal Kayla was particularly outraged and swore that if Abdul Ghafour were not incarcerated, even shedding the blood Muhammaduh and his entire family would not have satisfied him.

Muhammaduh was thrilled at the prospect of Abdul Ghafour Ashour's welcoming his son, so he could see the wounds flowing like rivers, mutilating his son's face and permanently altering his once-handsome features. That would leave them the unenviable task of searching for a solution to heal the injuries and restore their son's once-flawless skin.

Chapter 14

The wounds to Ibrahim's face and his father's imprisonment empowered Muhammaduh to pursue a goal that would be hard to achieve.

Since childhood, Omaima has held a special place in Muhammaduh's heart, as if she were a long-awaited dream.

Fatima's family had relocated to a neighbourhood near Al-Kahira cafe and the Nails stadium, known as "Namimina" by local Ethiopians. The area was infamous for the story of travellers passing through the port of Masswa, where there were frequent battles between Eritreans and Ethiopians.

Oft repeated tales speak of foreigners being killed and their money taken but these were only hearsay and not actually witnessed in the community.

After much thought, Muhammaduh made the difficult decision to abandon his association with the neighbourhood gang and rediscover his lifelong love of football. He found refuge in the corners of Namimina, where the sport he held so dear opened its arms and embraced him once more.

In this district were scattered wooden crates for the various local clubs. The president of each club played a vital role, ensuring that their team was well equipped for every match and practice session. They went the extra mile, providing essential services such as water and refreshments during games and rehearsals to keep the players hydrated and energised.

One of the presidents of the neighbourhood clubs was

"the Peeler", a former fish skinner who was rumoured to be gay and known for socialising with attractive young men. He transformed his room into a black market for selling alcohol and perfume, using the proceeds to fund "The Birds of Paradise". Despite his efforts, the team frequently lost matches due to the frailty of their players.

The Peeler had come across Muhammaduh and saw in him a defender for "The Birds of Paradise". As a result, he offered Muhammaduh the opportunity of a lifetime to take on the role of both captain and coach. Muhammaduh reminisced about the days he played with a ball made from socks and was delighted to belong to a team he called "house pigeons". With this fond memory in mind, he was eager to take on this new experience with the Peeler. Although Muhammaduh's age prevented him from joining a youth club, it now allowed him to play with peers of similar ages, and he was content to be serving as the coach. The match between the "Birds" and the "Night Lions" was heavily one-sided, with the "Night Lions" players tirelessly pressing forward and scoring goal after goal. The "Birds" were unable to put up much of a defence, and the final score was a reflection of the team's performance, as well as the lack of strength and physicality among its players. As the time for the sunset prayer approached, Muhammaduh shouted out that the goal of the sunset was considered to be worth ten.

Muhammaduh held onto this dream, and moved from his coaching position to that of a forward player on the field. He ran in all directions, determined to push the ball forward towards the opposing team's net. However, every time the ball came near him, it would slip away from his control, tripping him up and bouncing back into the possession of his opponents. The encouragement and laughter from the crowd grew louder as he continued his relentless pursuit. He was filled with determination, driven by his hope of scoring the coveted "goal of the sunset".

But just as he was about to reach his goal, disaster struck. A nail on the field pierced his foot, causing such intense pain that he felt like it had come out of his eye. He fell to the ground, groaning in agony. With one eye, he looked at the cheering and cynical laughter of the spectators, while with the other, he watched as the "Night Lions" scored the coveted sunset goal. The final score was 17-0.

****

As Muhammaduh lay on the ground groaning in agony, both teams gathered around him. The pain was etched on his face and his cries were so loud that they seemed to reach the sky. A nail was lodged in the sole of his foot, bent and protruding from the top.

Abdallah Abou Hadid showed bravery in attempting to remove the nail, asking those gathered to hold Muhammaduh's foot steady.

Abou Hadid stepped in to fulfil the task at hand but soon realised that removing the nail wouldn't be easy. It was deeply embedded between flesh, bones and nerves, making it difficult to remove without turning it and pulling hard. He needed the assistance of the strong players to hold Muhammaduh's foot steady while he worked.

However, as Muhammaduh lost patience and started to shout and curse those trying to help, the removal of the nail became even more challenging. Three people were needed to hold his body still while three others held his foot, making the operation even more difficult.

Muhammaduh was in agony, wishing for nothing more than to lose consciousness and escape the all-consuming pain. He was surrounded by a crowd of spectators, all staring at him with expressions of pity as he writhed on the ground in agony. He buried his face in his arm, trying to shut out the world, as water was poured over his wound in an attempt to cleanse it of his freely flowing blood.

The moment the nail was finally pulled from his flesh, Muhammaduh understood the true meaning of the phrase he had often used to threaten others with severe punishment; "to show him the midday stars". As the nail was extracted, he saw visions of every possible form of torture a human could endure. His mouth was dry from shouting and crying out for help, until he finally lost consciousness.

Abou Hadida was the one who finally pulled the nail, causing a spray of blood to cover his face and clothes. Muhammaduh's friends came to his aid, lifting his massive body between them as if it were a gigantic mountain.

****

For four sleepless nights, Muhammaduh was tormented by pain that seemed to come from every direction, particularly from the wound near his bones and nerves. His mother, Hajji Fatima Al-Muhajira, sought help from anyone who had knowledge or experience with herbs and medicine that might provide some relief for her suffering son, who was lying down in a wooden room, groaning and unable to find any respite from the pain.

THE CISTERN

Fatima's first attempt to treat the wound was by covering it with ground coffee. However, no matter how much coffee she applied, the blood continued to flow, spurting with each opening of the wound. Desperate, she then sprinkled finely ground salt on the wound in an attempt to stem the flow. The results of this action left her wishing she had never tried it. With a single monumental scream of pain, Muhammaduh lost consciousness. It was hours later when he woke up. Fatima was still suffering her own agony, tears streaming down her face as she prayed for her son's recovery.

Although Muhammaduh's wound was obviously horrendous, Hajji Fatima never lost hope of finding a way to treat it. She tried various remedies, grinding up herbs to use as poultices. She used ginger, hot pepper, yogurt, honey, cinnamon, garlic, onion, turmeric and olive oil. In her desperation, she even sought out herbal medicines from Chad, recalling that people of Aouzou used herbs believed capable of healing even the worst wounds or lion bites. Eventually, after several months, pilgrims brought her these rare and potent herbs.

Despite the wound appearing to have healed, it would still cause Muhammaduh immense pain whenever he walked for any moderate distance. As a result, he limited himself to visiting only a few specific places and would often sit in a chair outside his house. There greeted friends or watched the street bustle of vendors, service providers, cobblers, dentists, itinerant barbers and fast food merchants.

He yearned to see a smile that had eluded him for so long. After seeking revenge on Abdul Ghafour Ashour and his son Ibrahim, he thought that his passion for football would fade away. He would spend many days glue to the same spot on the long street, which connected the heart of the neighbourhood to the main road, just to catch a glimpse of the girls coming and going from school. Despite more than two weeks passing without an appearance of the smiling girl, he didn't give up hope. One scorching hot afternoon, she finally sauntered by, returning from school and spoke to him for the first time. "Follow me carefully," she told him.

Muhammaduh trailed behind her, leaving a bit of distance between them. She moved gracefully, like the gentle ebb and flow of waves. She turned down a narrower street and as she wove her way through the twists and turns between the cistern and namimia neighbourhood, she quickened her pace, heading towards a dead-end alley, waiting for Muhammaduh. Both their hearts were racing. And when she finally revealed her face, Muhammaduh was speechless at seeing her beauty. He froze. Only his eyes and ears were still alive.

She handed him a coloured letter, which was scented with a delicate womanly fragrance. Holding his hand, she gave him a warm smile before skipping away. Muhammaduh was unable to move. He followed her with his eyes, afraid someone might see him looking at her and rebuke him. He was also worried that the young boys in the neighbourhood might lose respect for her if they saw him following this paeon of beauty. The total of these fears was enough to make him turn around and go back, his hand still clutching the letter and its scent. The fragrance was like nothing he had smelled before. It made him dizzy with delight.

****

He returned home and made his way to a quiet and secluded spot, which was now his own private space after his family had been gifted a piece of land by Oqab ben Ali.

He sat inside a clutter of tools, scraps of copper and an assortment of broken and used devices that he had previously collected from various dumpsites. The treasures were stored in boxes of various sizes. Discarded and broken electronics, including radios, telephones, car parts, motorcycles. Even bits of bicycles.

The clutter was so chaotic he struggled to clear a space for himself, where he could sit down and read the letter he was holding. He pushed aside some objects and finally managed to access his chair; a salvaged car seat he used whenever he wanted to think, relax or bring some joy to his mind. As he sat down, he inhaled the sweet fragrance of the smiling girl's perfume. Only then did he open the letter and struggle to decipher its contents.

****

"May the peace, blessings and mercy of God be upon you.

"I hope this message finds you well. I find myself constantly thinking of you, even though I do not know your name.

"I was away for two weeks as my brother was involved in a fight that left his face severely disfigured. This has left me filled with anger towards the person responsible for inflicting this harm and the only person I could think of to seek justice for him was you.

"I implore you, on my behalf, to seek retribution for what has been done to my brother.

"My name is Omaima by the way.

"I am the sister of Ibrahim Ashour. Please keep this communication between us a secret, as well as another truth that I must share with you. I am deeply enamoured of your masculinity and virility.

"I implore you to take action on behalf of my brother and seek retribution. Do not let this matter slip from your mind."

****

Muhammaduh was overcome with a whirlwind of emotions. He was disoriented but stunned. Regret, heartbreak and sorrow weighed heavily, leaving him feeling like he was trying to piece together something that had been shattered, or restore what had been lost. An overwhelming sense of worry and uncertainty regarding the situation at hand.

Chapter 15

He knew it was her, Omaima, the one who had filled his heart with love since his childhood. Despite this, he couldn't shake off the memory of Muhammaduh, the little boy who had suffered at the hands of her father and she was the only living witness to the atrocity. He couldn't help but wonder if her tears were simply out of pity for the child who had had his face smashed against the wall.

The thing that pained him the most was the fact that she had forgotten about that child, the one she used to smile at every time he walked by their grand house. He felt regret for ever thinking that her smile, coming and going from school, was just a link to his childhood memories.

He was grateful, in a strange way, that she didn't recognize him or connect their past with the present. He thanked God that she didn't know who he was or what's his name, or that he was the one responsible for disfiguring her brother. His soul was torn between regret and gratitude.

He was powerless, unable to do anything but listen to heart-wrenching songs and sigh all day and all night.

Whenever his heart yearned to see Omaima, his mind would intervene and remind him to quell the internal feelings of love that had been growing for so many years.

The nights passed by, leaving him in a state of dilemma. Should he come clean and reveal to Omaima that he was responsible for the harm inflicted on her brother? Or should

he move forward with his patience, longing, and heartache? He struggled with his thoughts, asking himself,
 "How can I extinguish you from within?"

****

Muhammaduh was confined to his home, unable to step outside due to the wound that was impeding his mobility, it had grown infected, causing discomfort and a repulsive smell. He was unable to stop its deterioration and it continued to spread, attacking his cells and flaking his skin and nerves, ultimately destroying the bones in his foot. The smell from the wound was overpowering and suffocating, causing discomfort for those around him, including his mother and siblings. Out of consideration for those affected, he was moved to a location closer to the entrance of the house.

****

News of Muhammaduh's illness spread, with people confirming that he was unable to move, sitting like a camel with broken hind legs.

Despite the urge for revenge lingering in Ibrahim Ashour's mind, the news of what had transpired in the Tantabawi quarter of Mecca made it impossible for anyone to attack Muhammaduh among those of his own community.

He had to reconsider his actions, delve deeper into his thoughts and arrive at a belief that brought peace to his soul and made him wait.

****

THE CISTERN

Muhammaduh's wound was getting worse every day. He watched as numbness spread throughout his foot and was accompanied by unbearable pain and a constant urge to scratch. His skin turned blue and his foot swelled, pimples filled with pus appearing on its surface. The smell from the wound became so overpowering, not even Muhammaduh himself could bear it. He attempted to chase off the flies that were attracted to the smell, by using a more potent fragrance. But this only created a more pungent and choking aroma, which was even more overpowering than the smell of the wound. He had given up on patience and endurance and instead expressed his misery and frustration to anyone who thought of visiting him.

The wound was constantly getting bigger, spreading beyond his foot and shin towards his thigh, and seeking to consume more skin.

His friend Ajil El Wafi (known as Al Wafi "Perfect" for his many virtuous qualities) regularly enquired about those seemed to be missing, tended to the sick, sought to help those in distress, and cared for people facing difficult circumstances, taking part in both their joys and sorrows. Wafi saw that Muhammaduh was close to death, so he immediately sought assistance from his other friends to transfer him to the public hospital in Bab Sherif.

****

In the northern room on the second floor of Bab Sherif Hospital, four patients with tired bodies lay in humble beds in the bone department. Two weeks had passed since Muhammaduh was admitted to the hospital. He had become emaciated, his eyes sunken into their sockets, his eyebrows brittle, and his nose drooping like an old kufiya, needing someone to prop it up so he could breathe, his cheeks were pale and gaunt, his beard was curly and matted on his cheeks, and his thick lips were pale and thinned out from the intensity of pain.

Despite his sickly appearance, his African accent could still be heard resounding in the ward. When the effects of an anaesthetic had worn off, his visitors were at a loss to describe his reaction to discovering that his left had been amputated above the knee. As the anaesthesia completely wore off, he felt a sharp pain in the lower part of his thigh. After feeling the exact location of the pain, his hand reached into the void below his thigh. He moved the cover and saw a thigh without a leg, surrounded by blood-soaked gauze, with blood also seeping from the dressing at the site of the amputation. His reaction did not go beyond the initial shock, and his eyes remained fixed on his mother's face as she silently dried her tears, unable to speak through the heartbreak.

He couldn't bring himself to believe what he saw, so he tried to get out of bed, but fell with a thud. He had bruises all over his chest. His mother ran to support him but he exploded in anger, shouting a barrage of curses that could not be answered. Everyone in the hospital could hear him. Eventually, with the help of several nurses and the presence of the hospital manager, he was put back in bed. The doctor told him,

"You wouldn't have lasted another week if we hadn't amputated your leg."

To which Muhammaduh replied,

"I'd rather be dead than helpless."

THE CISTERN

Hajji Fatima tried to persuade the doctors to overlook Muhammaduh's unruly behaviour and promised to mediate between his anger and the hospital's integrity.

However, Muhammaduh's loud complaints continued to cause daily disruption, as he repeatedly demanded the return of his amputated leg. Despite knowing that the medical procedure was necessary, he clung to his stubbornness, still yearning for his leg.

A hope in his mind led him to imagine he could regrow his leg, even if it was damaged and foul-smelling. He stayed true to himself and remained upright.

As days passed in the hospital, he started each day leaning on a wooden support, wandering around the hospital's departments, searching for medical scraps that were no longer of use. With each round, he stood in front of the director's door, shouting and demanding to have his leg returned.

Hajji Fatima visited the bones clinic for a few days, trying to soothe her son.

Despite the wound becoming larger and the blood curdling from his daily walks, making it harder for the wound to heal, he was now demanding just to hold his amputated leg.

In front of the hospital director, he tearfully begged for an explanation for the amputation. The director explained that the procedure was necessary to save his life. The son struggled to understand and asked for his leg back to bury it. The doctor spent the day with colleagues from the bones department discussing the possibility of releasing this patient, who he considered to be "stupid".

At the beginning of the third week of Muhammaduh's hospital stay, before his discharge papers were finalised, the sound of his crutch echoed through the halls like the sound of tired horses with laborious steps. He showed strength and fortitude as he leaned heavily on the right side of his body, his mind searching for a hope that fades each day.

With his adeptness at overhearing, he uncovered a container filled with improperly discarded medical waste near the operating room. The container contained a multitude of used syringes, cotton, gauze, blood-stained specimens and decaying bodily remnants.

He felt frightened and sick encountering remains of human body parts haphazardly mashed together. The foul stench emanating from the decaying skin of amputated limbs was overpowering, causing those who smelled it to struggle for air and retch.

He saw only one amputated leg and after seeing a detail in the toenail, he realised it was his own limb. Carrying it was difficult but his large African robe provided some concealment. Before he could catch his breath, the hospital director asked for a copy of his medical record and promptly signed the release papers for the "stupid" patient.

Chapter 16

Muhammaduh will never forget for as long as he lives that fortune was not always on his side. He remained stubborn, which only added to his frustration and constant annoyance. He retreated to his wooden room to escape the chaos of his aunts and sisters in the yard, each with a never-ending list of daily chores such as laundry, cooking, cleaning dishes and pots, preparing and cutting wood to roast the peanuts, cleaning around the chicken coop.

He found his bed neatly made with a thick mattress and blue cover, some pillows at the head, and a headrest adorned with bright green patterns on a white background. A table stood beside the bed, with an old radio and a warm water dispenser on it. The window, which looked out on the yard from the southern side and faced the street outside, was open.

He turned on the radio looking for a song to distract himself but the host's voice came on instead, announcing the start of a newscast. The voice was shaky and the words struggled to escape the speaker's chest. He listened intently for the news of King Saud stepping down and King Faisal coming to power, based on the decision of the council of senior scholars.

He pondered how he could use this change in power to his advantage, with the intention of visiting King Faisal's palace to voice his grievances. The anger and frustration he felt over the director of the hospital amputating his leg while he was under anaesthesia in a deep sleep, still burned hot within him, causing his chest to heave and his nerves to feel like burning coals. His mind was consumed by a deep bitterness, like a lonely animal traversing a vast stretch of boredom.

Despite the distress he felt, Muhammaduh felt even more shame and self-disgust upon hearing the news that Ibrahim Ashour had dropped the charges against him for the damage he caused to his face. Muhammaduh saw this as an act of mercy towards a disabled person, and those who heard the news regarded Ibrahim as a noble individual.

Upon learning that Ibrahim had publicly announced his act of leniency towards Muhammaduh as a display of his mercy and compassion, Muhammaduh's grip on his cane tightened and he vehemently cried out,

"May God's wrath fall upon you, Ibrahim."

****

In recent days, Hajji Fatima struggled to come to terms with her son leaving the hospital carrying his amputated leg. She had planned a celebration for his return, and had also requested assistance from her neighbour's son Adam in bringing him back home from the hospital, and even hired a taxi, paying for it herself.

To avoid drawing attention to his amputated leg, Muhammaduh asked the taxi driver to pull into the yard of their home and covered himself with a robe that concealed his entire body.

The family gathered around the car, offering warm greetings and wishing him well. As Muhammaduh sat in the back seat, Hajji Fatima and Adam attempted to help him out of the car but he lost his balance and fell, revealing his amputated leg to everyone, when his crutch fell away from him. The sight and smell of the leg caused the taxi driver to become impatient and demand his fare in order to leave, while the family struggled to come to terms with what they saw.

None of the family wanted to touch Muhammaduh's amputated leg, and his young sister Aisha had the courage to describe it as repulsive whether dead or alive.

Despite the shock and horror of the situation, Muhammaduh was determined to stand up on his own, embracing his amputated leg like a newborn in need of comfort.

Upon Muhammaduh's return, Hajji Fatima tended to him with utmost care, recognising his broken spirit and working tirelessly to heal it. She offered guidance and support to help restore his faith in fate, and prevent him from sinking into despair. Mindful of their limited resources, she delegated Aisha with the task of washing the gauzes while she took on the responsibility of changing them.

Despite being faced with poverty, Hajji Fatima provided for her family, while handling any problems that arose with ease.

Muhammaduh wasn't bothered by his isolation in the wooden room, which had set up to manage the odour from his decaying foot before it was amputated. However, once he returned carrying the amputated limb, they put him back in the same room.

****

Muhammaduh barely slept before sunrise, and woke up with

a start. He had just made a promise to himself to go on a trip with Adam, who was waiting outside his house. Seeking his mother's aid, Muhammaduh obtained a bottle of perfume, which he applied to his amputated leg before wrapping it. He then set off to visit King Faisal, feeling remorseful for his tardiness.

Pausing near the palace, Muhammaduh leaned his crutch against the wall and raised his empty thigh, cautious of any movements that might cause him to lose balance and fall without anyone to help him up, he had instructed Adam and the driver to remain hidden.

Contemplating his amputated leg with sorrow, Muhammaduh noticed the skin had disintegrated, the bone was visible, and the nails were worn. He briefly saw worms slowly crawling towards his knee. The pungent smell mixed with perfume filled his nose, causing him to feel nauseous and turn away, seeking fresh air from the trees surrounding the palace.

He didn't hear the soldier calling out to him until he had reached the top The soldier noticed Muhammad's distress when he saw him leaning against the palace wall.

"What do you want?"

Startled, Muhammaduh swiftly covered his amputated leg.

"I want to see the king," said Muhammaduh.

"Can you see him at Qasr al Hokum?" the soldier asked

"I just about made it here, as you can see," Muhammaduh replied.

They chatted for a bit but the soldier eventually told Muhammaduh to leave. "You can't stay here," he told him. Continuing the conversation might have been possible but the smell from Muhammaduh's amputated leg was too much

THE CISTERN

for the soldier to handle, making him more firm.

"Write your request in a letter and it will be answered in detail," the soldier insisted, urging Muhammaduh to step back and leave.

The soldier couldn't help but look at Muhammaduh's face, stained with dirt, eyes filled with hope and a smile still on his lips, all while a bad smell came from his hands.

On his way to the car, Muhammaduh came across a beggar and was torn between hobbling to reach Adam or calling the man for help. He ultimately chose to keep hobbling. Two soldiers came out from the palace gate and as they approached, they were told to slow down. Muhammaduh stumbled, bending his body and declaring,

"I just want you to witness that my leg was wrongly amputated." He bent down further, removing the fabric that had been covering his amputated leg. He was revealing all black and foul-smelling leg to the soldiers.

The sudden movement piqued the soldier's interest and they approached Muhammaduh, blocking their noses with their fingers. declared,

"Thank God, there are three of you," said Muhammaduh. "I need two witnesses."

"They exchanged looks of surprise, clearly thinking Muhammaduh was crazy. The leader told him,

"Go back home, Hajj."

When Muhammaduh said he wanted to complain, the soldier instructed him to write a letter,

"Do you testify?" Muhammaduh asked them.

"Testify to what?" the soldiers replied.

"That I came here with my amputated leg," Muhammaduh answered.

The soldiers, as if trying to shake off the madness of someone with a fever, agreed and then urged Muhammaduh to leave.

"Don't forget, you're the witnesses," he reminded them before departing.

Muhammaduh placed the crutch under his arm pit and set off away from the gate. The sun had risen, bringing with it heat and sweat. Muhammaduh felt a twinge of regret for telling Adam to stay away, he saw the Qashla square as if it were miles away, even though he had crossed it on his arrival. He leaned on his crutch, eager to cross the green space and reach the Jaffali mosque. Standing alone, he gazed at the few cars passing and the blue ocean, where the waves were lapping playfully against the shore and pushing sea creatures away from the docked ships. Muhammaduh walked with care, focusing on his amputated leg and fearful of causing additional harm, and with a loud voice, called out to Adam,

"Hey Adam."

He collapsed onto his bed, exhausted. His mother had made the bed comfortable with fresh linen and provided a jug of water and some refreshments. He drank the water quickly, like a parched camel. Heavy drowsiness soon closed in on him and he surrendered to a deep sleep.

****

A rancid smell swept through the street, causing every person walking by to quicken their pace to escape the smell. Unfortunately for Mohammad Ba Sonbol, his pastry booth "Yoghmosh", was situated on the side. People started to spread rumours that he was using cat meat in his pastries, causing

THE CISTERN

Saadiya to confront him. She stood at her gate and yelled,

"Sonbol, wasn't it enough that our children were forced to eat cat meat. Now you're bringing dead cats from the dump too?"

The street was filled by outrage and, before a big crowd could gather, Sonbol placed the plate of Yoghmosh on his head, using a fabric cloth for support, and hung the metallic legs of the table over his shoulder as he fled to a different location. A group of boys pursued him, throwing rocks, whistling and shouting vulgarities. Even two days later, the putrid scent persisted and rumours spread that the cause was a dead cat or dog. Others claimed that Mariam Issa's sheep had died from hunger. To find the source of the smell, a group of volunteers bravely stepped forward to search. However, they were unable to go far because the smell was overpowering. They had to retreat due to lack of breathable air.

As Hajji Fatima returned from the bakery where she roasted peanuts, she saw and heard her neighbours gathered, searching the corners and nearby areas for the source of the terrible smell that had spread in the area surrounding her house. At this moment, Suleiman Abou Assida approached her asking,

"Hajji Fatima, may we search your house? It's possible there is a dead rat or dog on this side."

As Suleiman Abou Assida pointed towards Muhammaduh's room, Hajji Fatima was about to agree but she remembered the amputated leg and tried to remain calm, despite her heart racing.

People were moving about, trying to cover their noses from the foul smell. Fear and unease filled her heart but she held off telling everyone about the amputated leg. Instead, she went to wake Muhammaduh to tell him about the disturbance the smell was causing among the neighbours. Finding him in a deep asleep, she took the leg and moved it to her own room, before returning to the neighbours and asking them to search her son's room.

As Jamil Abou Samra entered the room, he found Muhammaduh sleeping and snoring in a clean and organised space. An incense burner with embers and incense was sitting next to his bed.

Jamil was covering his nose as he moved around the room,

"There's no doubt that a rat has died here, we'll search for it," he said.

Muhammaduh's family soon emerged from their rooms, disturbed and covering their noses with whatever cloth they could find. Abou Samra turned to Hajji Fatima and said,

"Poor creatures, they can't handle the smell."

Hajji Fatima feared that he had discovered the truth but as he moved towards the main door, she quickly jumped to her daughters and shouted,

"Don't you know how to be patient?

"The amputated leg will remain in this room until Muhammaduh's soul is restored and his well-being is improved."

The room was located in the centre of the space, so basil could be placed around it, and perfumes and incense used to keep the smell isolated.

****

As friends came to visit Muhammaduh and wish him well, he was not in good spirits, hardly speaking or smiling. He was lying on a low couch that was struggling to support his weight. His friends tried to console him, each offering their own words of comfort. Shaker Al Bati, however, was not mindful of his words, and they came out harshly,

"Has Muhammaduh become dependent?"

The atmosphere became charged with tension, and the air felt heavy. Shaker Al Bati's harsh words hit Muhammaduh hard and left a deep impact. He was consumed by thoughts of how to arrange for a decent life despite his disability and ensure that he wouldn't have the choice of begging or being dependent and penniless. He tried to think out his future and the steps needed to take to secure healthcare, an income, and mobility. One more consideration for Muhammaduh was the added strain his dependency would add to his mother's burdens.

He remained quiet, trying to rein in his emotions, but his friends were at ease, trying to lighten the mood. Feeling the heaviness of the situation, Adam steered the conversation towards humour, sharing details of amusing stories that made everyone laugh.

Despite all the commotion, Muhammaduh's determination to bury his leg remained steadfast. He ask his friends to join him for the funeral of his limb.

"Help me bury my leg," he told them.

To his disbelief, his words were met with laughter and mockery. The constant thought that weighed on his mind had become a source of ridicule and disregard. He was unable to suppress the loud laughter coming from his friends, leaving him with only silence and a lingering sense of anger.

Despite this setback, he couldn't shake off the thoughts that plagued him, thoughts that offered no solutions for his future. Eventually, his friends left one by one without his noticing their departure.

Chapter 17

The night went by and the friends went their separate ways after completing what they believed to be their obligations. The family was plunged into deep sorrow, each person sitting on a makeshift bed made from old pieces of sponge held together by fabric. Hajji Fatima, her eyes filled with grief, held her daughter Aisha close, who had become delirious from seeing her brother's amputated leg. She comforted her, tenderly running her fingers over her back and closed her eyes as she envisioned the wide open spaces of Chad. That was where she and her family would run behind her husband as he guided them to the Sudanese border. Despite a heavy lump on his left ankle that caused him pain, he pushed on, determined to reach the borders. He urged his family to be patient,

"We only have a few miles left," he told them. Any signs of weakness from his family were countered with his determination,

"I swear to God, we will make it. Don't let fatigue make you an easy target." Hajji Fatima smiled, her eyes still closed as she remembered the day when all of Chad ran behind them; the soldiers, the blue-eyed, the bandits, the horse and camel traders, the slave-seller snipers, all running away from hunger, thirst and fear.

She couldn't quite fall asleep as her imagination was still filled with the memories of crossing the long desert sands with her husband and the rest of her family.

She remembered those days and compared them to what had happened to her son Muhammaduh, as if sleep had trapped her in her memories. She felt the winds of the West Tibesti mountains blowing and pushing her towards the southwest, along with hordes of people making their way through the western desert, away from the Chari and Chad river towards the south of Sudan and safety.

The men in the convoy found solace in the voice of the muezzin calling for afternoon prayers in a small mosque just inside the Sudanese borders. With water in abundance, they rushed to clean themselves, washing away all the sand stuck to their clothes and bodies. Some of the boys roamed around the mosque, eating sweets they had acquired along the way, while others collected empty bottles, cigarette butts and empty rifle cartridges, avoiding the scattered human bones. The more they kept moving, the more content and peace they felt. Their hearts finally found rest in a green space filled with grass, where they picked mangoes, sugar cane and peanuts. A little distance away, there were banana trees with clusters of unripe, firm fruit swaying in the breeze.

They settled in a place that eased their exhaustion, hunger and thirst. Every time they glanced back at Chad, they saw the long trail of their journey and felt as though fear still lingered, trying to drag them back to the desolate sands.

Their entry papers had not yet been completed, as they lacked any official documentation, making the process of entering more difficult. And the border officials were confounded by the excuse given for crossing the border heading to Beit Al Haram, as they were escaping a devastating war that had left them no choice but to flee their home country.

As the night settled in, Moussa Jamnin's joints began to ache and the pain in his ankle became unbearable. Added to the physical pain was the uncertainty in his thoughts about what lay ahead in their journey. Fatima, his beloved spouse and the one who produced a son into his life after a series of daughters, was the only one who heard his groans. In an effort to keep his distress from spreading to the rest of the group, he tried to stifle his moans so that only Fatima would be aware of his suffering.

He was moving about, biting his lips and shutting his eyes as he leaned on his wife's shoulder. She was trying to alleviate his pain but could only resort to wrapping her head scarf round his ankle and murmuring prayers to comfort him. He listened to her assure him, and believed that what he was going through would ultimately lead to reward in the afterlife.

As he drifted off to sleep in her lap, she was fighting off a deep slumber that propelled her into an horrendous dream in which a ruthless hyena sneaked in from the nearby desert dunes to attack Muhammaduh. The hyena bit his leg and he awakened his parents with a scream for help,

"Where are you Mum? Where are you Dad?"

Hajji Fatima woke up with a start fearful for her son, whose groans filled the stillness of the night, scaring her daughter Aisha. She groped her way in the darkness, hoping Muhammaduh's pain and groans would subside and that he would be able to rest peacefully. The bite on Muhammaduh's leg was a distant nightmare but now it had become a harrowing reality.

****

THE CISTERN

On a night where sleep eluded Muhammaduh, his mind was filled with anger and frustration over his amputated leg being moved to another room. He was determined to have it returned close to him, and insisted on having his bed placed back on the floor. Yet, no one did anything to alleviate his suffering.

The room was brightly lit by a lantern, its light spilling through the broken pieces of wood onto the street. The door and windows were worn and weathered, barely able to withstand a strong gust of wind. The floor was attached to the glowing concrete walls and two empty sofas sat nearby. A mattress was laid on the floor, with a new crutch placed within easy reach for Muhammaduh. The relentless buzzing of flies and the overpowering stench of decay revealed the rotting and decaying amputated leg. The smell was a nauseating mix of rot, pus and perfume, causing discomfort for those unfamiliar with it.

As he struggled to sit properly, Muhammaduh's backside found a resting place on the centre of the bed. Beside him was a metal bucket filled with water, a copper soap container, a scattering of green jujube leaves and pieces of kafur tree. Shaking, he reached for the amputated leg, careful not to tear the skin and expose the bones.

With the utmost care, Muhammaduh placed the amputated leg that was missing a toe nail, into the soapy water of the copper container. The fragrance of jujube and kafur filled the air and he handled the limb delicately, mindful of any movement that might cause the hanging skin to come apart. The thought of massaging it crossed his mind but he was hesitant, again afraid that the bones might be exposed. Instead, he wrapped the leg in a new white cloth and carefully poured amber and oud onto it. Reciting small, reverent verses, he was consumed by sorrow, "You will be reduced to a burden, Muhammaduh."

Omaima felt like an extra wound. He felt as though she symbolised a loss that would be impossible to overcome and her presence reignited feelings of regret for his actions towards her brother. Thoughts of Abdul Ghafour Ashour, Ibrahim, Omaima, the hospital director, Ajil Al-Wafi, his mother and the poverty in which he lived all intertwined in his mind. He was plagued by self-doubt, questioning how someone as deserving as Omaima could ever love him.

Illusions are like memories that won't die or be forgotten.

He carefully examined the shroud covering his amputated leg, ensuring it was wrapped securely with no openings. Then, he patiently awaited the sunrise prayer.

****

The morning carried scents that mingled and fought against each other around the area of Hajji Fatima Al-Muhajira house. Every corner held a different aroma. The chicken coop was filled with chicken sounds and its scent mixed with the smell of the toilets that came in different shapes and sizes, and a strong stench came from the sheep shed. The guava tree retained its sweet scent, overpowering the smell of limes, and deep in the courtyard, Hajji Fatima gathered roast peanuts and removed baobab seeds from their fruits. She then rolled up the mattresses that were infused with delightful fragrant scents. Everyone awoke feeling drowsy.

The voice of Hajji Fatima echoed across the household, calling out loudly,

"It's time for prayer," awakening everyone from their slumber. They swiftly rose and began their morning ablutions.

She rushed to check on her son Muhammaduh. Finding him motionless, like an overlooked statue while he struggled to hold back his tears, she said through her own opening sobs, "My dear son, didn't you get any sleep?"

"How can I find rest when a part of me is yearning for a final resting place?" he replied, his voice heavy with sorrow.

After refusing to have breakfast, he put on the vibrant colours of the national costume with its intricate embroidered patterns. He meticulously arranged the trailing section of his blue turban at the back and applied a cheap perfume to his neck and clothes. He nearly lost his balance trying to stand up but his mother was quick to support him. He took the crutch from her hand and reassured her,

"I'll get used to walking with this crutch."

Hajji Fatima's heart was heavy as she watched her son put on his shoe.

He sat with a look of resolve, gazing at his single remaining leg, standing alone with nothing by its side. The other shoe was cradled in his hand, as he allowed a few tears to fall. He placed the spare shoe in his pocket, saying,

"I won't let my amputated limb go without the right shoe."

Pictures of his friends and enemies played in his head, and he realised his appearance made him an easy target for ridicule. He let out a bitter sigh, thinking,

"Everyone's going to take shots at me."

He swallowed hard, trying to steady himself, but then remembered Ibrahim Ashour's contentment and how he'd never find a smile as beautiful as Omaima's. The morning was calling everyone to get ready for a hot day ahead. Most people were already out, leaving few behind to brighten the streets with passers-by.

The children at school were confined within its walls, while the women inside their homes were either grappling with boredom or preparing for a gossip session with their friends.

It was almost as if the entrance to Muhammaduh's home had become the bane of everyone's existence, with no one daring to venture near it. He was confined to a tiny space, keeping a watchful eye over the street that led to Abi Khadach's meeting place, as if the only person allowed to come and go through the entrance was Muhammaduh himself.

Despite having friends who had promised to stand by him during his journey to the cemetery, he found himself alone at the door and realised no one would come to help lay his leg to rest. The morning was passing as he stood there, shifting between standing, sitting and lying down in silence, surveying the surrounding streets. His leg ached from the strain of standing and the other side of his body was rubbing against the walls and door as it opened and closed, causing even more discomfort. He maintained his stance like a seasoned performer, holding up his lifeless limb with effortless grace, before alternating between sitting, lying down and standing again. Despite his best efforts, he felt a mix of anger and sadness, with no clear solution in sight.

"Why have my friends abandoned me?" he pondered.

As the hours ticked by, his anxiety skyrocketed. His friends were nowhere to be found and the idea of sending his sister Zeinab to remind them about the funeral made him uneasy. He didn't want her to have to go door-to-door but he couldn't shake the thought. He felt terrible for feeling so low and he was biting his lip in frustration.

He didn't eat or drink, opting to stay on his crutch while the front door still felt like a nightmare to anyone who tried to approach. He kept his ears peeled, trying to hear any sounds from outside his window overlooking the street. He was exhausted from all the bickering with his sisters over silly things and searched for anything to distract from his constant worries.

Then, Hajji Fatima stepped in, calling for the family to accompany him on his final journey. She was insistent and took Muhammaduh's amputated leg in her arms, marching steadily like a soldier carrying a flag,

"There is no deity but God, there is no partner to him, he is the everlasting, he is the only one, he is the eternal."

When she discovered no one was repeating her words after her, she responded by shouting, "repeat with me".

Everyone repeated the chants after her, albeit totally devoid of harmony. The family set off in the funeral of Muhammaduh's leg, without a man, except the owner of the leg, whose heart was pounding. They went through cobbled streets to go out towards the port in the direction of the Al Seban cemetery. The scene was confusing, and comic at the same time. Some passers-by joined the procession, and the more they walked, the more other people came along, including some who wanted to help. Meanwhile Hajji Fatima was showing off the big number of people walking behind them in the funeral,

"You are blessed my son, all this great march for your amputated leg."

"There's only one God and he's eternal and unchanging."

Chapter 20

People marched in the funeral procession, parallel to the "Al Thaaliba" quarter, heading towards Al Seban cemetery. The women led the way, crying and ululating loudly, causing some to think the deceased was a baby being carried by the elderly woman in front.

One of the mourners said,

"You gifted her a heart, yet took one away God, show her mercy."

They walked faster than Muhammaduh, despite his strenuous attempts to stay in step with his mother. His crutch made it difficult to walk steadily on the uneven street. But as the procession quickened, Hajji Fatima slowed down to ease her son's mobility problem, muttering to herself,

"The burden of his disability is enough. It is also a funeral in its own right."

His gaze roamed over the mourners' faces. Not spotting any of his friends induced conflicting thoughts and emotions.

"They didn't mourn my lost limb, and their absence is proof. What if I were the one lying in the grave?"

The Al Siban cemetery was near the stadium with a vast space to the south, honouring the deceased on a patch of both hard and soft earth.

Footfall fans rushing and jumping over the wall to enter the stadium without paying for tickets, would sometimes spill over into the cemetery during game days, trampling on both wet and dry graves, causing many of them to collapse, particularly those near the west wall of the stadium.

Muhammaduh stood unsteadily, unsure of which grave to choose for his leg. The spot where his crutch touched the ground brought back memories of him jumping over the wall to watch the games. He gestured for his mother to move forward and stay away from the stadium wall, and he raised his crutch as a sign of his choice for the burial spot.

The wind was whistling through the deserted stadiums, where he used to stand cheering for Al Ittihad club, the crowd echoing songs after his hoarse voice. He once dreamt of running in Al Seban field with people cheering him on but this dream died when his leg did, leaving him with a heart full of sorrow.

Muhammaduh's family gathered in a semi-circle in the middle of the cemetery. Hajji Fatima was struggling to dig into the hard ground because of the rocks beneath. She used a sharp flintstone to make it easier but eventually had to move the location of the dig while offering a prayer of thanks to God. Aisha was removing soil and piling it up on either side of the pit, and whenever Hajji Fatima stopped digging, Muhammaduh urged her to continue, saying, "I want a grave for my leg."

Muhammaduh sat in front of the deep pit, which was equal in both length and width with the help of his aunt Baraka and carefully lowered himself to the ground. He appeared serious and resolute. His hands suddenly became stiff. He tried to shake it off by coughing and looking more intently at the pit which he asked to be dug deeper.

Hajji Fatima spoke a few words she had learned from her husband while crossing the Sudanese border, words filled with frustration,

"Comandi nima aabotma andio anda kuarne."

Suddenly, a very strange thing happened. The ground split open, revealing some worms. A strong gust of wind blew away some of the soil. The sky cleared, and a swarm of flies and mosquitoes descended, joined by beetles, red ants and weevils rising from the ground. The combined chirping and buzzing of the insects created a loud, unsettling symphony. Muhammaduh's family watched as a colony of red ants made their way towards the cloth-wrapped limb next to Muhammaduh. Auntie Baraka exclaimed,

"The ants have come to pay their respects to the departed."

Muhammaduh rushed to pull his leg out of the grave, brushing away the ants that had crawled onto the white cloth, a piece of Hajji Fatima's shroud that she had brought with her as they fled from the rebel leaders seeking to overthrow the Chadian government in the south, with the support of the French.

It seemed as if the grave had unleashed its ancestors, as all sorts of insects emerged from beneath the ground and swarmed the area. This creepy atmosphere made it impossible for Muhammaduh to bury his leg as he wanted and all his efforts to put it back in the grave were in vain. He couldn't bend down to reach the opening of the grave and after much effort he handed it to his mother to drop it to the bottom and quickly come out.

As they refilled the grave, a small mound formed. It was sprinkled with water and surrounded with small rocks, as the women tried to shake off the red ants that clung to their robes and dresses, each of them shuffling, walking jumping between the graves.

Not far away, the call for sunset prayer rose from Al Zahed

mosque, while the army of darkness prepared to cover the graves with mounds, except for the grave of the leg that had come as a visitor to the decaying bones that night, wishing for some rain to soothe its cracks.

The family walked back from Al Seban field towards the street leading to the black rail, returning to the neighbourhood, with Muhammaduh hobbling behind them on crutches, still haunted by Aunt Baaraka's words, "The ants have come to pay their respects to the departed."

****

All the women who had returned from the graveyard quickly took off their clothes and rushed to shower, trying to rid themselves of the ants that had clung to their clothes.

They dug small holes in the ground to send the insects back underground.

In Muhammaduh's chest was a desire he struggled to express to his family. He couldn't seem to articulate it, Sipping on a drink prepared by Aunt Baraka, with pieces of fermented pineapple, lemon, and apple sweetened with date water, he let his mind wander.

He finally broke the silence with, "I'm going to have a memorial service for my leg tomorrow."

Hajji Fatima put down the wool bobbin she was winding for her daughter Aisha to turn into a scarf that would be sold to raise extra money for her upcoming wedding with Adam.

"What's got into you, my son?" she asked him.

He didn't reply immediately, instead spreading out his healthy leg and feeling his thigh, knee, and leg. He tried to reach his toes without losing his balance, then moved his hand to his amputated limb. A tear streamed down his face as his throat tightened with sorrow. He gazed at his family, clearing his throat irritably,

"I'm going to spend the rest of my life mourning my leg. Is it not my right to receive condolences for what I've lost?" he asked, his voice choked with emotion.

Hajji Fatima did not want to bring up their financial struggles and the lack of opportunities for them to earn extra money. In this difficult situation, she thought of her distant cousin, Hajj Suleiman Kaido, who had come to Jeddah more than 20 years ago and worked for the Ghazzaoui family. He was diligent and obedient, which earned him their trust and he was given the opportunity to work in commerce. He excelled in this work, was given a large sum of money as recognition for his efforts and has since continued to expand his business ventures and attract others to join him.

Remembering him brought a glimmer of hope in a dark tunnel for Hajji Fatima. She viewed him as a shining light in her bleak night. She considered borrowing some money from him but her co-wife Madlia put a stop to that idea. Aunt Madlia was deeply affected by Muhammaduh's loss of his leg, as she herself was born with a birth defect that caused her to limp. Her empathy towards Muhammaduh made her go to Hajji Fatima and take off the only bracelet she had, which was her bridal dowry that was kept safe for future needs. Aunt Madlia said to Hajji Fatima,

"Let's sell the bracelet and have the memorial?"

Muhammaduh was grateful for Aunt Madlia's selfless act and the next morning he set about preparing for the memorial service. When word of it spread in the neighbourhood, people laughed and began sharing the strange stories he was known for. At sunset, the memorial service was held in an empty room lit by a few flickering lanterns. Square wooden chairs sat empty on the floor and a pot of coffee was brewing over a coal fire, with no one there to drink it. Boys peered in from the doorway as the reader, seated on a couch, recited verses from Surah Al Dukhan while swaying. Muhammaduh was both the comforter and the mourner.

Before Muhammaduh lost hope that his friend would come, something unexpected happened. As the call to evening prayer rang out, neighbours emerged from their homes and poured out from the alleys, shops and playgrounds to offer their condolences for the loss of his leg. There were so many mourners that he was asked to sit in a chair rather than stand on crutches that were hurting his armpit.

The mourners took their seats in the chairs that had been set out for them, and there was a solemn hush as each person grappled with what to say about missing the funeral. Tension was palpable as faces betrayed unease and some fidgeted with excuses. The atmosphere was heavy, as if everyone was holding their breath waiting for some terrible blow. In the end, they all rose, silently pretending to make their way to the cemetery, reciting the prayers usually said at a funeral. It was their way of acknowledging and making amends for not attending the actual funeral and to pay their last respects.

Muhammaduh was befuddled by the unexpected turnout at the late funeral, unable to comprehend the sudden throng of mourners and their frenzied actions with every prayer recited by the crowd.

However, seeing Youssef al Ejel among the mourners lifted his spirits. Youssef was a skilled communicator and had a talent for comforting those who were broken. Muhammaduh wondered to himself,

"What is the retribution my friend?"

Youssef took a seat in the second row of mourners, his eyes constantly scanning the crowd, revealing the true intentions of those in attendance.

Mansour el Najjar suggested they hold the prayer in the funeral room while they waited for dinner to be served. Everyone was rooted to their chairs, some even skipping the group prayer.

Muhammaduh was bewildered by the outpouring of kindness from his neighbours, especially after feeling so down, and dinner was like a satisfying release from the hunger that had been gnawing at the children's stomachs, who eagerly attacked their plates like eagles swooping in on their prey.

Some neighbours stayed behind to help tidy up, put the chairs away, fold the carpets, and turn off the fire under the coffee pots provided by the neighbours.

The memorial service was an emotionally charged day that weighed heavily in Muhammaduh's heart, leaving him deep in thought as he repeatedly asked his family members seated beside him in his room,

"I long to know what led everyone to attend the memorial service."

Chapter 21

Muhammaduh managed to overcome a heavy depression that had taken hold of hm, like a spider weaving its webs throughout an abandoned house. A short while after, he received a letter from the Ministry of Interior, asking him to visit their offices and explain the situation regarding his amputated leg. He remembered the numerous letters he had sent through the mail and delivered to the royal palace. He even became friends with the palace guards and every soldier who heard his story had a different reaction, but they all agreed to laugh in the end.

Muhammaduh was able to let go of the tightness in his heart but despite his efforts he never discovered the reason behind the outpouring of support he received at the memorial service. Fortune seemed to smile upon him, fulfilling his deepest desires, while thinking of Omaima, caused his heart to break with longing to see her smile again.

"Playing is like laughter, it can also be heart-wrenching."

This advice that Hajji Fatima constantly gave him was not concrete and felt like false guidance.

After accepting that he was no longer fit to play football, either as a player or coach, it was hard for him to remain in the afternoons near his house where the boys would run off to play on nearby fields. He would sit amongst discarded and broken pieces that he collected and used to fix but always failed. This provided him no sustainable income and made him feel like a burden to his doting mother. His heart was attached to the fields, where the team would gather after sunset prayers to talk, shout and blame each other. Although he was no longer playing, he was fully present in spirit and his imagination would allow him to participate in each story they shared. Every day he would listen intently until he had heard all the tales. He even began to finish stories that the others started.

In the midst of these thoughts, news arrived that he had been chosen to be the lead referee for the neighbourhood games. This recognition of his football skills boosted his morale and he felt grateful to the neighbourhood boys for considering him. On his first game as a referee, he struggled, using his crutch for support and with a whistle in hand. The players on the field could be seen trying to score on the goals without nets, with the boundaries of the dirt field drawn in lime paint and everyone in position, all of this could be seen by a referee who was unable to run.

Despite the limitations posed by his injury, the neighbourhood boys wanted to bring back some joy into his life by including him in their games. However, big dreams can become a trap for those who don't work towards making them a reality, and a deep sleep can be like a death knell for one's future.

The density of the crowd, the enthusiastic cheers, the piercing whistles, the dust rising from the field beneath the feet of the players chasing the ball, the fervour in the voices of the players who had objections, and the adrenaline rush of wanting to win the game, all of these things drove Muhammaduh to keep up with the fast-paced action. Despite his disability, he ran with his crutch in a way that was remarkable, given the circumstances. He fell several times, his face and clothes became smudged with dirt, and his whistle slipped from his grasp repeatedly. To the crowd, these instances only added to the excitement of the game and instead of just applauding the players, they cheered and clapped every time Muhammaduh stumbled and fell, while the players were always there to help him get back up.

****

As the game progressed, the crowd was in a state of permanent happiness watching Muhammaduh's unwavering spirit despite his repeated falls. He was determined to see it through to the end, as this was his last chance to be a part of a football match, a game that he held in high esteem.

Some neighbourhood boys gathered after the football match to mock Muhammaduh for falling into the dirt. They didn't take into consideration Al Mujaljel's reaction, who was furious with the boys, describing them as braying donkeys.

The neighbours had differing reactions to Muhammaduh's role as a referee, with his repeated falls causing a mixture of pity and frustration, especially for Al Mujaljel, who was given this nickname for his rough voice and tendency to argue until he ran out of breath.

Al Mujaljel was troubled as he made his way to his real estate office located near the sea port, feeling hesitant and unable to calm himself. At the door of the office, people scrambled to get permits for their clients' goods stuck at the port, causing chaos due to the owner's inaction. The horns of ships coming and going added to the already chaotic atmosphere.

Despite his uncertainty about whether to stay at his

current job or take a position at Al Ari Tourism Agency, Al Mujaljel opened the door to his office. A throng of irate individuals surged in and before he had a chance to take his seat, he was confronted by towering stacks of black-bound documents, jostling against one another and official forms requiring his signature. Some of the papers were frayed at the edges, others precariously balanced between files and still others lay scattered haphazardly about the room. Behind his desk, a row of neglected shelves with copper trim loomed, seeming unsure of their significance.

Al Mujaljel has long been plagued by chaos in his daily life. Whenever he needed a machine, official record, papers or a pen, he impulsively rose from his seat, causing items to fall and scatter around him without putting them back in their place. Each day, disorder and instability accompanied him to work, and the influx of people seeking his assistance only added to his feeling of being overwhelmed. The sound of their laboured breathing made the room feel cramped, and their constant demands for him to process their papers could be deafening. As his determination waned, he often daydreamed of himself as a rat being chased, frantically searching for a quiet corner to escape the turmoil. This image haunted him, and at times, he found himself hiding among the scattered papers, pretending to look for a lost document as a means of escape. Despite this, he showed a strong will to overcome the annoyance and pushed himself to remain calm, thinking "to escape all of this annoyance, tell them to come back tomorrow".

With his decision, Al Mujaljel put an end to the internal turmoil that had been building within him. The pressure and stress had become so intense that he lashed out, pushing someone in front of him and nearly caused a fight. The person stumbled and was nearly knocked off balance but was caught by others, and remained upright on his wooden leg, steadying himself amidst the barrage of curses and insults he directed at Al Mujaljel.

Feeling remorseful, Al Mujaljel apologised, offering gestures of peace as he turned his gaze towards the man with the wooden leg. It was a hot day, and the ceiling fan spun idly, unable to provide relief from the suffocating heat. The people in the room longed for a fresh breeze, their nostrils searching the air for any scent of relief coming through the window.

The door was opened wide to let fresh air in and break the thick, stuffy air inside, which was filled with the breath of all those present. Al Mujaljel received and processed some papers and promised to complete the pending ones. He deliberately made the man with the wooden leg wait, constantly smiling to keep him relaxed, signalling for him to wait until he had time for him.

Amidst all the chaos, complaints, scolding and apologies, the man with the wooden leg leaned forward and asked why he had been waiting for so long. He was wearing a short, white cotton dishdash, which showed off his wooden leg.

Al Mujaljel moved his fingers around his Parker pen on top of his desk, which was falling apart. "I'm not the one causing this," he said. "The Customs employees want more money." He addressed everyone present in his office filled with papers whose fees did not cover the office expenses.

He then called the man with the wooden leg and said something he wasn't expecting, "Where did you get this wooden leg from?"

The man felt a hint of sarcasm in Al Mujaljel's tone but

it vanished when he told him about Muhammaduh and his desire to buy him one. "The finest quality wooden legs come from Khartoum," he told him. They suddenly felt closer, and the man with the wooden leg promised to provide another one for Muhammaduh.

****

In the wooden room at the front of the house, Muhammaduh sat on his bed, cradling his amputated leg and extending the other one. He had grown accustomed to this position, and at times he would bend like a mast in the middle of a storm, clinging to his crutch that leaned against the wall beside his bed. His soul was in turmoil, swinging between feelings of frustration. He heard a continuous knocking at the main door.

"Open the door, referee!" a voice called out, and Muhammaduh detected a hint of sarcasm in the word "referee". It was Al Mujaljel, and though he wanted to ignore it, his mental state pushed him to talk to anyone, to lift himself out of the state he was in and raise his morale, even if he was the subject of ridicule.

He leaned on his crutch, which he had learned to handle, and made his way to the door. A group of hands were knocking, and he was surprised to see his close friends shouting at him,

"You'll never fall during a game again," they told him, having the man with the wooden leg as proof of how steady he could stand and move.

"In just a few days, you'll have a leg just like Al Morghani," they told him.

Al Mujaljel rallied his friends to provide financial support for buying the wooden leg for Muhammaduh, and with one round of fundraising, he had gathered enough to manufacture and purchase the leg, bringing the task to a successful conclusion.

They took measurements of Muhammaduh's amputated leg by removing the covering, and exposing the amputated part that looked like a pestle with extra bones protruding without any skin.

Muhammaduh's eyes were filled with a mysterious joy, and his cheeks were fresh like dark grapes. He was attentive to everything being said and had lifted himself out of the depression that had consumed him. He felt like spreading his hands to fly above his friends who were busy taking the measurements of the amputated part's circumference with the help of the carpenter Hassan to create an accurate mould for Muhammaduh's new wooden leg. Al Morghani provided guidance as they also compared the length and size of the amputated limb to Muhammaduh's intact leg. When it came time to send someone to Sudan with Al Morghani, they struggled to reach a decision and ultimately chose Jaleel Mansour, who was without employment at the time. They also split the cost of the trip.

Chapter 22

The arrival of the wooden leg was celebrated with the fervour of a wedding, bringing the community together in a festive gathering in the neighbourhood square. Excited chatter filled the air as music played and Yasser Mohbabi sang, adding to the celebratory atmosphere.

Despite the large crowd that had gathered, Muhammaduh couldn't help but be surprised by the number of people who had come to show their support, from the memorial service to the purchase of the wooden leg and now to celebrate him as if he were a revered leader.

The sounds of the celebration echoed around the square, coming and going amidst the commotion. Muhammaduh tried so hard to thank everyone who was there, his mouth always open like the gate of an old house unable to be closed against the strong wind, he also started expressing his gratitude through gestures, joining his hands on his chest to show the appreciation that flowed through his veins. His black eyes watched the joy on people's faces, looking deeply into each one who had made this happen.

Then, Al Mujaljel said,

"May God grant you happiness." This wish came from his heart like a flock of pigeons, spreading good spirit to all who were celebrating and dancing to the tunes of Al Bahri(s famous song,

"Why are you smiling Nile, while my tears are streaming?
"Me and my lover loved each other but now we are separated
"My beloved has gone, leaving me with sadness in my eyes"
The sounds of sorrow could be heard, as the crowd began to dance and toss their amamas onto the dance floor.

An image of Omaima from the past appeared in Muhammaduh's mind, with her confused smile as she used to walk by him like a graceful deer. His gaze wandered away from the lanterns, jumping over the walls and roofs, through the streets and shops, until it stopped outside Abdul Ghafour Ashour's house, where he waited for Omaima and thought to himself,

"Now that I have a wooden leg, would you accept me?"

This thought made him feel sad once again, and reminded of the feeling of inferiority he had experienced since he was a child and first heard the word "slave". He turned his gaze back, placed his hand on his heart, and said,

"If you can't find solace, may your sorrow be blessed."

His thoughts shifted back to the present and he reflexively placed his hands over his chest in a gesture of gratitude. He briefly wondered if the motion was for his own comfort or for the benefit of those at the gathering. But he quickly dismissed these musings and instead focused on the possibilities his new wooden leg would bring. He pondered if it would help him secure a job to provide for his family. Testing his newfound mobility, he stood and was pleased to find that he could move freely and maintain his balance. The sight of him standing on his own two feet – albeit one made of wood – brought tears of joy to those in the room. He stepped outside to share the news with his family, who rushed over to celebrate with him. His mother, Fatima

Al-Muhajira, cried tears of happiness as she hugged him, savouring the excitement that radiated from his being.

Yasser Mohnabi took a short break from singing and the percussionists put down their instruments, taking a moment to drink tea and smoke. The noise level dropped as Al Mujaljel walked amongst the crowd, his voice ringing like a bell. Muhammaduh's eyes scanned the area, imagining that Ibrahim was watching from a nearby distance, cleaver in hand, ready to disrupt the celebration of his recovery, even though he was now on a wooden leg.

****

The night was dark in Muhammaduh's yard when a fire started and cries for help could be heard above the roaring flames. The weather took a sudden turn, bringing with it a strong wind that was unusual for Jeddah. The people ran inside instead of enjoying the breeze. This was the first time that the winter had been so strong in Jeddah.

From behind the fierce wind that blew across the wooden houses in the neighbourhood, Muhammaduh's wooden room was visible. It was supported by slender wooden beams painted with a striking blend of bright red and yellow and was remarkable for its colours, furniture and shape. It was located close to the entrance door and was part of a spacious yard that housed multiple rooms for Muhammaduh's family. The land gifted to them by Oqab ben Ali made it one of the oldest inhabited places near the seaport. The yard contained four delicate wooden rooms with zinc roofs, and the fourth room was added at the end of the space when the stench from Muhammaduh's decaying amputated leg became unbearable.

Hajji Fatima arranged for him to move to this room, citing religious laws as the reason for the separation. However, the true cause was the foul smell coming from his leg, a fact that was revealed through the words and gestures of his sisters who often covered their noses and sighed in disgust. Muhammaduh was moved to this room and has lived there ever since.

It was midnight and before removing his wooden leg, Muhammaduh felt a rush of excitement from his straight posture, he stood before a tall mirror that stretched from the ceiling to the floor. In the dim light of an oil lantern, he removed his clothes, revealing his toned abs and chest. He took some oil and rubbed it over his upper body, admiring his own physique. The image of Omaima came to his mind, smiling and jumping like a pigeon. But she was absent due to circumstances, events, social differences and ongoing animosity. A heartbreak surged in Muhammaduh's throat as he thought about the injustice of life,

"A life of hardship puts your heart in a grave that has no walls."

He felt a complex mix of heartbreak, ecstasy, and bewilderment. He dreamed of soaring like a bird through the streets of the neighbourhood, greeting each day with a joyful trill, brimming with hope, if only Abdul Ghafour Ashour had not cast a shadow over his childhood, snuffing out his sense of pride.

When he was young, he was filled with pride, but the harm he caused to Ibrahim Ashour shattered his dream. Omaima remained a fading flower in his heart. He recalled the day she wrote to him, asking him to avenge her brother against his rival. The memory tore him apart and he wondered, "Does she know I am her rival?" Agony still lingered in his chest, escaping with every breath he took. On this chilly night, an old harp melody drifted into his mind, inspiring him to dance with his wooden leg to its beat. He sang,

"Float Jamal, come help me carry my burden
"On Noaman's road, look at me!
"I'll open the chest and dress her in fine silk...
"Me and my love, we fight with swords!
"I only love the one with the black kohl-lined eyes
"Oh, those eyes are a gift from the gods."

He paused at the final phrase "the black eyes", recalling Omaima's emerald green eyes, and rubbed his forehead as he muttered, "If only we could love with a pure heart, we would never lose a beloved." The night beetles roused from their slumber at the deep sound of his voice, and began to chirp in unison with Muhammaduh, announcing their presence. With his body brimming with confidence, he swung his wooden leg to the beat of the music as he imagined himself dancing at a "mezmar". The thought wouldn't disappear, so he left his room and gathered some dead branches from under the guava and lemon trees. He returned to his room, laying the branches out, and poured oil from his lantern over them, starting a fire that illuminated the entire room. Grasping his crutch as if it were a mighty weapon, he danced around the fire, clapping and beating a drum as loudly as he could, repeating the movements to songs that he knew by heart,

"I promise you, my dear, the fringes of the shawl brush against my cheek
"It's a vision of silk swaying in the breeze, oh my!'

"The corner of the shawl has ensnared me, I'm undone, I can't resist
"This was not in my expectations
"I never thought my heart would be tethered to the end of this shawl."

He spun and clapped around the fire, but soon realised his wooden leg was causing him trouble with its unsteady gait. He hopped onto his bed, removed the wooden limb and placed it next to him like a discarded shoe. As he lay down, trying to ignore the flickering embers in the middle of the room and resist the pull of sleep, memories of his dancing and singing at neighbourhood parties flooded his mind. The thoughts of Omaima, Ibrahim, and their father drifted into his consciousness, bringing with them a mixture of love and hate.

Chapter 23

Just before Abdo Jaber's call to morning prayer echoed through the air, a raging fire had taken hold of Muhammaduh's room. The flames were consuming everything in their path, like a ship being swept into a whirlpool by tumultuous waves, the wind howling, fanning the flames as if it had a mission to fulfil.

Hajji Fatima, while performing her ablutions, noticed the thick smoke billowing from Muhammaduh's room, black and red with the intensity of the fire. She quickly raised the alarm, and was soon joined by her daughters and the rest of the family as they raced to Muhammaduh's room. They heard him calling for help and without hesitation, Hajji Fatima instructed her daughters to gather some covers to protect themselves from the heat and smoke as they entered the room, remembering the time when the French set fire to the hay huts in a national army camp, and covers were used to rescue the survivors.

She was alarmed by the speed at which the flames were spreading throughout the room. Neighbours had come to help, trying to put out the fire with dirt and water from the tap. Chaos broke out among the rescuers as the fire had already eaten away the back of the room and there was a high chance that Muhammaduh would either burn to death or choke.

The women in his family were shouting, almost certain he

had been burned alive. They held the covers, standing there motionless, crying, shouting and calling for help.

Everyone gathered, praying to God for help, as there was nothing else that could stop the fire. They continued to pray and waited to see what would become of the room engulfed in flames. As the flames grew stronger, Hajji Fatima crumbled, seemingly surrendering to destiny with complete faith. She fell to her knees, praying, while Muhammaduh's friends gathered around her trying to ease her pain.

"It looks like she's given up," someone said.

Al Maskoun was agitated and terrified. He replied, "Help ease her pain." He stood tall and strong, the perfect candidate for a rescue mission. He took a cover from Aisha's hands and stepped into the flames that were everywhere, with smoke so thick it was impossible to see. He shouted out Muhammaduh's name as the latter lay there like a chicken waiting for his fate, unable to push away the fire that had surrounded him. The final moment had arrived. The fire had reached Muhammaduh's mattress, threatening to consume him. The furniture was collapsing and the fire was devouring everything in its path. The ceiling fell on the other side of the bed and Al Maskoun went straight to the bed where Muhammaduh was lying helpless like a wooden plank.

With determination, Al Maskoun navigated through the raging flames and, like a seasoned baker who knows how to rescue his dough from the oven, he lifted Muhammaduh from the bed and shielded both of them with the cover. Despite feeling the intense heat of the fire on his hands and feet, the two of them managed to escape the inferno. The family and neighbours cheered and whistled as Hajji Fatima fell to her knees in gratitude, giving thanks to God. She kept her head bowed until Muhammaduh reached out and touched her, lying beside her like a freshly peeled aubergine.

****

By midday on the day of the fire, Muhammaduh felt an immense sadness. A bed had been set up for him in his sisters' room, which now had more space as two of his sisters, Hawaa and Khaddar, had married and Aisha was about to be married. As he sat, he felt like a burden and began to dwell on the fire, focusing his sorrow on his wooden leg that had been damaged in the blaze. The fire had taken everything of value, including his crutch, which he had replaced with a branch from a guava tree. He asked everyone to leave the room, wanting to be alone with his thoughts and pain. He refused to dress his wounds or eat or drink anything. Unable to sleep, there was nothing left but pain and a faint glimmer of hope.

"They say money is a home but even this home has shut its doors on me."

He leaned to his right to reach his damaged wooden leg, he grasped it, and tossed it outside the room. This prompted him to realise the importance of two crucial things, obtaining citizenship and finding a job that accommodates his disability.

During a neighbourhood gathering at Abbas Halaawi's seating area, the men talked about Saadiya, the daughter of Jamal Khayrat. She had put an end to her struggles after her husband's death by visiting King Faisal's palace and having her children placed in an orphanage. Muhammaduh was on the periphery of the gathering but listened intently to the story, sensing that it might offer a solution to his own troubles. So he resolved to visit King Faisal's palace again. He couldn't help but wonder why he was denied entry to the palace and why the guards always laughed and asked him,

"Do you still want your amputated leg?"

and he would simply reply with an angry African accent,

"I just want citizenship."

His mind was in turmoil as he struggled with his helpless wishes. His mother tried to comfort him by saying, "Words are like birds, some of them are like chickens and don't have much worth, they just move their legs in the rubbish.

Chapter 24

Feeling defeated and ashamed, Muhammaduh found himself doing nothing and growing increasingly inactive, feeling trapped in his own body. Meanwhile, the women in his family worked hard to earn money, selling their goods and trying to ease their poverty.

Memories from his past pained him, especially those from his childhood when Abdul Ghafour pressed his earlobe between his fingers, swinging his life between existence and insignificance.

Suddenly, he had a flash of wisdom. However he kept it to himself, repeating the thought in his head,

"There are those who set traps for others, like snipers waiting for something to fall into their trap. It doesn't matter what is caught, just that something is caught."

Abdul Ghafour Ashour is a print that never fades, present in both his past and future. No matter how much he tries to erase him from his memory, he remains, a sniper laying traps for both good and bad birds alike.

The truth was that Muhammaduh was an unintentional victim, like bait on a fishing hook or a pawn on a chess board, pushed forward to be part of a game not of his choosing.

When Muhammaduh first heard the word "slave"," he understood that his skin and race were doomed. He was brought into this world to be humiliated, and used like a cheap currency that everyone accepts and uses.

THE CISTERN

The coastline of Jeddah was a melting pot of cultures, where people from all races coexisted without distinction. The streets, alleys, shops and cafes bustled with life, as people left their past behind, either carried away by the waves or distanced from their home country and its problems.

Every race lived in its own style, in palaces, homes, nests, boxes, on the streets, alleys, and pavements but only one was subjected to discrimination, the black race, marked by a curse since the beginning of time.

The incident involving Abdul Ghafour was a defining moment for Muhammaduh, one that was deeply ingrained in his memory. He believed that he was constantly pursued by several curses but none more significant than ethnicity and the colour of his skin.

Chapter 25

Anyone who hears this tale of Muhammaduh's childhood can ponder the question, ""Can a small grudge grow and become an inevitable fate for a family on the fringes of society?"

The country was peaceful, with no wars, no protests and slogans, no resistance, no demands, no arrests, no groups spreading rumours in the markets or holding secret meetings at night, no political parties trying to sway political decisions. It was a country as still as a mirror, where you could see an ant walking from one side to the other.

Only a few dared to break the silence of their days and explore what lay beyond it. One such person was Khairy Ashour and his son Abdul Ghafour, who found himself implicated in a situation whose main character was his father. Amidst this stillness, the people of the
neighbourhood lived their lives, breathing their air and paying no heed to the events outside, consumed by their own small problems.

The problems that led to Muhammaduh's failure lingered in his mind. He soon realised that Abdul Ghafour was the source of the curse that had plagued him and driven Omaima away. His deep yearning was simply a spell from which he couldn't break free.

Some individuals soar to great heights, while others are trapped in the mud. They linger in their misery and, if they dare to look up, all they see are shoes.

THE CISTERN

He calculated the gaps and barriers that stood between him and his aspiration – ethnicity, poverty, disability, nationality and Ibrahim's wrath.

He sat amid the debris, with nothing to do but to sift through the ruins. He was acutely aware that his own life was in a shambles and needed fixing. Losing his leg propagated anger in his chest and became like a refuge for a spider that couldn't distinguish between its threads.

Each day, his dreams became more modest, at first, he shook off his despondency and was determined to visit King Faisal's palace but as time passed he settled for a visit to the Ministry of Interior to answer some questions.

****

Muhammaduh suddenly lost consciousness and was taken back to his house. Hajji Fatima couldn't understand what had happened. She slapped his face to woke him up and her words echoed in everyone's ears, "I'll give my life for you, Muhammaduh."

Al Maskoun kissed her head, trying to calm her down,

"Don't worry, he'll be alright," he reassured her.

"What happened?" she asked

"Nothing, we were talking about who has left the neighbourhood, both now and before, and he suddenly fell. I thought his crutch failed him, but he wasn't even standing. We brought him back here straight away," he explained.

Once Muhammaduh regained consciousness, his friends left while his mother still didn't know what had caused this emergency. He had a frown on his face, making his mouth tight, and it seemed as if he was straying in and out of reality, repeating some words as if he were mumbling to himself.

Hajji Fatima went out to the yard to peel peanuts and break the seeds of baobab, thinking about a son who brought her nothing but a broken spirit. She wanted to be with Aisha, who was due to give birth, but she was assured both sisters were next to her and promised to take care of her.

Hajji Fatima left her chores and approached her son, trying to make him relax with conversation, laughter or doing things for him but she received very little response. Muhammaduh's gaze was distant and he was visibly shaken. What he had just heard was shocking; he wished he had been killed by Ibrahim Ashour a hundred times instead of learning the news that was worse than a mortal blow. The news hit him like a knife to the heart. Ibrahim Ashour had left the country with Omaima, promising that no one would ever see him again. Muhammaduh wilted like a branch without a root, wandering the streets and alleys in search of her.

****

It had been some time since Muhammaduh had seen Omar Al-Yaridi, and every time he remembered the night when he disfigured Ibrahim Ashour, he would secretly laugh, wishing he had decapitated Al-Yaridi instead.

But that wish had come too late. He was powerless to undo all that his family and relatives had gone through and never realized that Al-Yaridi was the main reason that it all happened.

"Life becomes bitter when we discover its secrets,"

his mother had once said in a moment of consolation and excessive remorse. With a deep sigh, Muhammaduh picked up the crutch that lay next to his bed, trying to shake off his sadness.

PAGES FROM THE LIFE
OF OMAR AL-YARIDI

Chapter 1

"For anyone seeking Al-Yaridi, they should check around Ashour's house."

Recently, Al-Yaridi had been seen sitting for long periods facing Ashour's house, which has sparked rumours among the neighbours. Some believed he may be in love with Omaima but the gossip was kept quiet for fear of upsetting Ibrahim Ashour. Another explanation given by Saliha Bent Issa was that his umbilical cord was buried near Ashour's window. When Al-Yaridi appeared distracted, it was whispered that he was in love and it had taken over his mind.

Al-Yaridi could be found sitting on a bench at the start of sunset, with his tea pot, a fire and some logs listening to the Sawt El Arab radio station while he sips tea. He didn't ask anyone to join him, preferring to stay by himself. Since he started reading "The Sun of Knowledge" nobody wanted to sit with him or talk to him any more. Whenever he walked by, people would

I'd shout his famous phrase, "I see you... I see you."

****

Al-Yaridi turned 50 and spent his dinnertimes learning how to summon Jinn and get rid of them, all the while sitting in front of Ashour's house, regardless of the weather. Other behaviour was also bizarre, like jumping on barbed wire and ignoring warnings of the danger. Al-Yaridi was stoic and uttered not a sound. However, his prolonged silence was eventually broken, making him the subject of ridicule and leading people to believe he had lost his mind. Some even condemned his actions. It was well-known that Al-Yaridi had a mercurial temperament, which was illustrated when Jamila Abou Setin scolded her servant Zahra for being late with dates she was supposed to bring. Jamila stammered her reprimand but her cruel words and curses caused Zahra to break down in tears. As Jamila looked at her torn shirt and bruises, she shouted,

"Who did this to you?"

Zahra stayed silent and did not want to talk about what happened. When Jamila insisted she explain it was revealed that Al-Yaridi was responsible. Jamila went around telling all the women about it, and in their turn they told their husbands. After this incident, Al-Yaridi was observed following African women trying to lure them into his company, It wouldn't have been so obvious if Al-Yaridi hadn't taken them straight to his secluded house on the corner. Barik Al Adani confirmed the rumours that Al-Yaridi pursued his desires without disturbing anyone. People questioned why Al-Yaridi was drawn to African women, with many women feeling sad that his beauty was being wasted on people who did not appreciate it.

Al-Yaridi would roam the city searching for African foreigners in need or who had become lost. He would take them to the ruins at the back of Ashour's house and carry out his reprehensible actions.

On arrival, the women would start shouting for help and neighbours would come to their rescue but the culprit, later identified as Al-Yaridi, had usually escaped by that time.

He was often in a state of delusion and madness, shouting obscenities and curses at the black race.

It was said that no African woman was able to avoid his harassment. He would not respond to women who tried to seduce him with a smile or by walking past him. The only person who had a burning love for Al-Yaridi was Fekriya Saabih. She made her feelings known to her friends, who started calling her the "Jinn lover".

It was also said that Al-Yaridi was infatuated with Jumana Ashour and that after she left, no other woman could capture his heart. Al-Yaridi's seductive tactics disturbed the neighbours, who approached the mayor to put an end to his behaviour. The mayor was angry with Al-Yaridi and hoped to catch him in the act so that he could discipline him, but before he could take action, news spread that Al-Yaridi had lost his mind. Despite everything he had done, people forgave him and prayed for his recovery. Some neighbours even asked an imam to offer a reading and prayer for Al-Yaridi but he refused. Hisham Mahlawi explained that the number of Jinn that Al-Yaridi conjured was too many for anyone to dismiss, and whoever tried to do so would be pulled into the seventh earth.

After the news of Al-Yaridi's madness spread, people were warned not to approach him as the Jinn that lived within him could transfer to anyone who was nearby. This warning resulted in people shaking their clothes and praying as they walked past him.

It was also believed that the Jinn had divided Al-Yaridi's body among themselves and kept him close by in case something troubling occurred. This explains why he was always seen near Ashour's house. Another explanation was that the Jinn lived inside the house and, as they could no longer fit inside, they took up residence in Al-Yaridi and kept him close to where they lived. They were still searching for a suitable room for him. It was also said that the Jinn were active at night, rebuilding Ashour's palace. The neighbourhood believed what Suleiman Al Matwaa' had sworn, that whoever sat next to Ashour's house or with Al-Yaridi would be inhabited by the Jinn.

Chapter 2

Whole days slipped away from Al-Yaridi's life with his gaze fixed on the pages of the book "The Sun of Knowledge". This transported him to a dark world, offering only a glimmer of hope of uncovering the truth. He constantly spotted new revelations in the book, such as the talisman's warning that choosing women was a costly mistake that took away his youth.

The heat of his body rose from under his arms to reach his cheeks, causing a burning sensation in his breath. He closes the book and bellows,

"I see you... I see you."

This warning was directed at any Jinn that may mean him harm, and as soon as he spoke, they disappeared and his state of mind returned to normal.

As the dawn prepares for prayer, all the creatures were moving around in their own private space. For those who had lost their mind, planets fall in their imagination until nothing remains in its place. Al-Yaridi's mind was a field for all planets to fall, each causing a blinding light.

All the passages to his inner thoughts were blocked, with the exception of one, which was consumed by various fixations, particularly the acquisition of a slave. This was prior to Al-Yaridi's descent into madness, or so it was said, when he made his way resolutely to the slave market.

He felt a deep sadness as the cries of the girls no longer

interested him, while he shuffled forward, muttering curses in all directions without speaking to anyone in particular. His mind was filled with people he couldn't see, whom he conversed with and cursed, for reasons he couldn't remember.

The neighbours grew used to him arguing with figures he imagined to be at his side, giving him compliments, and he would reply with shouting and intimidation,

"I will burn you all if you don't help me achieve my goal."

His loud outbursts inside the mosque made Imam Bilal wary of his presence among those in prayer. As his condition worsened, the Imam issued a Fatwa declaring Al-Yaridi unfit to pray with the community. Those who were praying rose to confront him, denying him entry to the mosque, which led him to become enraged and shout,

"Do you forbid me to enter the house of God?"

His objections, along with the muttering under his breath, were in vain, and like a fly in a jar of honey, they silenced him with disdain and forced him away from the gates of the mosque.

His actions drew laughter from the crowd, with the elderly attempting to stifle it and children openly giggling. As soon as Imam Bilal started the Takbir Al Ihram, a loud disturbance could be heard outside, followed by threatening voices aimed at all those who were praying. Al-Yaridi's voice echoed in the ears of those who pray, his body pushing through the crowd as he cursed the Imam and everyone who is praying behind him, declaring that the Imam was not speaking the truth. People cautiously glanced at him from the corners of their eyes as he stood before each row, shouting, "Here I am."

He persisted in his disruptions until he stood to the right

of the Imam, pushing away those in the front row and filling their ears with the most horrific stories and pressing his shoulder against the Imam. For a short time, he remained quiet, then he began speaking loudly, regaling the crowd with all the stories he knew about those who prayed in the front row.

In light of these events and in accordance with the Fatwa, the people who were praying met to find a way to prevent Al-Yaridi from entering the mosque, and agreed that one person would volunteer to stand guard outside until the prayer was over, ensuring that he was not allowed inside.

****

Before Al-Yaridi's mental state became severely impaired, he would walk around muttering words about a decision by King Faisal.

He became infamous for always repeating,

"If it weren't for Faisal, my dreams would come true."

People would shy away from him, fearing the consequences of listening to his rants, and those who felt sorry for him would try to silence him or cover his mouth, telling him how harmful his words were. This only made Al-Yaridi feel more hurt and resentful.

Feeling sorry for him, Al Massoudi sighed and said,

"The House of Ashour and the book The Sun of Knowledge have completely taken away Al-Yaridi's sanity."

At first, no one knew how Al-Yaridi obtained the book. But as his stories circulated among the neighbours, the truth was eventually revealed; Ibrahim Ashour was the one who brought him "The Sun of Knowledge" from Cairo.

Chapter 3

On a particularly stressful night, with the furniture in Al-Yaridi's small room shaking from a passing gust of wind, he was occupied with tidying the letters and numbers as per "The Book of Knowledge", desperately searching for any mistake that could explain why he couldn't find the treasure he was after.

As he scanned the pages, a loud voice echoed in his mind, "The condition is that of a slave who has not been weaned."

This was the answer he had been searching for and he felt a sense of relief when he found it. Although he was frustrated with himself for wasting time chasing African women, he felt a newfound determination to find this unweaned slave.

He dressed in his travelling clothes, his imagination running wild with thoughts of how he would locate this slave. He stepped outside his small room, where the light from the lantern shone bright, illuminating the cluttered and mismatched furniture that filled the space. Despite the shoddy appearance of his surroundings, he was driven by the newfound purpose that had eluded him for so long.

****

The dull yellow light of the rising sun illuminated the taxi rank, its cars and surrounding cafes and homes. As the sun climbed higher, people woke up and started going into their cars, filling them with passengers.

Al-Yaridi boarded the bus, taking a seat and trying to calm his agitation by moving his legs and tapping the seat in front of him with his fingers, humming a childhood song. Despite his off-key singing, he didn't mind until a passenger anxiously shouted at the conductor,

"When will the bus leave?"

The conductor smiled gently and replied,

"Just one more passenger" while hanging out to the bus door and calling out to those in the taxi rank,

"One more passenger, one more passenger."

The wait felt interminable for Al-Yaridi, as the minutes dragged by. To distract himself, he started to send pulsing through his brain words that had been pent up inside him, imagining the sounds of utensils. He emptied his mind of everything and all what was left was a series of fragmented words. He felt scared but he pushed the fear aside, reflecting on his past and realising that all he had collected were scraps, bad words, bad people, and bad luck. The only good thing in his life was the gift from Ibrahim Ashour, the "Sun of Knowledge" book, which he had spent years studying.

Determined to move forward, Al-Yaridi made the decision to close the door on his past and focus on the new information he had learned about "bringing the treasure." He vowed to make sure his future steps were flawless. Meanwhile, the bus attendant continued shouting,

"One more passenger, one more passenger"

until an old man in tattered clothes approached and was helped inside by the attendant.

"You're lucky to have bagged the last seat," the conductor told him, but all he received in return was a frown and fiery glare. The bus trundled down the streets on its route out of the city.

The driver navigated through the gates of the Grand Mosque and, on reaching their final destination, passengers started to disembark. Three passengers remained in their seats, and the driver shouted,

"This is Jibril Gate, our final stop". Before the attendant could move to assist, two of them got up and left the bus. Al-Yaridi, however, remained seated, arguing with the conductor.

"I told you to let me off at Bab Al Dariba," he complained.

"Everyone knows our final destination is Jibril Gate," the conductor retorted.

"But I specifically asked for Bab Al Dariba and you nodded in agreement," Al-Yaridi countered.

"Bab Al Dariba is not far. Don't taint the sanctity of the place by insisting," the attendant advised.

"And you don't taint the sanctity of the place by breaking your promise," Al-Yaridi shot back.

The driver turned around and confronted Al-Yaridi,

"What promise?" he asked

"Muslims are supposed to keep their promises, right? Before I took my seat, you promised to take me to Bab Al Dariba," Al-Yaridi explained.

The driver's anger boiled over and he cursed and shouted at the bewildered conductor, unable to shake off Al-Yaridi's complaints. As the passengers boarded the bus, eager to reach their final destination on time, the heated argument between the driver and Al-Yaridi caused a delay, so the passengers decided to switch to another bus. Frustrated by the delay, the driver turned off the engine and delegated the task of dealing with Al-Yaridi to his assistant.

As pigeons fluttered around the bus, he retrieved a bag of barley that he keeps next to his gear stick, and threw a handful to the birds, muttering a prayer for mercy. Small stones were entering his shoes through a torn patch, and he was feeling the effects of the hot air of dawn, while sweating profusely, so he used his scarf to wipe the sweat from his face.

As time passed, the driver felt a mixture of annoyance and anger and decided to address Al-Yaridi himself. He hopped on the bus and approached Al-Yaridi calmly, asking,

"What exactly do you need?"

"The slave market," was Al-Yaridi's reply.

The driver explained that his final stop was here and the slave market wasn't far but Al-Yaridi refused to leave the bus, stating,

"Even if it were just three steps away, I will not leave this bus until you drive me there."

Seeing no other option, the driver summoned all his remaining patience and took money from his pocket, offering it to Al-Yaridi and saying,

"Take your money back. May God forgive you."

However, Al-Yaridi refused to accept the money and stood firm in his demand,

"I insist on going to the slave market," he declared.

In an attempt to resolve the conflict, the only passenger who stayed in the bus approached Al-Yaridi and tried to pacify him with a gentle kiss on the head and a suggestion,

"We're at a sacred place, let's show compassion and move on."

However, the assistant's intervention only escalated the situation,

"Tell him to get off and go to Bayt Al Atik, there's no such thing as a slave market here."

This irritated Al-Yaridi even more and the driver in turn became increasingly frustrated, hitting one of the bus seats in anger and shouting at his assistant, "Who allowed you to speak?"

To diffuse the situation, the driver reluctantly agreed to pay a higher fare and kiss Al-Yaridi's head, who took the money with annoyance before getting off the bus. Despite the efforts of the only other passenger to intervene, the driver continued to berate his assistant.

Chapter 4

He ignited the streets with his unjustified anger…
People flooded the gates of the holy sanctuary, murmuring words of forgiveness. Despite the reverence of the place, Al-Yaridi's devilish anger was uncontainable and he ravaged the serenity of those who were walking. He rudely waved his hands in the face of anyone who tried to calm him down, shouting words that disturbed the peaceful atmosphere. This caused some of the pilgrims to become frightened and run to pray and ask for forgiveness.

In search of the slave market, Al-Yaridi approached some of the passengers. However, he found himself surrounded by people from India, Indonesia, Burma, Turkey and Africa, and his constant demands for information went unanswered as he could not understand their responses.

His anger was obvious and his frustration was growing as he continued to move from one place to another, piercing the crowd and searching for the slave market. He was like an inexperienced boy, holding onto his desire without knowing how to get his way. Despite his constant anger, he failed to arouse any sympathy from those who passed by. Eventually, he moved to the other side of the main gates in search of the information he sought.

After each prayer, large crowds of people poured out towards the nearby homes, markets and shops, like hard working ants, making their way up the mountains to their homes, or down steep paths, or walking in straight lines, always clear on their destinations. The whiteness of the passengers' garments dominated the many colours of the workers' and vendors' everyday clothes. Pilgrims and pigeons filled the streets, and along the pavements and alleyways were groups of people joined by ethnicity, skin colour or purpose.

The shrine brought peace and satisfaction to the souls, making the atmosphere calm and friendly. However, Al-Yaridi's negative emotions accumulated inside him, as he walked around with only one goal in mind, haunted by his own thoughts. He was thrashing about, as if the devil had written a curse upon him.

The further he got away from the shrine, the more he was embraced by the busy markets and busy streets, where the calls of sellers overpowered everything else. He found himself surrounded by chaotic and disordered stalls, where sellers exhibited their food and drinks, and those who couldn't shout loudly were still able to attract customers with the smell of their offerings. The stalls were arranged in two parallel lines, adding to the bustling atmosphere of the market.

Al-Yaridi's very soul was longing for a plate of Takatii with ground garlic, vinegar, lemon slices and onions. He watched intently as the cook expertly stirred the pot with a wooden spoon, adding spices with flair while shouting,

"Don't keep your customers hungry." The chef's assistants then served plates of Takatii and liver to the waiting customers.

Al-Yaridi was eager for breakfast to restore his composure but his need to reach the slave market before it became too busy outweighed his hunger. He asked for directions to the market but the busy cook and assistants couldn't help. Finally, a nearby vendor pointed down Al-Shamiya neighbourhood, telling him to follow Kabat alley to reach Al Dekka square, where slaves were bought and sold. However, Al-Yaridi was insulted by the vendor's gesture and snapped, "Do I look like a female camel to be led by its reins?"

He kept using foul language, loudly complaining about people he deemed inferior. Everyone who passed by heard his insults,

"All these animals roam the earth, knowing nothing but how to bray."

He let out an obscene laugh that echoed in the air. He had a secret desire he kept to himself, imagining tomorrow when he finds the treasure and buys and sells many slaves, then everyone will know where the market is.

As he walked, he encountered an Aga walking in front of him, dressed in bright white clothes with a green and gold belt, surrounded by admirers who showed him reverence. Al-Yaridi felt a surge of anger towards the Aga's calm confidence and steady steps. In his rage, he started shouting at the him,

"Hey you slave, you slave."

In his frustration at being ignored, he repeated loudly,

"Hey you castrated people, you unwhole men."

Two of the men accompanying the Aga stepped back, and one of them grabbed Al-Yaridi by his robe, pulling him forcibly,

"Behave," the man said.

Al-Yaridi jumped back, outraged, and challenged the man, "What if I don't?"

The man then lifted his leg and stamped down hard on Al-Yaridi's toes with his heavy shoe, causing him to cry out in pain, preventing him from pursuing his enemy or his followers, so he sat on the ground, shouting threats at them as they got further away from him. He then realised that cursing was the best way to relieve his frustration.

Chapter 5

Facing "Bab Al Dariba," one of the main gates of the shrine, there is a narrow alley that goes down through Al Shamiya neighbourhood, ending at a square with a wide platform in the middle, rising two feet above the ground and measuring nine feet in width, covered with a shiny coat that masks the darkness of concrete, and to the right, a few steps that the slaves take up when the show begins.

As the dignitaries gather, looking to buy slaves or domestic workers to trade in other cities or find a beautiful slave to enhance their mood, all eyes are on the head of the brokers who keeps his wealth hidden around the corner, starting with the slave warehouse and ending with the bikes leading to the platform.

In the midst of this crowd, the wait and anticipation, the head of the brokers moves about with delight, approaching those who wish to attend the haggle and witness the slave show. He encourages the hesitant and truly deserves his title, able to sell dirt as gold.

As he steps onto the platform, he calls out to the auction with words that are like traps set for unsuspecting birds,

"Today is unlike any other day that has passed."

"How?" The crowd inquires, some ask to no purpose, while others question within themselves, to which he replies,

"Wait and you shall see."

Like a rehearsed show, the head of brokers made a grand

entrance, decked out in a fine outfit, and accompanied by two slaves carrying a large ostrich feather fan to keep him cool. The group that surrounded him was in sync, moving in a circle as they followed their master's every gesture. He had his back to the platform and was carefully surveying the crowd's reactions, eager to announce the surprise of the show. He made it clear that only the rich would appreciate the surprise and called out to any dignitaries who may have left.

His words were filled with drama as he described the slave, saying that such a pure, beautiful and shining being had never before passed through there. His descriptions caused a stir among the audience, with people jostling to get a better view. Finally he turned to the crowd and asked,

"Shall I start the show or should we wait so that none of the dignitaries miss the chance to own a slave from heaven?"

The crowd was divided, some eager to see the slave and others content to wait. The head of brokers, sensing the tension, signalled for a group of slaves to separate the wealthy from the less affluent. The dignitaries and their slaves with umbrellas took the front row, while the head of brokers grew increasingly eager to start the show.

"Let's see whose lucky day it is," he declared, and all eyes turned towards the narrow path leading to the slave warehouse. The crowd held its breath as a beautiful black slave appeared, making her way up the stairs to the platform. The crowd became agitated, with many expressing anger and disbelief.

The head of the brokers raised his hand, trying to calm the situation,

"This is her courtesan," he explained, "and the slave comes with one condition, whoever buys her must also take on her courtesan."

The statement caused the dignitaries to voice their disapproval and Sheikh Salem Afandi declared, "Even slaves have conditions now?" Salem Ben Ali, the head of the brokers, realized he had stirred up the crowd and tried to correct himself,

"This is the playful charm of the beautiful."

The dignitaries' objections grew stronger but before they could become too loud, he signalled for her to come forward. The crowd hushed as she made her way to the front, her black dress emphasising her stunning complexion and captivating everyone with the grace of her movements. When she finally removed her scarf, many were awestruck and exclaimed,

"God the Glorious creates what He pleases," Salem Ben Ali's grin was like that of a wolf who had reluctantly given up its prey.

He proudly proclaimed,

"Did I not tell you that no one like her has ever been seen in Mecca?"

The eyes were wide open and the people were taken aback, their mouths agape, stunned by the beauty that God had created in this slave. In the silence, Salem Ben Ali excitedly proclaimed, "Mecca has never seen a woman as beautiful as her since God created humans." No one in the crowd was bothered by his statement except for Omar Al-Yaridi, who stood at the back, his voice of protest lost in the crowd pushing forward to get a closer look. If it weren't for the line of slaves blocking the way, people would have rushed forward to capture the slave or get as close as possible to her beauty that had blinded them. With grace and agility, Salem Ben Ali jumped down from the platform, asking her to come down. He held her soft hand and they moved together left and right while people drooled and gasped in wonder. The tongues were wet and everyone wanted to drink from this flawless glass. Sheikh Muhammad Momina could not contain himself and shouted,

"Let the bidding begin, and the winner will be one of you who came here today."

Salem Ben Ali realised the crowd was eager to begin the bidding. Before Sheikh Youssef Kerdi arrived, the slave went back onto the platform to flaunt her posture, her confidence, her charm and her grace. The broker began to highlight all her various assets,

"A woman of Anatolian descent, she speaks Arabic fluently and has a talent for poetry, music and the oud. She is joyful, playful, flirtatious, obedient, and free of any trouble. And that's not all..."

The Aga interjected, "That's enough. Let's see her up close."

Omar Al-Yaridi was livid and pushed his way to the front, against the will of the slave who was tasked with keeping order. His voice mixed with the voices of those eager to examine the slave but no one could hear what he said, "What does this castrated man have to do with slaves?"

The Afandi, Mahmoud Bachata, Muhammad Mo'mina, and the Aga went up, each holding the hand of the valuable creature, their eyes alight with the desire to start bidding.

To obviate any false buyers from claiming interest, everyone on the platform returned to their seats, leaving the stunning slave to captivate the hearts of all those in attendance.

Salem Ben Ali announced with authority,

"Let the bidding commence. Who would like to start?"

Mohammad Momina took the lead, offering a hundred gold

pounds without hesitation, disregarding the objections from other dignitaries who asked for a slower pace. He declared,

"I came here to purchase, and anyone who wishes to bid higher may do so." Mahmoud Bacha raised the bid to a hundred and fifty gold pounds. There were complaints from the crowd about the high prices and the behaviour of the wealthy in blocking others from bidding. Jalal Mogharbel, frustrated at pushing from the crowd behind him, retorted,

"This slave is not for people of your means. You don't even have ten gold pounds. Keep quiet. Hold your tongues."

A curse came from an unseen person in the crowd, and Jalal realized it was the Aga who had just increased the bid to two hundred gold pounds.

Omar Al-Yaridi, upon hearing the soaring price from the Aga shouted once more, "What does this castrated man have to do with purchasing a slave?"

The bidding continued until it reached an impressive sum of one thousand three hundred and fifty gold pounds, which was won by the sudden arrival of Youssef Kurdi. To appease the slave, he added another three hundred gold pounds for her courtesan. As soon as the slave was taken away in Youssef's car, the dignitaries dispersed from the market, with a throng of onlookers trying to catch a glimpse. Omar attempted to keep pace with the car, unable to believe that the slave was none other than Jumana.

Chapter 6

As the dignitaries left with regret for missing the chance to purchase the stunning slave, Salem Ben Ali, the head of the brokers, took control of the situation. He realised that the best strategy was to sell the more desirable slaves before moving on to the less valuable merchandise. Despite blaming himself for losing such a valuable opportunity, he directed his frustration towards his subordinates, pushing two of them to open the gates and allow the remaining slaves to take the stage.

A procession of slaves emerged, lined up by height with both men and women in the four rows. Salem Ben Ali began to recite each slave's assets, though his presentation lacked the passion and excitement demonstrated for top selling star attraction. He tried to mask his disappointment with a show of politeness but it was clear that the events of the day had taken their toll on him.

Omar Al-Yaridi stood close to the platform, observing the sale with a heavy heart. His mind was preoccupied with thoughts of Jumana, recalling the sight of her as she walked in and out of her house.

He struggled to reconcile those images with the newly sold slave he had just laid eyes on.

To refocus on his mission, Al-Yaridi pushed aside all thoughts of Jumana and concentrated on the task at hand, buying a newborn slave. He made a loud commotion while bidding, which caught the attention of Salem Ben Ali,

"What do you want? I've been hearing you shout all morning, but I haven't seen you make a bid," Salem asked, clearly irritated.

Al-Yaridi was momentarily speechless but soon regained his composure and replied,

"What I want isn't on the stage."

Salem was getting more frustrated by the minute. "I've already sold the most beautiful and the ugliest slave, the strongest and the weakest," he said.

"All that's left is on the stage, so choose whichever one you want," he told him, growing increasingly frustrated.

Al-Yaridi stood firm.

"What I want isn't on the stage."

Salem was close to losing his temper, but his confusion in the face of Al-Yaridi's determination made him pause and ask once more,

"For the last time, I ask you... what do you want?"

Looking Salem in the eye, Al-Yaridi replied quietly,

"I want a newborn slave."

****

Al-Yaridi was forcibly removed from the slave market and given a beating as a warning not to approach again. The workers, who were from various African countries and spoke different languages such as Swahili, Gujarati, Rundi and Fula, made communication with him nearly impossible. Whenever he attempted to get close, he was overpowered and thrown out of the market. With their muscular bodies standing tall, feet firmly planted on the ground and heads scanning the bidders still left, the workers/security guards were a formidable force.

At one of the auctions held in front of the stage, the head of the brokers was absent, which resulted in the oldest of the slaves being put in charge. Al-Yaridi was upset by the mistreatment he received from the slaves tasked with guarding the stage. Despite his attempts to communicate his desire to buy a newborn slave, he failed to reach an agreement with them.

They didn't understand Al-Yaridi's persistence in staying to check the slaves warehouse. As his behaviour grew increasingly aggressive, so too the workers became hostile towards him.

He repeatedly harassed them by making suggestive gestures with his hands, uttering vulgarities, whistling and clapping loudly near their ears. Although the security guards pushed him away from the place where they were trying to take a break, Al-Yaridi continued to misbehave by tossing cow manure into their rest area.

He also disrupted their meals by pretending to vomit and he repeatedly blew his nose in their direction, spraying mucus on their plates of food. That was the last straw. One of the bigger guards dragged Al-Yaridi to a side alley, where he pinned him against a wall and rained punches on him, complemented by severe kicks to his shins. There was no pretend in this attack as the guard covered Al-Yaridi's clothes, face and hair with sick.

The violence and vomit was interrupted by the voice of a woman, who carried a baby on her back in a big, brightly-coloured shawl. Although she spoke in a language Al-Yaridi did not understand he thought she knew he wanted a baby.

THE CISTERN

Or even if she didn't, the seeds were being sewn of a good opportunity to get one.

She and the attacker exchanged a few words and gestures from which Al-Yaridi understood she was willing to part with the newborn. The thug, perhaps the father of the child, seemed to agree with that idea.

Her quavering voice had contained a heavy slice of begging and, much to Al-Yaridi's delight, put a stop to the assault on him.

The victim's understanding of the crude communication between mother and thug was aided by a rough translation from a man in the crowd. The attacker, initially called a "pig" by Al-Yaridi but now identified as Bakr, stormed off to the market after speaking with her. The mother, named by the translator as Khaddar, had been pointing towards the baby on her back in her conversation with Bakr.

Al-Yaridi was lying on the ground like an old, soiled rag with only two clear words, in his head – Bakr and Khaddar. And one idea in his mind: there was a newborn here for the taking one way or another.

****

Almost automatic were thoughts of revenge for the beating he had just taken. As he stumbled after the woman who had saved him from an even worse beating, his mind turned to a more practical and more attractive idea. The thought of owning a newborn slave, particularly if the baby was related to the monster Bakr, filled him with a deep sense of pleasure.

The woman took various routes but never strayed out of Al-Yaridi's sight. She walked quickly, with the baby's head bobbing in continuous vibrations and constantly crying. Al-Yaridi was about to approach her but before he could she entered a large yard surrounded by houses on the highway where people of her own race had gathered. The yard was packed with women and children, as well as men trading goods.

Al-Yaridi was filled with mixed emotions and conflicting thoughts. Heavily influenced by his bruised and painful body, he abandoned any idea of punishing Bakr. The thought of acquiring possession of the baby had far more allure. He surveyed the bustling scene in front of him; a marketplace cluttered with bodies, simple goods and food that was exposed to flies and handled carelessly. He was overwhelmed by the cacophony of voices speaking different dialects, shouting and arguing with one another. Despite the chaos around him, his gaze was fixed on the woman with the baby. She was weaving her way through the crowd, zigzagging to avoid various gatherings before finally taking a seat along the wall that overlooked the Ba Atiya woods warehouse behind the yard.

As she soothed her crying baby, she undid the fabric around her waist and took the newborn from her back. Khaddar cradled him and unbuttoned her shirt, exposing her breast to feed him. The baby eagerly took it into his tiny hands and began to suck. This was the moment Al-Yaridi struck, like a savage and hungry wildcat, pouncing on the opportunity laid temptingly before him. With all the courage he could muster, he approached the woman and snatched the baby, tossing fifty riyals in her direction before sprinting away down the twisting alleyways. The cries of a woman pursuing him were lost amid the shouting of people seeking their share of the meat that was being generously distributed.

THE CISTERN

Al-Yaridi reached the taxi rank in Jeddah after a long and arduous journey, cradling the newborn carefully in a multicoloured shawl. Despite the newly fed newborn's baby's calm, Al-Yaridi's insides were filled with a mix of anguish and fear, compounded by the sight of vomit still fresh on the shawl.

The passenger next to him kept eyeing the shawl, making Al-Yaridi uneasy. To ease the situation, Al-Yaridi told him his wife had died and that he was on his way to have his sister raise the baby. The passenger expressed his condolences and even asked the other passengers to do the same.

Al-Yaridi remained quiet, avoiding eye contact with the other passengers, especially the one sitting next to him who wouldn't stop talking. He was afraid the baby's dark skin would show through any small opening in the shawl, and that the man sitting next to him would ask more questions, so he made sure the shawl was wrapped tightly, obscuring any details, and offered the baby some sugar on his fingers to keep the infant quiet and content.

At the taxi rank in Jeddah, Al-Yaridi pondered his options for transportation, trying to decide between motorcycle and car. As he surveyed his surroundings, he took in the sights and sounds of the busy cafe filled with travellers, observing the signs on the lamp poles, the dirt and grime on the buildings, and the colours in the eyes of those passing by, still avoiding direct eye contact with anyone. He did not want to get involved in a staring competition.

As he waited in the cafe, his nerves started to get the best of him. The cries of the newborn in his arms made him anxious but he acted to calm the baby by giving it some sugar to lick. Drinking a cup of tea, he grew increasingly agitated by the laughter and noise from a group playing cards and smoking hookahs in the corner. He was eager to leave the cafe and the taxi rank as quickly as possible.

Determined to avoid as much attention as he could, Al-Yaridi waited until nightfall to leave the rank, when the darkness would provide him with a greater sense of anonymity. When it was time, he climbed into a decrepit taxi and pretended that he could barely speak, eager to disappear into the shadows of the night.

He dashed into his home, collapsing onto the couch in the living room, completely exhausted.

The darkness enveloped the walls of the house and with great effort managed to rouse himself enough to light the lantern near the door. The night's events weighed heavily on him; freeing himself from the clutches of a monstrous slave, pursuing the woman and abducting the baby, running through the streets of Mecca and boarding a bus to Jeddah. It all required a determined spirit to achieve what one wants.

He removed the shawl and laid eyes on the newborn, whose dark skin was covered in a small white shirt. As the night began to wane, he opened "The Sun of Knowledge" book, and copied a talisman he had underlined from previous readings. He armed himself with a dagger and a bright light powered by new stone batteries, then set about feeding the baby from a bottle of milk he found in the bottom of his fridge. Realising the task would take a while, he added some sugar to the baby's mouth and wrapped it in a dark fabric, covering its mouth and chin with tape. He nearly forgot to summon the Jinn but retrieved an anklet in the shape of a snake from his closet, adorned with turquoise stones for eyes, and placed it around the newborn's ankle as a condition for offering sacrifices to the Jinn.

He had four anklets remaining in the box, making him feel that his mission was still incomplete. He closed the box and cradled the newborn, hastening through the narrow streets shrouded in darkness even though a thick robe concealed his identity. He made his way towards the ruins of Ashour's house.

As dawn broke, the neighbours were shocked to discover the mutilated body of a newborn, its neck savagely slit and its head still hanging by a thread.

Chapter 7

He slunk back home, his steps heavy and unsteady, disregarding caution and carrying his robe under his arm. His mind was consumed by obsession, so much so that he walked right past his house in his distraction. The reality was a far cry from what was written in "The Sun of Knowledge".

His agitation at that moment prevented him from noticing the blood on his hands or fixing the image of the brutal killing in his memory, or the struggle he endured before disposing of the body in the dump.

The sense of failure was overwhelming and thoughts raced through his mind like a string of beads. He licked his moustache and furrowed his brow in frustration,

"Was the blood of the slave rancid?"

He felt a surge of anger, as he reflected on how he had forsaken his family in pursuit of an enduring treasure. He had dedicated himself to the pursuit of knowledge through worship and study, aspiring for a state of spiritual elevation. But in a moment of weakness, he gave into temptation and committed a serious transgression, the Jinn then guided him towards the search for earthly riches beyond the realm of ignorance. He became consumed by magic books and tirelessly sought guidance. His hope was reignited by Ibrahim Ashour's regular visits to Egypt, as he implored him to bring back books such as "The Sun of Knowledge" and "Wisdom" from Cairo.

THE CISTERN

Although there were no verified accounts of his encounter with Sheikh Al-Jilani during his pilgrimage from Morocco, he was the only one who believed in this meeting. He proclaimed himself as one of the chosen by the Sheikh and spun endless tales, if others didn't believe him. He entertained himself by imagining strange events, regaling himself with the fantastical stories he had created.

He was well aware that he had distanced himself from his family and tribe and was now a lone branch, walking the streets of life with exhaustion from his parents and relatives. His goal was to guide people and lead them under his shadow but he felt no emotional attachment to his family. He was lost in dreams, not knowing what he was searching for, and in his latest quest he was met with fear as his dreams crumbled before him.

As he walked through the dark streets, the distant barking of a dog could be heard and all the doors were closed with no light coming from outside lanterns. The only source of light was a dim lantern hanging on the door of Ali Al-Hodrami's shop. Despite his determination, he could not even make it to the nearest wall.

He was eager to get home and delve into his book, searching for the reason behind his failure to retrieve the treasure of Ashour's house. He went over every step he had taken to ensure he had followed the instructions precisely. After spilling boiling blood on the specified spot, the book's directions were clear – a dead tree with a hole beside it and two alabaster stones that had fallen from a nearby castle window frame. The hole was shaped like a vulva and went deep into the earth's veins, much like a canal with thin sides and a deep interior. He had learned the teachings.

Start by lifting the intertwined roots and pouring blood into the deep canal, placing the turquoise anklet at the point where the blood met the roots that connected to the earth, muttering unintelligible words, and wait, hoping for the gold to shine and the earth to open its core as a sign of accepting the first sacrifice and revealing its treasures.

Every time he remembered the ritual of slaughtering and pouring blood into the canal, reciting the talisman and waiting, and nothing appearing,

He felt a growing sense of despair. The absence of any sign of the treasure made him feel as if he was going mad. He constantly questioned what he may have done wrong but could not bring himself to doubt the prophecy he held so dear, convinced that the treasure was meant for him.

Chapter 8

In a secluded house that stood on two corners, the door was tightly shut and he struggled to figure out the mistake he had made.

As he lit the entrance lantern, the mystery of his failure to uncover the treasure consumed him. The air was thick and humid, making it difficult for him to breathe, even as he tried to calm himself by saying that it was too early for the earth's treasures to be revealed.

His eyes were fixed on a photograph of himself that he had taken when he first arrived in Jeddah. He gazed deeply at the picture, as if trying to read a prophecy written by Sheikh Jilani.

He often told himself and anyone who would listen stories from his imagination, becoming so engrossed in them that he would forget about Sheikh Jilani entirely.

When he arrived in Jeddah at the age of eight, from Kadid valley in Mecca, he was quickly absorbed by the community. He worked at various jobs, including baking, where he prepared thousands of loaves of bread. The heat from the oven darkened his skin and turned it red, and he would reach deep into the oven to touch the hot coals, performing a show that earned him admiration from his customers. This became his favourite act, as it brought him so much praise.

Omar worked for Othman, who sold beans, but he soon discovered his talent for baking "tamis" bread. This skill brought in more money and Othman would often praise him in front of customers, claiming that they were earning more because of Omar's baking. The tamis bread from Al-Yaridi was renowned for its delicious taste, even more so than biscuits. The tamis dough would run out, while the pot of beans was still half-full.

On a rainy morning, however, they ran out of everything, after cleaning and closing the shop as instructed by Othman, Al-Yaridi relaxed on an old chair. As he ate the sesame seeds stuck between his fingers, the memories from his village in the Kadid Valley began to overwhelm him. The exhaustion, combined with these memories, caused him to fall into a deep sleep. His head kept nodding, causing him to wake up every time it fell onto his chest but he would soon fall asleep again, swinging between these two states. Suddenly, Sheikh Jilil approached and tapped him on the shoulder, saying,

"I want breakfast."

Al-Yaridi, half asleep and with a faint voice, replied,

"We have nothing left."

Al-Yaridi awoke to the sight of a green mantle covering a thin figure. The person donning the mantle had a glowing face with eyes as clear as a mountain stream. High cheekbones and a thick, well-groomed beard only added to the striking appearance. This person was often seen among customers, speaking little and simply indicating what they wanted to buy. They would pay for their bread and beans and then leave.

As Al-Yaridi's grogginess faded, he sat up and apologised for having nothing left to sell. Suddenly, he noticed a pile of dough and on stirring the pot, found it overflowing with beans. Al-Yaridi was stunned. Just before the Sheikh left, he fixed their gaze on Al-Yaridi and, in a deep and resounding voice, declared,

"You are the one who was foretold."

With this prophecy, Al-Yaridi abandoned the bakery and followed the man, later known as Al-Jilani, on his journey to the upper echelons of Sufism. Al-Jilani walked with a slow, peaceful pace, his large rosary hanging from his hand. He exuded an aura that was a mix of reverence and a warm smile, and his green mantle made him stand out in the bustling streets. He would begin his daily journey just after dawn and return after evening prayers, like a bird returning to its nest. The entire neighbourhood sought his blessings, and soon it was said that he possessed "Karamah", leading people to witness the miracles he performed. Eventually, Al-Jilani disappeared, leaving behind a legacy shrouded in mystery and reverence.

Al-Jilani was known for his ability to uncover hidden talents and that was how he stumbled upon Al-Yaridi one morning. As the tamis baked, Al-Jilani spoke a prophecy that left a lasting impression on Al-Yaridi, who was determined to see it through. Al-Jilani words "You are the promised one" echoed in his mind. Sheikh Barakat Al-Jilani was renowned for his understanding of Sufism and the desires of the soul. He lived a humble life with few material possessions. Despite his wisdom, as he once said, his fate led him down a path of darkness.

At his council consisted of no more than five loyal regulars, of whom Al-Yaridi was one. Al-Jilani was giving the impression he knew the location of the island where the false messiah was imprisoned. One night, during a conversation about the treasures of the earth, he recited a hadith, saying that the False Messiah would come across ruins and say,

"Let out your treasures" and the treasures would follow him like a swarm of bees. He then looked to his loyal regulars and explained that it was his destiny to extract the treasures from every ruin in the world, so that when the false messiah arrived, he would find none and feel regret and helplessness.

As his friends surrounded him, Sheikh Al-Jilani entered into a deep meditation, and words flowed from his mouth without finding a mind to interpret them. "What you keep hidden with your knowledge, I am aware of with mine. And what you conceal with your eyes, I store in my heart. I have found you, an eye, a heart, and a hand, and I have everything. So if I will it, you will be my will, so be it, so it is."

He pounced as if someone had thrown a bucket of cold water over him, his eyes fixed upon the five individuals sitting across from him. His gaze was intense, scrutinising each one for a few seconds before moving onto the next. He continued this pattern for several moments, the only sounds being the soft mutterings from his lips. He then straightened himself, pointing directly at Al-Yaridi and declared,

"You've got a look about you that can't be mistaken."

Al-Jilani silenced any potential interruptions, his mind overflowing with thoughts as he spoke,

"The world is a test for the steadfast, so embrace it like a feather floating on the breeze, a flame burning bright, or a breath-sustaining life. Let your soul soar free. You are nothing but a universe in disguise, so respond, lest you fall into the pit of Harut and Marut where even repentance cannot save you. Remember, this game is eternal, and you are a part of it. Stay with it always."

With a steady thumb, Al-Jilani pointed at Al-Yaridi's face, causing him to shiver and stammer,

THE CISTERN

"Me Sheikh?"

"You shall be the keeper of the world's treasures, and the first one you'll uncover will be hidden in a house shrouded in darkness," the Sheikh told him.

He pulled on his green mantle, stood up and instructed that he was not to be followed. He then addressed Al-Yaridi, saying,

"If it's not yet clear to you, try to understand it now."

Al-Yaridi's mind was consumed by his quest, and he travelled from one country to another, giving his body over to the journey, in search of the earth's treasures. Despite his efforts, he was met with disappointment time and time again, until he had a dream that was as bright as a new dawn.

"Return to your roots, the treasure you seek lies within the cursed house."

He saw a neighbourhood in Jeddah, where the Jinn held darkness captive, like bats, hanging upside down, that even a flicker of light would make them jump at any intruders, be they man or wind. He saw himself hanging alongside them, attacking every face that came near.

He caused events to unfold that went against the words of his Sheikh,

"He who ceases to learn, ignorance will consume them?"

For years, his heart was set on finding the treasure, promised to those who shed the blood of newborn slaves as an offering to the guards tasked with guarding it.

He arrived at the Cistern, just as he had seen in his dreams, standing before Ashour's house, taking the lives of innocent newborns without knowing the exact number demanded by the Jinn to unlock the earth's riches.

In his quest for more victims, he was constantly met with death's shadow. He understood that the courage required to reach the necessary number of sacrifices was immense.

The African community in Mecca became his source for stolen newborns, and he avoided taking babies from Jeddah to avoid detection. He left money behind in an attempt to make it appear as though he had bought the babies, granting him the power to do with them as he saw fit."

****

Since his first attempt at kidnapping a newborn, Al-Yaridi's fate changed and he was consumed by the quest to uncover the earth's treasures. He was careful to maintain secrecy and avoid suspicion, putting on an appearance that kept him from arousing any suspicion. He even joined his neighbours in condemning the kidnapper of these innocent babies, and the community whispered that these infants were nothing but Jinn who had defied Ibrahim Ashour's commands and were now being punished.

Like water that flows through the dirt and is eventually covered and disappears, only one anklet was left in the box, for the final victim whose blood was needed to open the earth and reveal its treasures. Al-Yaridi feared that he would not be able to abduct this last victim, worrying that the book had set a specific time for the shedding of the treasure blood; it was to occur between the ascendant Aries and the new moon, with the promised one fasting for three days.

He found it difficult and he got busy studying the signs and their influence, and how the Aries moved during the new moon.

Chapter 9

Al-Yaridi was determined to fast and knew that the new moon would arrive in the coming two nights. He had no option but to break into the African boys' warehouse, as he had called it after obtaining four newborns from there. He believed that the one who would uncover the treasure must come from that very yard.

****

As the road to Mecca welcomed the journey of Muhammaduh's family to celebrate their daughter's first baby, Al-Yaridi found himself on the same bus, making sure that no one, especially Muhammaduh, spotted him. He covered himself in an orange shawl and kept his gaze lowered from the back seat.

The passengers gestured to Muhammaduh who struggled to board the bus, leaning on a cane that pained his arm. Hajji Al-Muhajira had invited close neighbours to attend a party thrown by Adam to celebrate Aisha giving birth and his new fatherhood.

Al-Yaridi mingled with the guests, hoping to obtain his last victim and put his mind at ease. He remained quiet, carefully observing his surroundings.

Mecca is renowned as a city of atonement and spirituality and even during family visits, people engage in sacred prayers that bring peace to their minds. As soon as the bus reaches the Jibril gate, the passengers alight and are greeted by a refreshing breeze that carries the fragrant scent of the shrine to all corners of the city, reaching even the deeper neighbourhoods of Mecca.

The shops surrounding the shrine gates are brightly lit, welcoming pilgrims to their holy journey. The pristine whiteness of the Ihram attire is a striking sight to behold, leaving a lasting impression on all who see it.

The flowing Zamzam water refreshes the skin of the travellers as they complete their pilgrimage and enter the sanctity of the shrine.

Al-Yaridi was happy at news of Muhammaduh's family celebrating the birth of a newborn, and he decided to join them, disguising himself among the well-wishers, as he knew that the same location was the warehouse he used for acquiring newborn slaves, and he hoped to escape detection should he be discovered.

Upon the arrival of the family, the yard gate opened, and the joyous emotions of the well-wishers overflowed. The crowd was a mix of men, women and children, their voices raised in song and celebration. The drums echoed through the yard, as the crowd turned in a circle, singing in a harmonious blend of Hijazi and Chadian dialects, clapping, humming, and crying out in ecstasy, punctuated by fits of laughter and jubilation.

Aisha was brought to the centre of the gathering, cradling her newborn baby, dressed in a vibrant dress with a red cover that blazed like fire at its corners, enveloping her entire body. She swayed gently to the rhythm of the music, her newborn dressed in pink. The crowd moved in unison, as one.

Muhammaduh was unable to join in the dancing and

celebration, his amputated leg preventing him from moving. Hajji Fatima took charge of her grandchild, freeing Aisha to carry on dancing, she proceeded to the room where the children of the women participating in the celebration were.

Al-Yaridi remained hidden in the background, observing the scene with a watchful eye. Despite his nervousness, he maintained his composure and followed Hajji Fatima through the crowded room to the area where the newborns were left. The cries of the babies filled the air, creating a chaotic and discordant atmosphere due to their neglect. Some babies were feeding, others were trying to shoo away flies, or crying helplessly.

Hajji Fatima placed her grandchild near the door and cleared a pile of worn clothes to make a makeshift bed. She retrieved a roll from within her chest, with an amulet made from goat skin, which she gave to him, and recited Surah Al-Falaq. Before leaving, she noticed that the amulet had become dislodged from the baby's pink shirt and quickly hid it back in place, tucking the black thread that hung from its shoulder to its chest. She then returned to the dance floor.

Al-Yaridi was bold, disregarding the potential dangers that lay ahead. His imagination gave him a false sense of security, as it had before. His sleeping soul failed to warn him of the dangers he was about to face, Despite the ominous circumstances he found himself in, which could have easily invoked the harshest of curses, if he were to survive.

****

As he snatched the newborn, another memory came to mind. His imagination began to revisit events that took place more than two years prior.

"To conquer your fear, remember all your crimes."

Al-Yaridi believed that God had imparted this wisdom to him, so his impatience was kept in check as he muttered to himself, "The abduction of the fifth child will not be any more difficult than what you have already accomplished."

****

His heart was pounding and fear was building inside him as he approached the turn for Bab Al Dariba. His steps were uncertain, as if he was trying to delay the ominous thoughts that filled his mind. In that place, he had once survived a harrowing experience that left him checking to make sure his neck was still attached for a long time afterwards.

Two years had passed since then and he needed that time to come to terms with those events, and to correspond with the instructions to locate the treasure once again.

Despite the passage of time, he couldn't forget about the woman or the moment he took her newborn away before it could even feed. His motivation was to make a sacrifice to Ashour's Jinn treasure, and at first, he had no intention of kidnapping a newborn, if it weren't for

Bakr the monster who caused such heartbreak for Khaddar.

Two years had gone by, and while time moved forward, the events still remained etched in his memory like old furniture that would still exist regardless of what you did with it. The material world tires us before it withers away and only by burying the heart can a heartbreak go away.

Al-Yaridi struggled to reconcile his feelings as he faced the reality of his isolation from family and loved ones, which left his heart indifferent.

THE CISTERN

The unsteadiness in his steps as he approached the slave market tested his mental toughness. The first experience was not a rehearsal but a manifestation of his desires and failures.

Fear was knocking at his door, and he fought to keep it at bay, making one final push to overcome it before he succumbed to weakness, for he knew that weakness was the death of dreams. He found the courage within himself and approached the stage with purpose.

His thoughts were carefully guarded as he concealed his fear, not letting it show.

The voice of the soul often determines your path in life and Al-Yaridi clung to his resolve, walking steadily forward.

People were still like ants, busy with their own pursuits, indifferent to the noise and commotion around them. Humans are self-absorbed, never venturing beyond their own world unless it serves to enhance their existence. It is only sane to view each person as their own world, with everything else revolving around them.

This feeling was shared among people, though unconsciously, and what diminishes its emergence is your presence among people who you believed were preoccupied with you.

The footsteps echoed down the crowded street, teeming with men, women, boys, vendors and those just passing through. The air was alive with talkative, laughing, indignant, silent and threatening voices, each carrying something; goods, pots, wooden planks, metal poles, and a range of emotions; anger, pain, happiness, indignation and satisfaction. Fear gripped Al-Yaridi's chest, propelling him forward.

The slave market had undergone a transformation. The once expansive platform was now marred by uneven floors, collapsing in places and the cement that once shone was now dull. No longer were curious eyes fixed on those who entered from the back street and the stairs leading up to the stage were now broken.

The platform had become a hub for all, those who lived there, those seeking work, or just a moment's respite. Time had erased the faces of those who lingered there, preventing the common people from advancing and competing with the wealthy who sought to purchase a desirable slave. Two years had changed the place beyond recognition.

"Time has a voracious appetite, turning satisfaction into decay and eventual degradation."

Al-Yaridi surveyed his surroundings, looking for someone who could tell him what had happened to the slave market. He had saved enough money to buy two newborn slaves, if only Salem Ben Ali, the head broker, would agree to work with him. He was prepared to offer more money than the cost of even the most expensive slave.

As he walked, the bustling crowd jostled him, pushing him and asking him to move out of the way. He tried to keep his cool, not wanting to reveal his infamous foul mouth, which had once earned him a beating from the notorious Bakr.

"Where can I find the head broker?" he held back his question but the answers he received only added to his confusion,

"Which one are you looking for? Fish sellers? Groceries? Industrial?"

"I'm searching for Sheikh Salem Ben Ali, the head broker of the slave market," he said, struggling to hide his surprise when he heard that slavery had ended. He was stunned. The responses he received only added to his confusion.

"How did slavery end?" he asked, bewildered.

The turmoil in his mind caused him to sit down on the stage, deep in thought. "Is there no treasure left?" he pondered.

He remembered that he had only made one offering to the Jinn guards. His thoughts were troubled, and he made his way to a small cafe in the eastern part of Al Tantabawi neighbourhood. He pulled up a chair, ordered tea and water, and sat down.

For the first time, he felt the urge to talk about slaves and the end of their time. He was a scrap seller who only visited the poor, and he kept his eyes trained on someone, moving around the room, inquiring about the slave market and where the slaves had gone.

He gathered bits of gossip from the various people he spoke to, all pointing to the government as the cause of the end of slavery. If the conversation continued, they would say that King Faisal had forbidden the sale of slaves.

Anyone who said goodbye to Al-Yaridi at the slave market, whether through words, glances or handshakes, could tell that he was a man with a torn soul. He was burning with anger, letting out heated sighs and grinding his teeth. He was absent-minded, clenching his fist and hitting anything he saw, be it a wall, a chair, or a wooden or metallic structure. He walked around aimlessly, repeating the same phrase over and over,

"I am not going to let anyone stand in my way to the treasure. I am the chosen one."

Chapter 10

Al-Yaridi arrived at King Faisal's palace gate as the convoy was leaving and shouted loudly, "Why did you stop the slave trade now?" The outburst seemed to have driven him to madness, as everything inside him was released in that cry, If it weren't for the fact that he had lost his sanity, he wouldn't have returned to the corner near Ashour's house.

He searched for reasons why the slave trade was banned but there were many things he didn't understand. He heard some words about human rights and a war with Egypt, but he couldn't grasp the meaning of them, especially the words of Jamal Abdul Nasser.

If Al-Yaridi had not been seeking the reasons behind the ban on the slave trade, he would have remained unaware of the conflict in the southern part of the kingdom. On his third visit to the king's palace, he realised the risks posed by his words, as the soldiers were polite but ignored him, telling him to leave.

Muhammaduh and Al-Yaridi visited the palace gates repeatedly, each time placing themselves in danger of being arrested. Being so deeply engrossed in the surrounding neighbourhood, they were ignorant of the events outside, leading them to utter ill-suited words in a location that called for only the most proper of language. The head guard, displaying firmness, handled each of them based on their level of comprehension. Recognising they were venturing into uncharted waters, he advised them to write a letter outlining their requests. This was their final chance to depart the palace gates before the head guard's patience ran out and they were taken into custody.

Neither Al-Yaridi nor Muhammaduh were aware of each other's presence at the palace gate, and both struggled to put their thoughts into words. Their burning desire was to meet King Faisal and pour out their hearts to him, expressing their sadness in whatever words they could find.

****

From the moment the first newborn slave was abducted, Al-Yaridi was driven by the desire to provide the guards of the treasures with pure, untainted blood. The news of the end of the slave trade hit him like a hammer, depriving him of the opportunity to own a newborn slave, and he was willing to do whatever it took, no matter how impossible, to open up the treasures of the earth. However, he soon realised that all avenues were closed, so his only option was to go to the yard, as a last effort to appease the spirits of Ashour's house.

Chapter 11

Has time become stagnant? The heavy weight of stillness pressed down on Al-Yaridi's chest like an immovable boulder, unyielding to sighs, fear or anxiety.

Al-Yaridi had honed the art of abducting newborn slaves and on his latest mission he felt the riches of the earth were within his grasp. He felt a wet, invigorating sensation, which turned to a sense of triumph when he reined in his imagination on seeing the false messiah, vainly calling for the earth to give up its treasures.

He felt that he was promised both the treasure and the false messiah's humbling defeat. He told himself,

"This wouldn't have happened to anyone unless it was a Karamah from God."

He was filled with certainty at these thoughts and turned to see the newborn who was to bring him glory and sovereignty. However, he was irritated by the baby's cries and repulsed by the mucus smeared on his chest. In his repeated abductions of newborns, Al-Yaridi had taken to keeping sugar cubes or grains on hand, just in case the baby began to cry.

Al-Yaridi was torn between two options – to silence the crying baby or remove the mucus from his chest hair. He decided to stop the crying and rubbed sugar on the baby's gums. The cries temporarily ceased, only to start again, causing Al-Yaridi's face to become hard and his eyes to disappear behind a frown. He watched as the baby cried and tears streamed down his face, this newborn was plumper than the others he had slaughtered.

Despite his efforts to calm himself with his usual words, Al-Yaridi couldn't escape the baby's cries and was still burning with anger. He lifted the baby from his chest and looked at the little face, feeling doubtful of his own hardness as he saw the light from the baby's eyes and tears. He was afraid he was losing his edge and succumbing to soft feelings. In an attempt to avoid falling into this pit of childish tears, he jerked the baby's hips and pulled on his arms. That's when he noticed the leather talisman peeking out from under the baby's pink shirt, stuck between his armpit and shoulder, with a black thread hanging from his neck that had deeply cut into the baby's skin.

Thoughts of him and Hajji Fatima Al-Muhajira filled his mind but they didn't bring any compassion, despite Fatima's radiant smile and goodness, Al-Yaridi doubted she had seen him take her grandchild from the room. He tried to ignore the weight of this thought and was grateful for the shawl tightly wrapped around his face, hiding him from view.

The clock ticked slowly, unable to keep up with the frenetic pace in Al-Yaridi's veins. A beautiful joy swelled within him as the promise finally came to fruition. In his hand, he held the fifth soul, its blood untainted and chosen by the veins of destiny to belong to the Jinn of the Ashour.

Anxiety gripped him whenever he thought of his fourth sacrifice, the one that failed to reveal the hidden treasure. The memory of the ritual was clear in his mind – the newborn, the dead tree trunk, the two alabaster stones and the vulva-like hole that opened up deep into the earth's veins. He remembered following the instructions to the letter, reciting the talisman and placing the turquoise anklet between the blood and the roots. Despite his efforts, the golden light failed to appear.

The night was dark and overcast, the thunder rumbling like a female camel in labour, the lightning tearing through the sky with a wicked grin. As the slow hours passed, Al-Yaridi made his way back to the neighbourhood, finally reaching the comfort of his own home.

In his room, Al-Yaridi was filled with a mixture of joy and anxiety. The prophecy of Al-Jilani was finally within his reach, and he held the newborn close to his chest, trying to stop its cries with sugar. However, the baby's wails only grew louder, causing Al-Yaridi to utter a frustrated exclamation. He quickly took back his words, realising that the newborn was sacred, its untainted blood crucial to unlocking the treasures of the earth and preventing the false messiah from claiming it.

He then set about retrieving the last turquoise anklet from the box but to his dismay he found it was missing. He searched the house from top to bottom, turning everything upside down and checking every nook and cranny but the anklet remained elusive.

Just when Al-Yaridi was about to give up, the anklet reappeared before him, its faded golden shine and coiled snake design catching his eye. However, as he reached for it, he was suddenly struck by the fear that it might have been stolen. He checked the lock on the box, but it was still secure, and there were no signs of forced entry.

Despite the lack of any concrete evidence, Al-Yaridi's mind raced with the possibility that he may have taken the anklet with the fourth sacrifice and placed it in the deep feminine hole. But he refused to let that thought crush the dream of the prophecy, determined to keep the mission alive, even if it meant risking everything he had worked for.

Al-Yaridi found himself in a state of distress as the newborn had wriggled out of the shawl, and as he tried to steady himself on wobbly legs, he rolled onto his back, his pupils bulging with panic. The tape over his mouth and the clogged nose from the cold made it difficult for him to breathe, causing Al-Yaridi to quickly remove the tape, freeing the baby to let out a loud, piercing cry, he impulsively tried to silence the child once more, only to resist the urge to curse the innocent newborn.

Al-Yaridi was torn between his desire to find the missing anklet, his need to attend to the crying baby, and the urge to go out in time for the new moon and ascending Aries, completely unaware of the chaos brewing outside, as the city was about to be turned upside down in a night that would be remembered for years to come.

He quickly gathered his things and left, telling himself that he had most likely taken two anklets for the fourth sacrifice, this provided him some solace.

He rationalised that the earth not opening to reveal the first sign, the shining of the gold, was simply because the two anklets were in the same place. However, each time he tried to confirm the prophecy, new questions and possibilities arose. It had been some time since the last sacrifice and anyone could have found the anklet and taken it. But this thought was dismissed by Al-Yaridi, as the guards of the treasure forbade anyone from removing the gold and silver, with the exception of the promised one.

He prepared for his journey, feeling a chill in the air and so he dressed warmly, took a small torch and rubbed sugar on the baby's gums before covering its mouth with tape, feeling his breath, he almost hesitated but his dark imagination urged him to finish the task as quickly as possible.

"The baby is dead," he thought, "so what does it matter? The important thing is that its blood is still flowing, so when it is sacrificed, the guards of the treasure will be satisfied."

He set off towards the ruins of Ashour's house. The sight of the sky being consumed by dense black clouds engulfing the moon, and the frequent flashes of lightning punctuated by the sound of thunder disturbed him deeply.

"There is no moon" weighed heavily on his mind, and he hastened his pace, in a race against time to spill the final drops of sacred blood.

As he walked, the weather appeared to be gearing up for its barren dance.

Chapter 12

Winter arrived in the city of Jeddah meekly, not causing any harm to the inhabitants. But this night, it defied the old ways and let loose its full fury. The atmosphere grew increasingly ominous, as the night approached, signalling death and igniting fear in all who felt its presence. With each passing moment, the day was slowly overtaken by a malevolent darkness.

The night descended into a tempestuous storm, with howls resembling those of a wounded wolf. It wreaked havoc, destroying everything in its path. The trees bent under its force, their roots torn from the earth. The fragile, dilapidated homes of the lower class shook, their doors and windows rattled, while bird's nests and lamp posts crumbled. Nothing was left untouched by the fury of the storm.

The anger of the city was obvious, stirring the land and sea. The waves rose to discipline those who had forgotten its power, crashing against the shore and inundating the beach. The sea raged, throwing its waves against the city, as the sky unleashed rain and the land poured forth its torrents. A flooding unlike any other took hold, with no one to prophesise its end. And so the city of Jeddah was brought to its knees, overpowered by the force of the storm.

****

The piercing howl of the wind brought deserted roads with people compelled to take refuge in their homes. The wavering light of the torch stumbled through the scattered darkness as Al-Yaridi made his way towards the ruins. The sky was tumultuous, with claps of thunder and flashes of lightning dominating the atmosphere. Al-Yaridi, along with everyone in the neighbourhood, felt that this was a dark night like no other.

In Al-Yaridi's arms, the newborn was trying to release cries from behind a sealed mouth. Instead, it used its legs to kick Al-Yaridi in the waist, who was occupied with the quest of finding the missing anklet. Despite the darkness of the night, Al-Yaridi was familiar with the path to the ruins and moved with stealth, like a giant who had taken advantage of the darkness to go back home.

As Al-Yaridi approached the ruins, a damp and revolting scent hit him, carried by the wind. Suddenly, his foot struck a wet body and he stumbled, with goosebumps covering his skin as he stepped over it. He then tripped over a pile of wet bodies and for the first time, he was scared.

Al-Yaridi was stunned as he realised his legs wouldn't move. He took a deep breath, trying to calm himself and steady his nerves. As he walked carefully through the debris and ruins, shining his torch ahead of him, he kept his eyes peeled for any sign of life or movement. The numerous holes in the walls around him made him feel as if he were surrounded by unseen creatures. He felt like he was on the verge of uncovering the secret treasure guarded by the Jinn, as foretold by the long-awaited prophecy.

His heart was pounding with fear as he wondered what the Jinn would look like. Would they be soft or hard, or perhaps even insubstantial like smoke? It had been so long since he had seen spirits or communicated with them. Despite the constant rumble of thunder, he hesitated to uncover the wet bodies blocking his path. He realised with a start that he had forgotten to recite the talisman that would summon the Jinn.

Gripping the wall for support, Al-Yaridi stood up straight and took a deep breath of damp air, preparing himself for any surprise. But the foul stench was too much and he had to cover his nose with the shawl wrapped around the newborn.

Feelings of anxiety and confusion washed over him as he thought about the missing anklet, hoping to find it in the ruins. The newborn's angry movements and muffled breathing only added to the terror. Al-Yaridi trembled at the thought that the Jinn might have emerged, ready to claim their final victim.

Al-Yaridi stood firmly, clinging to the wall for support as the outside world was thrown into turmoil. The wind howled, thunder roared, lightning struck and in the air hung a deathly silence, broken only by the occasional crash of stones from the castle. Al-Yaridi was filled with dread when he saw the shapes of figures getting closer, uncertain of their location inside or outside the ruins. In an attempt to shake off his fear, he began to move around, pondering if the guards of the treasure had accepted the sacrifice without the necessary anklet.

With a single movement, the tape that had been covering the newborn's mouth came loose, and the baby let out a powerful scream that echoed throughout the ruins, drowning out the darkness, thunder, storm, and fear within Al-Yaridi. He stumbled and felt his shin collide with a wet body, nearly shouting out in unison with the newborn, "They're here! They've arrived!"

He recited prayers of exorcism, his words coming out stammered as his jaw quaked and his teeth gritted. The trembling ran through every fibre of his being, and the torch in his hand flickered as he struggled to keep it steady and catch a glimpse of the first Jinn to emerge. Al-Yaridi prepared himself to utter words of welcome be fitting for the creatures although he was unsure what these spirits would prefer to hear.

The cold air was bitter and the sky thundered with a vicious roar, followed by a flash of lightning that illuminated the surroundings. Al-Yaridi was horrified to see that he was standing among dead dogs, all of which were bloated and emitting a foul smell. The sight made him unsteady, and everything around him was shaking.

Confused and unable to focus, Al-Yaridi's only thought was to get away and defer the final sacrifice for another time.

The heavy rain made it almost impossible to see if there was a new moon, a necessity for the sacrifice to take place. He quickly secured the newborn's mouth with tape to stop cries that overpowered the madness of the sky.

Al-Yaridi ran to his house as the rain poured down, and the voice of the muezzin, Yahya Kassel, echoed in the background, repeating the same sentence, "Pray in your homes, pray in your homes."

Chapter 13

On a sodden morning, the neighbourhood was awash and the heavy rain had settled on the streets. As the rainwater mixed with clay, small deep pools had formed that young boys used as impromptu swimming holes. Meanwhile, men and women were busy trying to dry out their homes but the overflowing drainage channels made the task difficult. Mosquitoes thrived in the stagnant water but the boys still ran around, laughing and splashing in the pools, shouting as their heads hit the bottom.

After the downpour, tales of the storm circulated in the excited neighbourhood. The danger was real for the houses and the community rallied to divert the flow of water in different directions. However, it was challenging because of the damage to the cistern, which was releasing a torrent of water with extra power due to the steep slope of the ground.

Men laboured throughout the night to build earth dams and dig intricate canals to contain the flood. When the sun rose and the first rays of light penetrated, they were amazed to see shining gold coins glinting in the canals they had dug. They rushed to collect the coins while shouting,

"The treasure of Ashour's house has appeared."

Chapter 14

"The passage of time teaches us that we were stubbornly standing in the wrong place."

Al-Yaridi's mind couldn't grasp the meaning of this saying but time gradually revealed the truth to him and the other residents in the neighbourhood.

Nature can be unpredictably wild and irrational, as evidenced by the scent of the damp earth that wafted through the air on a wet morning, triggering memories of the tumultuous events of the previous day. People who pass through the area will not be able to witness the craziness that took place but the evidence remains in the form of everything being knocked over and the ground becoming soaked with water that leaked into houses.

During the storm, the darkness intertwined the earth and sky in a brutal battle, with the outcome in favour of those who stood tall. The commotion and noise created by the chaos ended just before the darkness dissipated, and the voice of the muezzin calling, "Pray in your homes," served as a dividing line between the turmoil and the ensuing peace.

As the sky's anger dissipated and the rain stopped, the earth started to fix its torn robes and restore its shape. The moment of calm was marked by the sky ceasing to pour rain, the sea calming its angry waves, and the morning breathing a sigh of relief as the last of the rainwater flowed away.

Al-Yaridi entered his home, trembling and uncertain of

what to do with the crying newborn in his arms and how to keep his secret until it was time to carry out his plan. He gazed on the baby's delicate limbs and the tears rolling down its face, thinking about removing the tape sealing its mouth that yearned to suckle or taste sugar. "If I don't carry out my plan, I will lose everything," Al-Yaridi told himself.

The day began brightly, with the previous day's rain gone and the smell of fresh earth in the air. People were still trying to save their homes from water that had seeped into the corners, and children were playing in the muddy puddles that dotted the landscape.

People basked in the good weather, the soft breeze caressing their bodies like a physician confirming the trembling in their hearts was pure joy.

Signs of winter's arrival could be seen, with a cold wind infiltrating the bodies of those outside, urging them to put on warm clothing. People walked the streets, congratulating and blessing each other for the mercy of God that had descended upon them. In this peaceful atmosphere, a sudden disturbance arose, voices rose high and news quickly spread. Al-Yaridi's ears perked up as he listened to the various voices relaying the news,

"The treasure of Ashour's house has been found!"

Al-Yaridi was stunned by the news and thought that all the recent changes in the weather were a sign that the Jinn had given up guarding the treasure after the promised one arrived and fulfilled their duty. He recollected that the storm had come to an end just as he arrived home, carrying the final sacrifice with him.

Despite some dark thoughts, questions started to race through his mind seeking answers,

"How could this have happened?" He was troubled by these questions, wondering why things had taken place before their time, when so many thing were still missing; the lack of spilled blood from the last victim, the missing anklet, the absence of the golden light, the failure of the Master Jinn to show up and give him the keys to the treasure, and the collective death of the dogs.

All added to his confusion.

In an effort to keep his joy from dissipating, he tried to reassure himself that the dogs were simply the guardians of the treasure and had died once their duty was fulfilled. He didn't want to dwell on these thoughts for long, so he started to jump for joy to ease his anxieties,

"This is how miracles happen. They don't require explanation, only faith."

The newborn let out a piercing cry that drowned out the sounds of the neighbourhood. In a moment of panic, Al-Yaridi scrambled to find something to soothe the baby and quieten its cries.

****

During the night the floods receded as water flowed towards the sea, leaving streams and brooks on its seaward journey. Locally the residents of the neighbourhood had redirected the stream in different directions, causing some of it to lose its way and flow into the alleys of the neighbourhood, settling into small scattered pools that provided delight to children who splashed in them or pretended to dive in.

The treasure began to appear in the rain, with a gold coin falling into the flooded hand of Saleh Antar, who was searching for his house key that he had dropped while redirecting the stream away from his house.

At the first scream announcing the appearance of the treasure, the neighbours started calling each other to come outside, and the streets were soon filled with people who were eager and greedy, searching for gold said to be carried by the stream's water. They ran round all night, following the water, but eventually returned to the side of Ashour's house, where Abdul Shakour advised them, "The gold deposit is in the ground, it doesn't run with the water, go back and search there."

The fervour of the search for treasure was met with resistance by the older residents of the neighbourhood, who were working tirelessly to redirect the water flow. However, the discovery of a glimmering piece of gold by one of them caused everyone to scatter in different directions in pursuit of more.

As they searched, their eyes were fixed on the stagnant pools of water and the rays of the cold yellow sunrise helped them concentrate. When the sun reached its peak in the sky, the excitement grew as both kids and adults caught sight of the gleaming gold and silver coins reflecting from the corners of Ashour's house.

****

The gold captivated everyone's attention as it glimmered in the rushing water. Word of the treasure hunt had spread far and wide, igniting the excitement of both young and old in the adjacent communities.

As dawn broke, casting aside the shadows of the stormy

night, people flocked to the streams and cisterns in search of the lost riches. The ground was thoroughly scoured as they followed the flow of the water, looking for any sign of gold, silver or other precious metals.

Each coin was unique, with a different shape and inscription, telling its own story. Some were round with a hole in the centre, others were hexagonal or square, and some were adorned with primitive drawings or inscriptions.

Omar Al-Yaridi stormed out of his home, shirtless, with a towel wrapped around his waist and a shovel in hand. His anger was directed towards the people collecting coins, whom he cursed individually,

"You bloody mongrels, offspring of curs, this is my money," he shouted. "I've been guarding it for years, and now you want to steal it?"

As he approached each group, they would scatter and run away from him, frightened by his threats of violence. He brandished the shovel in front of everyone, nearly striking Salem Al-Yamani's forehead in the process.

Before the situation could deteriorate any further, Jalal Al-Samkari intervened, taking hold of Al-Yaridi's hand and whispering to him,

"These are Jinn who have taken on the shapes and forms of your neighbours to help you gather your money, don't scare them."

Al-Yaridi's grip on the shovel relaxed, and he asked Jalal,
"Are you telling the truth?"

"Yes," Jalal replied confidently. "Who do you think I am?"

"You're the filthy mongrel Jamal Al-Samkari;" Al-Yaridi spat out.

"No," Jalal countered, "I am the Master Jinn. I have come

to you in the form of Jalal, Order me, and you will see."

Jalal then called out to everyone,

"Dear Jinn, all of you have come here to help Al-Yaridi recover his treasure. So, dig every inch and you will find the gold we brought out with the rain yesterday."

Everyone listened to Jalal and laughed. They dug more every time they found a coin and shouted in excitement, "Here is the treasure each time they uncovered a stash of coins. The area around the cistern was a maze of holes, with dirt scattered everywhere. Women were sifting through the soil, searching for hidden coins among the piles of dirt.

****

Al-Yaridi strode over, carrying a large box, and stood between the holes and the piles of dirt, shouting,

"Jinns! Gather all the coins you've collected and put them in this box."

He moved among the holes, confused, as he watched the people around him smile and wink at each other, despite clapping and calling out for Jalal Al-Samkari,

"Master Jinn! Master Jinn!"

No one answered or placed any coins in the box. His frustration mounting, he shouted,

"If you don't make them put the treasure in this box, I'll burn you all."

The laughter only grew louder, causing Al-Yaridi to feel foolish. He brandished a metal rod, threatening anyone who didn't put the coins in the box. Those nearby caved in to his demands but when Hussein Zubeidi refused to follow suit, Al-Yaridi yelled in anger,

"You're a rogue Jinn."

He was about to hurl the rod but he was stopped by Salem Al-Yamani and three other people who restrained him by tying his hands and feet. Despite his curses and loud threats, he was unable to escape their grip. Upon seeing Jalal Al-Samkari, his anger only escalated, causing him to thrash about in the mud in an agitated state. Foam was starting to form at the corners of his mouth as he descended into a pitiful state. Jalal approached him, trying to calm him down,

"Master, we Jinn can only carry the treasure to your house at night," Jalal said. He ordered Al-Yaridi's restraints to be removed and sat beside him, gently washing his face and calming him until he was breathing normally and his tensed muscles relaxed.

"Take it easy and when night falls, you'll find a hundred Jinn waiting to transport the treasure boxes to your house, just calm down."

Al-Yaridi was soothed by Jalal's words. He put his knees to his chest, giving in to Jalal's comforting pat on his back. He lay down on a pile of muddy earth, covered in dirt and with blurry vision. From time to time, he gripped Jalal's hand.

"Master Jinn, beware the night thieves. They might have overheard you speaking," he warned Jalal.

"Don't worry, we'll guard the treasure and make sure no one takes it," replied Jalal.

Al-Yaridi was no longer nervous. He kept watch, alternating between gazing at the back streets and the yard of Ashour's house where the gold coins were being collected. He felt shattered as he entrusted Jalal Al-Samkari with the money,

"Master Jinn, I entrust you with this money, and I still have your last sacrifice."

He remained quiet, with a gleam in his eyes as they darted back and forth.

"If you are sincere and bring the treasure to my house tonight, I will slaughter the last sacrifice for you and offer you its blood with my own hands, for you to drink," he told Jalal.

Jalal realised that Al-Yaridi was in a dire state. So he patted his shoulder and ordered two of his friends to take him home, reassuring him,

"Wait for me tonight."

Jalal did not intend to keep his promise and deliver the coins to Al-Yaridi's house.

****

Before Al-Yaridi's mental condition declined, he was widely revered and believed to be guided by prophecy in his thoughts and words. His friends went to Sheikh Al-Jilani and proclaimed,

"Just as the earth produces a reformer every hundred years, the sky sends down blessed protectors, and Al-Yaridi was a shining example of this divine grace."

Jalal Al-Samkari, however, understood that the praise being heaped upon Al-Yaridi was false.

People were attributing wise proverbs and sayings to him, despite his inability to distinguish between the scent of onions and mint.

Chapter 15

The excavation sites were scattered all over the neighbourhood, causing much noise and chaos as people from nearby areas flocked to see the treasure and claimed that it was a gift from the earth and therefore belonged to everyone, given the absence of its original owners. This passionate argument made Abdullah Al-Barakati's eyes fill with tears. He sighed deeply, his heart heavy with sadness, and said,

"Where are you, Ibrahim?"

He imagined what had been said about Ibrahim and Omaima's departure, "One who is forgotten by people is remembered only by the soil."

The digging continued, and a substantial amount of money had been gathered. Jalal Al-Samkari promised to distribute it equally among all those who participated in the search and excavation. His wisdom was accepted but people from other neighbourhoods who sought a fair distribution put the responsibility on Al-Yaridi to resolve a conflict that was about to break out. With no other choice, Al-Yaridi asked the mayor for help, who came to a crowd people on the brink of violence. However, their tensions eased when they saw him. They welcomed him, eager to hear what he had to say, but he mockingly asked,

"Has Al-Yaridi infected everyone with this madness?"

Before they could respond, he raised his hand and continued,

"I have brought Sheikh Abdul Ilah Anwar with me to

speak to you about what you believe to be a treasure. He is one of the first residents of this neighbourhood and knows all its secrets."

Sheikh Abdullah approached the crowd, where people had gathered. His silver beard and bright white attire radiated an aura of light, as he leaned on his oak wood cane, its golden bent head shaped like a hoopoe. His calm, reassuring face belied the deep, hoarse voice that was about to shock everyone,

"These coins have no value," he declared.

For a moment, the crowd was stunned into silence. Sheikh Abdullah then picked up a few coins and examined them, flipping them in his hands.

"As you can see, they are of different shapes and materials, but they are not gold. They are made of copper and other metals, some of which are coated with fake gold. Even if you take everything you've collected, you wouldn't be able to trade it for a single riyal," he explained.

A voice from the crowd asked, "Then why did their owners bury them if they have no value?"

Sheikh Abdul Ilah had anticipated this question. He cleared his throat and gazed upon the crowd,

"They were not buried," he said simply.

There was a long silence as Sheikh Abdul Ilah smiled at the crowd, he pointed at the Cistern and asked,

"What do you call the upper part of this structure?"

When no one answered, he repeated the question,

"What do you call it?"

Abou Zabida, agitated and angry, said,

"We call it 'the drowned'. What does the name have to do with what's happening here?"

The Sheikh smiled and adopted his deep, almost aggressive voice again,

"Despite living next to it, none of you knows the history of the Cistern or anything about the 'drowning'.

"Let me enlighten you. The city of Jeddah has limited water and during the time of the Turks, they collected water in cisterns to combat this problem. The floods at that time were severe, coming from the south-east, so they built cisterns in various locations. The Cistern in our neighbourhood was built on the eastern side with six side openings to collect the torrent, the water is stored in a large, brown, round tank made of stone excavated from the sea. The tank is shaped with a deepening lower part and raised upper arches that end with openings used like well mouths."

A voice from the crowd shouted,

"Sheikh Abdullah, why do we care about how and why the Cistern was built?"

This led to an increase in murmurs, and the mayor's face turned pale due to the increasing agitation. He snapped back,

"For those who don't want to hear the rest of the story, I will teach them the importance of listening over speaking."

He raised his cane in the air and received nods and hand gestures of support from some dignitaries. He then corrected his stance and signalled to Sheikh Abdullah to continue speaking,

"The Cistern was a stop for many pilgrims on their way to Mecca, providing a necessary source of water for those who would spend a day or less before continuing their journey. However, one fateful day, a female pilgrim was mugged and felt so ashamed that she threw herself into the Cistern. The other pilgrims rushed to save her but she was clinging to the inner part of the Cistern, insisting that the loss of her money was a sign of God's anger. To appease her, the other pilgrims started throwing their own money into the Cistern, trying to make up for what she had lost. Despite their efforts, before she could be rescued, she fell in and drowned, leaving the Cistern filled with a foul smell for some time thereafter.

From this incident, the Cistern became a place where every year, pilgrims would come and throw coins around or into it as a charity for the soul of the woman who died, hoping to prevent any thieves who might consider stealing from the guests of the merciful. It's said that a merchant from Turkey heard the story and made a contribution of a large part of his wealth to the Cistern and many other merchants followed suit. Whenever a pilgrim visited, they would throw coins of various currencies, making it a religious ritual for pilgrims from Turkey and Eastern Asia to visit the Cistern and spend some holy days there, which they called "Days of the Drowning".

Sheikh Abdul Ilah Nawar concluded his story by emphasising that the coins collected over the years have been there for a long time and are no longer considered a valid currency. He pointed out that whenever a torrent comes and uncovers these coins, people who know the story ask for mercy for the woman who died. With a sudden triumph in his voice, the Sheikh exclaimed, "Do you understand why we call this place 'The Drowning'? People used to come from all corners of the earth to throw their coins so that there wouldn't be a thief, and now you want to fight over some money that has no longer has any value?'

Chapter 16

What caused Jamal el-Samurai to fulfil his promise?

As the night fell, a procession of ghosts moved among the mounds of dirt, dressed in black and using small torches to light their way as they accompanied a group of individuals carrying boxes filled with gold coins they had collected. The group had agreed to maintain silence and Jalal el-Samkari would speak only if necessary. They were making their way to Al-Yaridi's house.

From inside the house, Al-Yaridi's angry voice could be heard. "Who's at the door?" he asked. The crowd remained silent. Al-Yaridi growled,

"I'm not opening the door, I'm waiting for someone."

He looked around the door, his eyes settling on the newborn with tape over his mouth, whose expression showed he was in a bad condition.

The knocking at the door persisted and Al-Yaridi continued to curse those outside. But then, Jalal declared,

"Open, I am the Jinn Master."

Al-Yaridi was taken aback,

"The Jinn Master?" he whispered in awe.

What happened next, Jalal Al-Samkari would never forget. He would recount the events for the rest of his days, unable to believe something he imagined could never happen. Al-Yaridi threw a cotton cloak over his robe, wrapping a dirty scarf around his head. He carried the newborn to the inner room and returned to the main door. He thought the squeaking of the door was the baby crying and considered going back to stuff the baby's mouth with sugar.

His emotions were in turmoil and he didn't know what was happening. He muttered to himself,

"The Jinn Master himself is delivering the treasure to me."

He tried to make sense of his confusion with the intention of showing gratitude to the King by sacrificing the newborn and giving him its powerful blood.

When the door opened, Al-Yaridi saw a group of individuals hurrying to get inside. He was shocked to see they were dressed in black and felt their bodies with curiosity and fear,

"It's the first time I've known Jinn to have bodies that can be touched," he exclaimed, letting out a hearty laugh.

"The eyes can make what we hear seem untrue. And here I am, finally seeing you after hearing about you for so many years. I've tried to summon you, but to no avail."

He greeted them with a warm smile and led them further into the house. He was filled with great optimism, which allowed him to welcome them with open arms. He showered them with kisses and affectionately held the hands of each person carrying a box,

"If only you knew what I had to do to get to this treasure," he said.

He extended his hands with confidence, "I am the promised one, just as Sheikh Al-Jilani told me. It was difficult to summon you, but I never lost hope.

"You must have seen what I've done for this, I'm sure of it," he added, as some of them opened boxes, shining their torch lights on the contents, Al-Yaridi laughed loudly at the gleam of the copper coins. He took a stack of coins and threw them high into the air, causing them to fall back down and hit the heads of those nearby. Despite the pain, his joy was clear. Jalal Al-Samkari approached him saying,

"This treasure was gifted to you by 'the drowning'."

Al-Yaridi's reaction was aggressive.

"Where is the treasure of the House of Ashour?" he shouted. The group found itself in a difficult situation, trying to calm him down as he became more agitated. Jalal spoke up first. "Take a deep breath," Jalal advised Al-Yaridi. "The Drowning is one of us. She's the queen of Jinn and she has safeguarded the treasure of Ashour for you." Al-Yaridi put his head in his hands, trying to make sense of it all.

"Now I understand why the anklet vanished and the shining gold didn't appear," he said. "It's 'The Drowning,' she wants the final sacrifice for herself. Where is she now?"

Jalal approached him, unsure of how to ease the tension,

"I'll bring The Drowning to you, just try to calm down," he said.

"Okay," Al-Yaridi replied. "You stay here. I'll show you in a moment that I kept my promise, just as you kept yours."

Anger began to bubble up and curses slipped from Al-Yaridi's lips as he shouted at the others,

"Leave, leave."

The group started to make its way to the door, cursing Jalal Al-Samkari for involving them in a never-ending joke. Al-Yaridi quickly blocked the exit telling them,

"You're new Jinn, how can you exit directly through the door? Go through the cracks in the walls and ceiling or I'll burn you."

The group stood in stunned silence, unsure of how to

escape Al-Yaridi's instruction. Jalal grabbed his shoulder, telling him,

"No human can see us, let them leave through the door."

The joke was far from over. The baby's cries marked the beginning of events where fate collided, bringing the true prophecy to life,

"Your friend eats the bird from its head."

****

The raging waters converged into one river mouth, and the fates of Ibrahim, Muhammaduh and Al-Yaridi flowed into a grand courtyard in Mecca, which had been waiting for them for a long time to gift them with the collection of fates it held for them.

MUHAMMADUH

"MY LOVE BROUGHT ME LUCK, NOT MISFORTUNE."

25

The heart of Muhammaduh is consumed by fire, and no cure or remedy can heal it except the power of love's testimony. O Muhammaduh, pray, "Oh, God, love has claimed me, and Your compassion is unmatched. In my weakness and brokenness, I implore Your mercy."

IBRAHIM ASHOUR

CROPS SOWN IN FAR-OFF LANDS BEAR ONLY DEATH AS A HARVEST.

Chapter 30

The streets were devoid of Ibrahim Ashour's footsteps and the last person to witness this was the taxi driver "Abou Al-Aynayn", who had dropped him and his sister Omaima off at the bus stop. It was then that he heard a heart-wrenching sentence from her,

"Where are you taking us, Ibrahim?"

AL-YARIDI

THE MERGING OF GREAT SECRETS MARKS THE FINAL END, LEAVING NO MYSTERIES UNTOLD.

Chapter 17

The piercing cries of the newborn baby brought all of the police officers to Al-Yaridi's house.

The city was in a state of shock as they witnessed the tiny infant, whose stomach had exploded from the intensity of its cries, while Al-Yaridi was brandishing a dagger with a thin blade, holding the baby so tightly that it seemed as though he was trying to crush it within his own ribcage.

"You won't take my final sacrifice from me," he yelled.

Hajji Fatima and her daughter Aisha were the only ones begging Al-Yaridi, with tears streaming down their faces, not to carry out his gruesome plan, crying bitterly, pleading with him to spare the innocent life in his grasp.